MW01278374

Legends of Celosia: Origins

Hellhound Saga, Volume 1

Moonlight Soldier

Published by Moonlight Soldier, 2023.

This is a work of fiction. Similarities to real people, places, or events are entirely coincidental.

LEGENDS OF CELOSIA: ORIGINS

First edition. April 5, 2023.

ISBN: 979-8223901631

Written by Moonlight Soldier.

For my mother and father, who taught me to stand tall when things were hard. For my best friend, my gaming brother-in-arms, who stands by me. Finally, for pup, my angel, who's love and devotion allowed me to push forward for my dreams.

To Michael

from Corey. U

the Moonlight Soldier

Chapter 1

As the setting sun peeked between the trees, citizens of Celosia were either finishing their day's work or beginning their nighttime business. The lumber town of Floraine would see merchants and lumberjacks returning from deeper in the woods where the twin city Huntersden lay. Floraine would use the fertile soil they cleared to grow crops and herbs for medicinal purposes to ensure any injured hunters could be taken care of.

A young merchant girl with long brown hair tied up in a ponytail jumped off of a wagon she caught a ride on, returning home after selling the medicinal herbs to Huntersden. She was dressed in simple cream pantaloons, a red and blue shirt, with knee-high brown leather and cloth boots. With a light and cheery sigh, she took off her shirt, exposing her torso and moderate breasts to the late-summer air and packed it away into the rucksack she had with her. Slipping the pack back on, she picked up a pole with hooks on either end to hang baskets off of.

Approaching her home, the girl passed by a number of villagers finishing up errands, wearing nothing but boots and shoes. A few of the older people would have a light jacket to help keep the wind off of their skin, and other merchants like herself would wear full outfits to stand out of the crowd of normal villagers. A pair of militia passed her by from the direction of her home, the female guard topless with a bandage wrapped around her torso and leather-lined, thick cotton pants. Her companion, wearing a full set of leather armor and carrying the top half of her uniform, commented when he had gotten shot in the leg by accident. Seeing the healer's daughter, the pair nodded "Evening Lethia!" Lethia responded with a polite nod and a wave as they passed. With the pantheon promoting that nature should be cherished, people only wore clothing for protection or status, never to hide what is only natural.

Finally, Lethia saw her home coming up, breathing out slowly in anticipation of getting to relax. She could see the last of her mother's patients standing in the doorway. From what she could tell, it was a family, the grandfather, his daughter, and granddaughter. Naked in the doorway as Lethia's mother finished tying off a bandage on the younger girl's thigh. "There, now be careful when you follow your mother in the woods. We don't want you to fall into anymore thorns." Lethia's mother said softly, the young girl riding her grandfather's shoulders nodded, hugging his head.

"Thank you for looking after her, Amelia." The mother replied before taking a pouch, held by a small belt that hung loose on her hips. She pulled out a few coins and gave them to Amelia, and the three of them wandered off home. Lethia looked at her mother with a happy smile, the only parent she remembered having. The tender healer took off her slender gloves, then finally noticed Lethia approaching her.

"Lethia! Welcome home~" Amelia steps out of the doorway to meet her daughter part way to the house, hugging one another tightly. Lethia had always loved hugs from her mother, warm with affection. "Dinner is just about ready, put your things away and I'll get the bowls out."

"Sure mom~" Lethia replied as Amelia turned back inside the house. She was in pretty good shape as a single mother, a soft figure with moderate hips and lengthy brown hair. Lethia preferred to keep her hair shorter than her mother's lengthy straight flowing hair, yet at times she wondered how she looked if she let it grow out like her mother.

After putting away the basket and pole, Lethia pulled off her boots and shimmied out of her pants. Stretching her legs a bit, toes wiggling free from the confines of her boots, Lethia made a light, hopping jog to the kitchen where her mother was scooping out a bowl of stew. "What took you so long to get home today, Lethia? I know sometimes sales are a bit rough, but this is getting to be a little bit too common." Her mother's voice was thick with concern, but Lethia waved it away.

"How can sales ever be rough with YOUR plants of all herbalists here, mom? A Huldra druid trained you!" Lethia exclaimed, chuckling at her words to try and hide a nervous twitch in her tone. Her mother gave her a look and a small smile.

"Don't dodge the question, Lethia. These late excursions are getting a little too common. I know the road between our two towns is short, but I do still worry about you. Bandits and Were-" Lethia's mother shivered for a moment. "Werewolves have been caught along the road before."

"Yeah, they've been caught, Mom. With so many hunters and militia from the Blood Blades patrolling the road, what could possibly happen to me?"

"Your father happened," the tart reply came, which caused Lethia to blush and look down. Her mother wordlessly looked over to a framed painting of a man in studded leather armor, the standard affair for town militia. His face had been ripped off, and in the bottom right corner was written 'For Amelia'.

Amelia took a shallow breath. "You were only two years of age, too young to really remember your father or what happened. Now, why don't you just tell me why you've been getting home late?"

Lethia took a bowl and helped herself to her supper with a resigned sigh.

"Some of the hunting boys were flirting with me again, saying they had managed to catch a massive boar. Apparently, the beast had smashed through a few wagons along the roads beyond Huntersden. They wanted to take me to the local tavern and celebrate with drinks."

"Mmm... drinks paid by whom?" Amelia asked, making Lethia flinch.

"They paid, Mom, I promise. Though I did want to buy myself some more. I just didn't have any money aside from the profits from your flowers."

Lethia felt anxious over some key details she was leaving out. Her mother turned and offered her hand, palm up, and Lethia responded by putting the profit's pouch into her hand. She quickly calculated the coins inside of the purse and their weight. Satisfied it was as accurate as it should be, she put the pouch down on a nearby table.

"They did invite me to be at the tavern tomorrow as they are going to be serving the boar in a celebratory feast. They even asked me to invite you as well," Lethia offered.

Amelia softly puffed her cheeks, blowing out air as she took a small log and fed it to the embers below the cooking pot.

"That's sweet of them, really, but I'm not able to go. You know I have to stay here and tend to my plants and people who need medical attention. Make sure you tell them I am flattered by the offer."

Amelia stood back up, "Now, why don't you eat your dinner, then go up and get yourself washed up? It's late, and you need an early start for tomorrow. I'll have all your things ready for the trip in the morning. Gunthor wrote to me. He needs to leave just after dawn tomorrow as he has to receive orders from his customers."

With a simple nod, Lethia quickly made her way to the second floor of the wooden cottage they lived in.

The upper floor consisted of a single tub with a secondary fireplace for warming water for baths and a bedroom where the two slept in separate beds. She set the embers ablaze to warm the bathwater while she finished her meal. With a relaxed sigh, she undid her ponytail and lay in the water for a little while.

She did feel bad about the white lie she left her mother. She was given extra money from a customer, and she felt she deserved a reward. *She* was the one who made the long trek to the neighboring village every day to sell the medicine her mother grew. Rain, snow, sun, or fog, she would make the journey by tagging a ride with a wagon if she was lucky, but when the roads were too muddy for reliable wagon transport, she had to make the trek on foot. "I march between the villages, through rain and snow. I should have some kind of treat, right?" she mused. "We live comfortably here, making enough money to afford what we need. Everyone here treats us nicely."

Looking down at her reflection in the water, she laughed at herself as she reached for the soap to wash. "Yeah... everyone treats us nicely because of my uncle. Besides... some of the hunters are kind of cute... maybe I wanna decide to... stay the night." She chuckled to herself. "Yeah, that would go over well with Mom. 'Where did you sleep, Lethia?' 'Oh, just with some boy.'"

"I better hope the boy is both cute and a proper gentleman, then," her mother responded as she turned into the bedroom, leaving a startled and embarrassed Lethia curled up in the bathtub, her face warm enough to heat the water. After a moment, she looked back out of the tub, a thought creeping into her mind about the topic of meeting boys.

"Hey, Mom, how did you meet dad?"

Amelia poked her head through the doorway, surprise clear on her face at the unexpected question.

"I mean, like, I guess if we're talking about meeting boys, how did you meet him?" Lethia continued, seeing her mom's look of discomfort as she closed her eyes. Amelia took a slow breath and walked into the bathroom.

"He was on patrol when he found an injured wolf pup and brought him to me. I was so used to soldiers and mercenaries having too little care for life. Your uncle and I always cherished life; as you know, he became a mercenary to protect people rather than just for glory." She sat on the edge of the tub and watched her own reflection. "I was so moved that your father, clad in armor and armed with tools of death, would take the time to rescue a wild animal which, in the end, had no impact on his life. He even knew a little bit of medicine himself, something so uncommon in mercenaries these days. Talisan approved of him very quickly, the charmer." Lethia smiled, enjoying the idea that she came from such a loving lineage. "It still hurts to talk about your father," she added before standing up and adding fuel to the water furnace. "If you're done, I think I'll have a turn now in the bath."

Lethia left her mom to relax in the warm waters. As she crawled into her blankets, a howl echoed out in the night. She sat up and looked out the window towards the sound. "Weird... it sounds almost musical instead of feral." As the howls died out, she shrugged, lying back down and allowing sleep to overtake her.

As the first light cracked the night sky in half, Lethia could feel the first early rays strike her face. With a yawn, she sat up, looking out the window as the blankets slid off her frame. She sat there for a moment to enjoy the feeling of the morning sun along her naked olive skin, stretching a little bit to help get the tiredness out of her body. Her mother walked into the bedroom, boots gently knocking on the floor as she had just come in from the garden.

"Morning sweetie, glad to see you awake on time. You need to get going," she said softly. "I made some porridge for you before you go, and... sweetie..." Amelia walked up to her daughter and hugged her tightly, which Lethia returned with a light giggle. "Just remember Lethia, I love you dearly, and always will. Make sure you come home safe for me today, okay?"

"I know you do, Mom, I'll make sure I'm home safe and sound as always," she replied as she slowly pulled away from the warm embrace. "Though if I'm going to catch Gunthor, I do need to get dressed and get going."

With a nod, her mother headed back downstairs to tend to her fields while Lethia finished getting dressed. It was moments like these that reminded her why she needed to make sure to be home: She was the only family her mother had left.

While going through her dresser, she paused to decide what to wear. The celebration was tonight, maybe she should wear something a little more flirty. She had a cute skirt designed by a Huldra seamstress, a gift from her uncle. It was a long skirt with a slit running up the left, straight to the hip, coloured a soft moss green. Parts of the skirt had material that was rather transparent, showing some more thigh and curves without exposing herself. She smiled as she imagined herself in it, before remembering she still needed to be walking all through town among horses and other beasts. Putting it away and grabbing her favorite pair of tan breeches, she remarked to herself, "Kind of like pants more anyway, even if those skirts make me feel pretty."

Once she had everything together, she raced down stairs and powered through her breakfast, to the amusement of her mother. They shared one more hug before Lethia bid farewell and ran off to find her ride.

Clouds had moved in, turning the bright morning dreary. That didn't sour Lethia's mood as she ran towards the carpenter's workshop to meet up with Gunthor. Spotting Lethia, the burly, older gentleman gave a nod and slapped the back of the wagon, where Lethia hoisted herself up.

A nearby journeyman was bringing out goods to load into the wagon and saw Lethia jump in. "You get what he means? I was just sent here from our original masters from the capital to learn from him. Why is he so silent?"

Lethia blinked at the journeyman. "You were never told? Gunthor's a mute. Some grey Mercenaries attacked a long time ago and his throat got slashed open, or so I heard. My mother was able to keep him alive until a priest healed him, but he wasn't able to heal him completely. Since then, he's been unable to speak. Us locals learned to interpret what he means, though."

"Your mother must be a talented woman to be able to have kept him alive. Even with healing magic, something like that should have been lethal." The man glanced at his boss. "Blood healing can't fix something like that normally, right?"

"It depends on the person, actually," Lethia began to explain, remembering her Uncle's lesson. "Someone in a status of wealth and power requires far more blood to heal. Gunther here is a simple carpenter, so it's much easier to heal him magically. It's hard to explain, I don't study magic, but the stronger and more influential someone is, the harder it is to heal them. However, to bring someone back to life, it would take all the blood from someone to do it, so the person reviving someone who died, would just die in the process."

"So the priest just sealed the wound instead of fixing it, huh?" he asked, looking her over. "You seem to know quite a lot for a simple village girl."

Lethia smiled at the inquiry, leaning forward from her seat. "My Uncle is the leader of the Silver Shields. He's told me about life outside of the twin towns, so I'm a little more aware of the world than most." A crack of the whip, a jolt from the wagon, and Lethia flinched as it was pulled along.

"Well you certainly seem like a good travel companion. Have a safe trip with the master!" The journeyman called after Lethia.

The trip through the woods was expected to be uneventful, but not long after they left town, someone else hopped onto the back of the wagon. Lethia blinked at the stranger, confused. He didn't seem to realize the company at first, or perhaps he was just being aloof. It wasn't unheard of for people to catch rides along the roads.

He was a curious gentleman in a flamboyant set of clothes with an array of different colors: blues, purples and some yellow accents. He sported pantaloons and some slightly curved shoes more designed for appearance than travel. He also carried a flute on his side, and a pack filled with papers, scrolls and other writing odds and ends. He looked over towards Lethia and gave a curt nod as a greeting, long tail wagging on the other side of his body.

"Hello there, young lady, heading towards Huntersden as well?" he asked, his voice light and playful, whimsy at its purest. "If so, then maybe I can help pass the time with a song, a ballad or a story of the recent times while I've been about. My name is Howard the Minstrel, wandering around to find stories so I can let others know about the tides of towns." He gestured his hand in a dramatic flair; a showman indeed, and a quick talker.

"Lethia Azalea, pleasure to meet you," she replied with a nod towards the rambunctious individual. Upon hearing the name, his eyes lit up like candles, tail swaying rapidly with interest.

"Do my ears trick me? Azalea? As in related to the legendary leader of the Silver Shields Talisan Azalea? Pardon my excitement, but I feel like I just ran into a celebrity by sheer chance! Yet I have to wonder. Why does a relative of such a prestigious man live so far out of the way? Surely he would treat even his extended family with part of the royal fame he has earned, would he not?"

"That was mostly due to my father," Lethia explained. "I was told he was a town guard and he wanted to live a more simple life out in the frontier, where he met my mother. He disappeared a long time ago when I was too young to know him, but my mother tells me stories about him. No one told me what happened to him, though."

"Oh ho, so the request of the dearly passed, I see. Forgive me for being so tart, if I had known... Well, such a statement is crude when one cannot know. We cannot read minds, and I'm certainly no magic user who could. Would you like to hear more news of your uncle, my sweet Leth?" he offered as he pulled out his flute, giving a quick test on it. Lethia noticed the flute had a rather ornate wolf design to it, piquing her curiosity. The head of the wolf at the end gave it the sense of howling when Howard played the instrument, or maybe a wolf trying to sing.

"As you may know, the famous Guild Competitions are starting, and the Silver Shields are poised to once again take the top spot. Talisan continues to lead them into glorious victory, though with his standards of recruits the way it is, it's little surprise. He only accepts the best of the best because he wants to be sure they can keep up with him. Though how one can keep up with his unorthodox way of fighting with a shield, well..." Howard gave a brief laugh before continuing. "They have a new recruit as well, a lamia who is the first one to have ever joined a guild in all of Celosia, or more appropriately, the Northern Commonwealth. Everyone knows the military in the Land of the Three Kings employ's lamia's as well, but in the commonwealth where the plight of their struggle is strong, it's a significant stride towards fixing it. They say she is an absolute powerhouse who can use the stumps of trees as clubs and can even pin down two Draconian all on her own. Certainly a significant advantage to have in any military or even a sports event. Their rivals of course have been working on their own secret weapon, or so I hear. As to what Hicoth the fire wyrm has been planning, I do not know. He's been quite secretive about it."

The news made Lethia chuckle softly as it certainly sounded like the determined Red Draconian. She'd heard a few stories of him from her uncle when he'd come to visit.

"Well, it certainly sounds interesting," Lethia said. "One year, I'll have to try and make the journey to the capital so I could watch the games instead of hearing about them. Who do you root for yourself?"

The minstrel smirked. "To be honest, not the Silver Shields. Sure they are famous and for good reason, but I'm a little bit of a gambler at heart. No, I like to vote for the Northern Pride, the survivalists of our wildlands. I'm always surprised to see them do so poorly in the games. They don't focus on combat as much as the other guilds, so you would think they would have a more robust skill set."

"My uncle says it's because their guild leader isn't very competitive. She's more sympathetic, and while she does allow her guild to compete, she's far more interested in saving lives over having fame and fortune. Most of her guild feels the same way, which is weird considering the name of their guild. I mean, the merchant republic isn't the most sympathetic government body."

"Aah, but the current leader did inherit the guild, so perhaps the original goal of the guild is lost from the passing of generations," the minstrel supplied, which made Lethia pause to consider the fact.

"Well what about news of the other guilds? I hear news about Minerva's Blood Blades easily enough. They supply the patrols and town militia all over the Northern Commonwealth. They keep wanting to recruit my mother as a temple healer. We joke about how they act like she could heal gods." Lethia laughed, remembering how many times her mother had had to strong arm a priest out of the house.

"The other two guilds? Not much more different than what you may know perhaps. The Shadow's Ally, secretive assassins as always. Hearing news about them is like finding gold in the swamps. You're likely to drown first.

As for the Iron Drakes?" He paused, as if recollecting something that had slipped his memory. "Oh, I remember, they have been experimenting with Nephele and artillery. They believe they could recruit the Nephele spirits into those new cannons to produce mobile artillery. Living artillery, walking, talking and completely independent. Raw magical devastation from above! Imagine it, raining down thunder, lightning and fire!"

Lethia's eyes lit up at the thought of raining literal Armageddon down upon an enemy army. Howard began to play to pass the time, satisfied enough with the conversation as the wagon continued onward. After a while, he looked Lethia over while fiddling with his instrument, taking in her features.

"A lovely lady lass, baskets filled with pleasant smells.

Sits beside me on this wagon, oh how swell.

Hair as pure as earth and a smile filled with fire.

Of Silver lineage she was wrought.

A humbling life of a healer was she brought."

Lethia blushed heavily at the song the bard made for her. Howard simply continued on playing his flute the rest of the way.

The journey itself lasted a few hours, and the wagon arrived at Huntersden before noon. Hopping off, Lethia bid farewell to her travel companions. Taking a specially designed pole Gunther left for her, she took her mother's herbs and placed them in hanging baskets. She put them on hooks on the pole and eased it onto her shoulders to hang from, then casually rested her arms along the top half of the pole as she wandered through town in the morning.

While the mainstay of her home was mostly farmers, carpenters and lumberjacks, Huntersden was home to foragers, breeders, leather working and of course, hunters. Similar to back home, the only people who wore clothes were merchants, to help stand out, hunters leaving for the daily hunt, and the standing Militia. With the town being a little richer than Floraine, few people would wear silks to accent curves and jewelry to show off status. Silver or gold headpieces, jangling bracelets and jeweled thigh bands or silken garters.

After selling a number of herbs, she looked at the sun and saw it was approaching noon. Inside the tavern, she met the local bar keep, trading a basket of herbs for food. They had an agreement her mother made so Lethia could always have a meal while working.

The rest of her day went by pretty normally, switching from free-selling herbs to delivering packages meant for specific people and regulars. She approached a house which sat just beside the guard post near the rear of the village: a regular customer who required a specific kind of herb which helped curb a terrible allergy he was born with. He was in charge of skinning and preparing the hides the hunters would bring back, so he would get a lot of news. Lethia gulped nervously; he was a gruff, tough love kind of man who always seemed to have something to say. It didn't help that he could see through a lie as if it never existed.

As Lethia approached his home, the door opened, and the sickly looking man gave her a rather nasty glare, made worse by the naturally sunken features he wore, accented by the massive overcoat. Lethia felt herself shrinking under his gaze as she fiddled in her pack to get the herbs he required. "So I heard you spent some time at the local tavern yesterday," he started as Lethia's motions slowed down and her face went pale. "Had a little bit of fun with some of the money I gave you?"

Lethia felt hot shame in her cheeks. She hadn't even said anything, and he already knew. She pulled out the herbs and sighed in defeat. "I... I did, yes... Mr. Juria" she admitted, holding the small flower in her hand. "It was supposed to be for my mom, not for me and... I... wanted to treat myself since I do all the running around for her."

"You do all the running around sure, but Amelia is the one who puts her very life into these plants. These same plants allow people like me to survive in these environments, Lethia. You shouldn't be taking advantage of her and of the good faith of her customers. Of *your* customers, I should add." His words lashed at Lethia like a bullwhip, making her wince at them and feeling the wretched sensation of shame inside of her chest. The sickly man sighed and rubbed the bridge of his nose. "Look... I won't tell anyone what you did, this time. But only because I know some of the younger hunters are a bit rowdy; not that you're much better, it seems. It's also supposed to be a celebration today, and I don't want to spoil the mood any more than it already has been."

"Wait, it's already being spoiled? What do you mean?" Lethia asked, having snapped out of her guilt enough to hand over the Druidic flower.

"Bandits struck at dawn. Nothing serious, thankfully, but a lot of the town guard chased after them to try and root out their camp in the woods, so a lot of people are not in town, and we're left with a token patrol. We still have the hunters in town and they make decent militia, but our grand celebration is going to be missing a handful of people." He pulled out a small pouch filled with coins and put it in Lethia's hands. "This is for today. No extra this time, and if I do hear about you spending your mother's earnings again, I will spread the word. You're a good woman, Lethia, don't make me think otherwise," he warned her, giving her hand a light slap before taking his medicine and going inside. Left at the front door, chest tight with regret, she put the money away and walked out.

"I just wanted to live a little bit... what's so wrong with that?" she argued with herself as the voice in her head responded, 'I still took advantage of someone's trust and good intention, and for what? A few pints of alcohol and some flirting with a few boys? Is it really worth ruining my own reputation?'

"No it isn't, yet it felt nice to be able to do so," she answered herself, rubbing her arms to comfort her hurt morals. Thankfully, the rest of her normal customers hadn't heard a word as was promised, and her day went by smoothly enough. After finishing the rest of the deliveries, it was finally time to head to the tavern for the promised celebration.

As Lethia approached the tavern situated at the heart of the village, she could already see lots of people filing through. Men and women laughed as they walked through the door held open by a tavern girl wearing a flower-lined skirt and festive tops representing the pantheon. While all the skirts worn by the male and female staff were the same, every top was different. A few of the men and women wore vines, hardly hiding their chest to represent Damien and Gaia, the father and mother of the pantheon. Following them, some wore simple studded or hardened leather to represent Minerva, who protects them. To represent the god of disease, people would slap on body paint, mostly purples and greens for Borus. Finally, those who chose to represent Hilgith wore a veil over their eyes and strips of black cloth hanging off of their bodies.

Lethia helped herself to a bench as people filled the tavern and the staff quickly bounced from table to table. A woman dressed in Hilgith's rags approached Lethia, grinning as she put on a mockingly wispy voice. "What shall be the lady's final drink of the hour?" Chuckling, Lethia waved a hand to turn down the offer.

"Aaah, staying pure before your final judgment, how admirable," the waitress said in a husky tone, before breaking into laughter. "Ah, I just can't hold that tone. Don't worry, hun, I'll get you some water." With that, she wandered back behind the ever expanding crowd.

Not being from town, she didn't get to take part in the grand carving of the boar, though she could certainly see it. The boar had to have been a Nephele monster; it was as big as a small horse. She remembered Talisan telling her when monsters died, their bodies would melt, so this creature had to have been naturally made. Yet the sheer size of the creature felt far too mythical, perhaps a rogue wizard's experiment.

Singing snapped Lethia out of her daze as a few of the musically talented locals started up a song while the servings of the boar began to be sent out. Suddenly, wafts of wonderfully prepared food aromas filled the room as the doors to the back kitchens opened. It was difficult to smell anything with a large crowd blocking the way, yet the powerful and delicious scents from the kitchen powered through even to the back. She almost missed the song starting up, wrapped up in all the delicious smells. A woman's voice cut through the crowd, bringing the laughter to a brief pause.

'There once was a lady who grew a tree.
She would weep all day to feed it water.
The only thing so sad she could give to thee.
Was the grief of a barren mother.
Along came a man whose vigor did flow.
He saw the woe of a weeping willow.
He picked her up, to bestow his love and plow.
Siblings three were born to follow.
They each took tools to carve the lands.
The once barren tree had life in which to grow.
The family came together and laid out plans.
Today our homes shall prosper both high and low.'

With the poem sung, Lethia suddenly found her table filled with food. Her eyes grew wide at the assortment before her. Roast boar sliced into hearty pieces with fire roasted vegetables and potatoes. A large pot filled with hearty stew was placed at the center for everyone sitting by her to enjoy. As the hungry girl tore into the food, she could feel how soft and tender the boar was cooked. She could swear she could have cut it with her fork. Savory herbs and sweet honey danced on her tongue with every chew, warming her face. Taking a bowl, she filled it with a stew, smelling of rosemary and fruit. Chunks of dried berries had been stewed with boar meat and potatoes. Breads and cheeses were being offered regularly, and the out of town girl ravaged down every helping she was offered.

The taps flowed, booze being slung around like entertainers' kissing lips. A hand rested on Lethia's shoulder as she was nursing the bowl of soup. Looking over her shoulder and up, she saw the hunting boy from the other day, clean shaven and hair combed. His face was a soft red, warm from alcohol as he leaned down. "Lethia, I was hoping to see you here." Lethia blushed, put her bowl down, and leaned back just a touch. The scent of booze on his breath was the only thing marring his charisma. "I was hoping, perhaps you would like to avoid the long trek home and spend a warm night here."

At first, Lethia was going to deny the offer of having him buy a room for her. Then she noticed the lust in his eyes, and her cheeks began to match his own. Her eyes trailed down, and she could see the fuzzy chest and toned abs of someone who hunted for a living. Licking her lips, she quickly grabbed her mug of water and took a drought, cooling herself for a minute. "I'd love to, but I promised my mother I would be home tonight. I've been getting home very late the last few days, so today, I really should be home on time."

"Aw, come on, one night is not going to be a problem. You show up in the morning, tell her you stayed the night, and it's no big deal."

"No!" Lethia replied harshly, causing a few people to look. Laughing nervously, she adjusted herself. "No, sorry. We talked about my dad, and I'm all she has. If I don't return home today, she is going to go mad with worry."

The hunter's expression softened into a gentle smile. "Then perhaps spare me a kiss for the road?"

Lethia relaxed in his arms, happy that even when a touch drunk, he was listening to her.

"Alright, one kiss, though I'm sure you get enough kisses from your hunting friends," she replied before leaning forward to kiss his cheek. The hunter laughed at the remark, pulling back. He took Lethia's hand and kissed the back of it, bidding her farewell with half-lidded eyes. Lethia watched him vanish into the crowd before noticing the sun through a window. "Damn, time really does fly by fast. I gotta get home. Can't miss the last cart."

As she passed by the bar front, the chef spotted her and waved her over. "Lethia, wait a moment." He called out, causing the girl to pause. "Let me give you some food before you go. There is far more than enough for us here. Your mother would love all of this. Call it my thank you for everything you do for us." Lethia brightened up and opened up her empty rucksack. She imagined it would be a small helping of food, but she buckled when the chef dropped a couple pounds of meat and vegetables, still warm, into the bag.

"By Minerva's blood! That's so much, thank you!" Lethia gasped, putting the rucksack back on. "This would keep us fed for weeks easily."

"Just be sure to tell the pretty lass hello for me," the chef said. "Now go to the inn and get yourself a room."

"I can't stay, sorry, I need to get home today." Lethia interrupted him. Without waiting for another word, she hurried out the door, the chef calling out to her, words lost in the din of celebration.

Making her way to the gate, she rounded the corner to find all but a single wagon was gone. "Wow, guess I wasn't the only one to leave early," she huffed in frustration.

She found the driver of the wagon, passed out in his seat, a mug of booze and a bowl with scraps of food left. His horse sat nearby, grazing on random tufts of grass in the ground. "Well... guess he's not an option. By foot it is."

Walking to the town gate proper, there was only a single guard standing watch. Smirking, Lethia continued to walk forward until the guard stepped forward. "Excuse me, ma'am, I'm going to have to stop you there."

"Not a chance, friend," she countered, grinning to herself as she leaned forward, ready to run. The guard blinked in confusion before taking another step toward her.

"Ma'am, I'm serious, no one is allowed to-" By impulse, Lethia began to sprint quickly, making the guard panic from her actions. She noticed he was holding a spear in his left hand. With a sudden motion, she stepped to his weapon arm instead of his open hand. As she suspected, the guard didn't know whether to drop the spear to grab her or reach with his other arm, instead flailing as she ran by. The guard turned and yelled out after her, "Stop! It's dangerous in the woods, there's been a report of werewolves!" But the words echoed back to him as the road stood empty once again.

It didn't take very long for Lethia to start regretting her choice to leave town the way she did. It had already been over an hour into her journey, and the sun had set a little faster than she remembered. "Must be approaching the cold seasons already... just my luck." She sighed, hefting her backpack on her shoulders. She began to wistfully think about the one hunter who had asked her to spend the night with him. He certainly seemed like a cute boy, maybe a few years older than her, but there wasn't anything wrong with that, right? He was a hunter, so he had a fit body, strong arms, and a well-groomed face that made him look rugged yet refined. Though coming from a duram father, it looked weird for a human to have two differently coloured eyes.

She was so lost in thought, she didn't notice the curious sound of music in the wind until it sounded quite close. A smile spread on her face as she turned towards the music floating on the breeze to see Howard. "Thank goodness, a travel companion." She chuckled with relief. "Here I thought you would have stayed in Huntersden. Enjoy traveling at night as well? It's a glorious full moon, I've always loved watching it."

Suddenly, she felt a strange fear grip her heart as she noticed he wasn't playing his flute, yet she could still hear a whistling howl in the distance. In spite of the fear in her heart, she let Howard approach her, who gave the lone woman a smile. A smile which made her skin crawl.

"Such a bold, young woman, traveling between the towns all on her own with most of the militia occupied with bandits. Did the guard not warn you? There was a werewolf spotted in the woods," he said, his voice still as upbeat and musical as in the morning.

Run.

"No? My, oh my, such a silly thing not to tell a lovely lady such as yourself. Alone and oh so vulnerable in the forest." He picked up his flute and played a few notes. The howling sounded like it echoed from all around Lethia.

RUN.

"What's the matter, Lethia? You look like you're seeing a monster," Howard said, his musical tone turning malicious. Raising the flute to his lips, he played a few more notes which carried on the breeze. "Or is it that you guessed who I am... oh don't fret about me, I'm no beast... but my companions are, and in return for my safety, I agreed I would be a scout for them. After all, I need to stay alive. How else can I travel the roads in these dangerous times as a rare male Huldra? All I need to do is find foolish people who travel on their own."

Having heard enough, Lethia turned on her heel and sprinted down the road. She barely saw a rock flying at her in time for her to dive off to the side, dropping the pole she carried, watching the projectile soar by her head. As she turned back, Howard had a sling in his hand, and from behind him, a werewolf was galloping her way, quickly gaining on her.

She pushed herself back onto her feet and sprinted into the nearby woods. On the open road, she stood no chance at outrunning the werebeast. She had to rely on her knowledge of the nearby woods to try and out maneuver the charging beast behind her.

It was at this time Lethia was very thankful she was wearing pants instead of a dress. The werewolf was out of sight, but Lethia knew she was not safe yet.

Hopping over a root, she remembered the food in her backpack. No wonder the sense of danger she felt wasn't fading; the werewolf had a scent to easily track. Thinking quickly, she slipped the backpack off, gripped the handle and flung it in the opposite direction she was running. The distraction seemed to have worked as the sounds of branches snapping faded in the distance and came to a brief stop, while she herself ran for some distance. She didn't know what direction she was going in anymore, all she knew was to just keep going. Werewolves were deadly and efficient hunters. The distraction may have bought her time, but not much.

A blind turn around a large tree sent her hurtling off the edge of a small hill, landing on a branch which broke from the impact. The sound of the breaking tree limb, and of the breath leaving her body, felt too loud to her ears. Lethia's head spun, throbbing from the impact, and her vision blurred. Grabbing the tree limb, she used it to hoist herself up and onto her feet as she picked up the sounds of heavy breathing. It found her trail! In a panic, she ran again, desperate to find something to hide in.

Sliding on the soil and fallen leaves below her, she turned sharply towards what looked like a cabin just as the werewolf plowed through the woods right behind her. She hefted a branch and swung as hard as she could. The mangled, heavy end collided into the werewolf's face, gnarled and twisted wood digging painful into his face and the weight briefly disorientating him. The branch itself snapped from the impact under its own weight and the sturdiness of a werebeast, though it bought Lethia precious seconds to clear the field and into the cabin beyond.

Open and shut, the door groaned in protest at the sudden and rough handling. The house itself seemed to creak and groan in response, as if annoyed someone had used it with such carelessness and force. Lethia spotted a bookshelf with moldy papers and collapsing tomes. Thinking fast, she ran to the other side and pushed the heavy bookshelf towards the door, barely getting it secured before a heavy slam caused her to cry out in panic. Splinters flew from the hinges of the door, and while the extra weight stopped the initial charge, it was very clear it couldn't hold for long enough. Running short of ideas, she ran deeper into the house where she came to a large room. She scrambled around, trying to find something, anything she could use as a weapon. This was a logger's cabin, was it not?

A loud crash signaled she was running out of time. Spotting another door way across the room, she made a dash towards it, ignoring what she was running over. The dust was disturbed below her which revealed the etchings of a demonic ritual. The werewolf bound through the entryway, around the corner, and spotted Lethia. Ignoring everything else, it ran right for her and intercepted her in the center of the room.

Pain fired through Lethia's torso. Fur, blood and the thunderous shock of fangs in her abdomen roared in her vision and in her head as the full weight of a werewolf tackled her. The splatter of blood hit the ground first, sent as projectiles from the sheer force of the beast's bite. Upon a bright flash, excruciating heat radiated around them, as if falling into a volcano or into the maw of a dragon about to breathe its flame. A scream of pain echoed through the woods before it was cut off and silenced.

Moments later, the bard and his werewolf companions found nothing but a few drops of blood and the demonic sigil burned into the floorboards.

Chapter 2

Word of Lethia's disappearance traveled fast to the leader of the Silver Shields. After all, she was the only child of their family line. Talisan was more than invested in her well-being and wasted no time when he heard the news, hurrying towards the twin villages in order to try and track down his niece, sparing no expense. He traveled dressed in silver-lined chain hauberk, a thick leather and cotton over shirt with steel-plated breaches. Two swords were slung across his back, one crafted of silver, another of steel. On his arm was his custom kite shield with the corners lined with sharpened silver. The grip had a mechanism with a chain, allowing the seasoned warrior to throw it like a lethal discus. His dark, earthy brown hair, opposite of his sister's light brown flowing hair, tousled in messy locks from the wind.

The wagon bustled and creaked in agony as his ruby red lamian companion hauled it as fast as her lengthy body could move, which, while not as fast as a horse, could go for much greater distances than any stallion could even dare attempt. The powerful serpentine woman cared deeply for those younger than herself, having once been in charge of protecting the young of her tribe from poachers. After hearing the paternal love her leader had for his niece, Ember had volunteered to help track her down. Alongside the two of them was a Huldra draped in cloaks of rotten leaves and furs, a cow like tail the only indication of his race. Normally very social people, this Huldra male, a rarity of his kind, lived the life of a ranger before being recruited, secluded and alone. He became far more attuned to the hunter's instincts, demanded of any beast living in the wilds, and promised his stalwart leader the best he could provide.

Soon, the grim trio arrived in Floraine where Talisan spent the day trying to calm down a frantic Amelia. No one wanted to say anything, but her mental health had been hanging on Lethia's safety. When he rejoined his companions at the tavern, his face was dark and stern.

"How is the poor woman?" Ember asked softly, looking over his shoulder as if trying to see Amelia behind him. There was a sigh, and a slow shake of his head before he silently gestured for a serving girl and signaled for a pint of beer. "She's not taking it well at all, is she?"

"For someone who has now lost everything she held close... no, Ember, she isn't. I might have to assign someone here to look after her for good. Maybe see if an old friend from the caverns can do it," he said as he looked up towards the ranger, who nodded. "I'm not telling you to go back to your home, Autu. I know you're not exactly keen on returning. But this is something personal. She needs someone, maybe a younger girl to at least let her feel like she's raising someone, though I'm also afraid she might become unpredictable."

"That sounds like you're already assuming the worst, Tal. We haven't even begun our search," came a tart response from Autu as the waitress brought the mug. "What makes you think she's dead from the start?"

"I know my niece. She's stubborn and a little foolish at times, sure, but she's a smart girl and can be quick on her feet when she needs to be. We got the news she was missing about a week after, and it took us nearly that amount of time to get back here. That means she's been missing for two weeks, and there's been no sign of her. What would you think after such a length of time?" he asked, taking a long drink from his mug. "I gave Amelia hope, but it's false hope at best. I don't even have hope she can be found. That doesn't mean we are not going to try at the very least."

His two companions exchanged weary glances before Ember moved away from the table.

"Do you wish for me to stay here and keep your sister company?" she asked.

Talisan looked down at his drink before giving a brief nod.

With a pleased smile, Ember made her exit from the tavern and headed towards Amelia's house.

As Ember went about town, she couldn't help but feel self-conscious about people looking at her. Most were not used to seeing a lamia in society, but she was usually accustomed to it at this point. Her people would sport tattoos, usually signifying their passions and skills. Her body was covered in the tattoos of plants and thorn bushes wrapped around her arms, which signified her as a warrior. On her back were the coat of arms for the silver shields, a Kite shield with the holy symbol for Minerva and Hilgith, a bloody sword and Scythe crossed over.

She knocked on Amelia's door before opening it up, her frame blocking the doorway entirely. "Hello? Ms. Azalea? It's Ember from Talisan's guild."

There was no immediate response. Lowering her torso, Ember had to turn her frame in sideways just to fit inside the door. She avoided the stairs, afraid her bulk might be too much for the support structure of the house. Luckily, she didn't need to go upstairs as she saw Amelia rigorously cleaning dishes.

On the table were a bowl and a spoon, untouched. "Lethia! Come down, sleepy head, your breakfast is ready!" Amelia called out before turning and spotting Ember. "Oh my, Lethia, puberty was good for you. You're going to make your mother jealous with such a figure."

Ember paused before looking back at the bowl on the table. The food was moldy and rotten, untouched for a few days.

Meanwhile, Talisan and Autu left the tavern to begin their search for any clues they could find about where Lethia had gone missing. While any ordinary hunter would be unable to find where the trail-leads after two weeks, Talisan had faith Autu would be able to use his connection to nature in order to track her down. Sure enough, as they walked the road between the twin towns, the ranger came to a stop.

The leaves on his cloak rustled as he pointed off the path where Lethia had sprinted off, and walked over towards it. Kneeling down, he placed a hand on the bushes, studying them. "She was chased... She ran through here. The bushes have some damaged branches..." Upon looking closer, he spotted a small tuft of fur which had been caught in a small branch. "Werewolf... the last of his shedding... month turned, probably his first solo hunt. Lethia might have either been singled out, or had bad luck. Packs normally scout out an easy target for their newer members."

"Seems like a family curse. Can't avoid encountering werewolves out here," Talisan commented as he walked over, Autu passing the fur to him so he could inspect it himself. "This pack must be quite old to be this sophisticated... or very foolish. If they scouted Lethia, they may have figured out she's related to me. I don't know any pack that would willingly try and chase down someone in my family."

"Unless they were trying to ensure your family would end here," came a harsh response from the ranger.

With a shared glance, they continued forward, picking out the path the chase had taken. Talisan spotted the abandoned rucksack, noting it was emptied and how it lay in the opposite direction. She had tried a distraction, but if it had worked, she would have been safe.

Finally, the path led them to the cabin, the door left as nothing but splinters and hinges bent into angles not fit for their purpose. Talisan walked in first, drawing the silver blade, padded boots making only creaks on the tired old boards below. The pair came to the main chamber, where the burnt sigil remained.

The ranger continued onward to inspect the rest of the house while Talisan studied the room. He noted the collapsed bookshelf, and the papers scattered and ruined along the floor, all up to where the circle was. Anything inside of the circle was pristine, almost too clean, as if the floor had vanished and reappeared. "Minerva's blood, Damian's strength, keep this place pure," he whispered as he knelt down to inspect the circle. "It's been opened... but no signs of anything coming out... no scorch marks aside from the circle... the portal was made, but no summoning spell was placed, like whoever made it only wanted a portal to look into, or use as a method to destroy secrets and documents."

"There are signs of other werewolves exploring the hut, but nothing traces back to the original hunter, or any sign of Lethia leaving this room, on her own or dragged otherwise," Autu said as he returned to the main room. "I'm sorry Tal... nothing is here. All the evidence here suggests she never left." They looked at the circle together. Talisan stood up for a moment before nodding. A sensation of dread dragged through his torso, like tar forced down his lungs.

"Lady Hilgith, Lady death. I beg you to find my ill-fated niece... and bring her back to the heavens where she belongs." With Talisan's prayers spoken in a nearly breaking voice, the pair share no more words as they travel back to the village. They were unable to save Lethia, yet they were able to find evidence of the werewolves who may have been responsible.

Talisan planned to bring justice to them and prevent another tragedy at the very least. He however wished such knowledge could bring peace to his sister who would now know her only child was lost forever, if she was even able to comprehend it.

A messenger galloped on his horse and ran through the open gates of the Silver Shields headquarters. The horse reared back as her rider pulled on the reins to make her come to a sudden halt, then leapt off the brown and white mare to hurry inside. Rain muddied his vision and dampened the cloak he kept on, though it had long soaked through. A duram stable hand hurried over to guide the mare beneath a stable that had been made out of twin oak trees, druid magic making them bend and twist together to form a roof above.

Talisan sat in his office looking over maps of the forests in the Northern Commonwealth, ink and quill nearby as he had been marking locations of different werewolf and undead sightings. He made his name by hunting down creatures unholy or unnatural, something only made more complicated by events passing day by day. "We live in turbulent times..." he said to the discordant pile of documents before him. "Things were simple when it was just the ordinary undead. These days, we have bandits who turn Nephele spirits into monsters, and to top it all off, there is-"

"Another hellhound attack!" The messenger cried out as he burst through the door. "It's nearby, in the town of Meltior! Gather your men quickly!"

Talisan's eyes widened before knocking his chair over in his haste to stand.

"Go get my lieutenant, I need to dress for battle," came the fast order from the guild leader, making the messenger nod and run off to do as he was ordered. Four months since his niece vanished. The Huldra girl stationed to care for his sister informed him that his sister's sanity had indeed been broken. She would function, but she would need supervision so she wouldn't harm herself or forget to take care of herself. Now on top of the hunt for the werewolves who started all this, a new monster seemed to have manifested from seemingly nowhere. The first few claims were of a Nephele gone rogue, but as more reports came in, it became clear this was a demon.

The guild leader slipped on a leather cuirass and thick cotton gambeson with straps along the sides. The overcoat was designed to be too deep for the creature's claws to reach his skin, and if it were to catch fire, he could remove it quickly. His guild responded to numerous different monsters, so he took painstaking effort to research different ways to protect his team. Grabbing his sword and shield, he hurried outside to see a dozen grim faced members of his guild ready to go.

His lieutenant, a yellow Draconian named Yurith, saluted him. While uncommon in Draconian society, they were not as rare as other coloured variants. Talisan marched past the towering eight foot lieutenant. "Ready to get a move on Talisan, sir! Emergency response has already gone ahead. The Duram twins should be able to begin evacuation, and Toshiko Hamada has already begun making the emergency tunnels."

"Perfect. Shields! We will not ride to the village. We need to hurry. The twins should be opening up the way portal soon, and when it opens, our first priority is to minimize the damage. Get the civilians to safety, and try to draw the demon's wrath away from anywhere it has not struck. People's lives come first. We know this demon uses fire and seems to be immune to it. Do not engage it directly, and if you must, fight defensively." The guild members saluted in response while the portal opened up. "Right, Minerva, keep us all safe." With those words, he was the first through the portal, followed by his Lieutenant and the rest of his guild.

Stepping through the portal, they were faced with two Duram, Felky and Telky. The petite creatures had cat-like ears poised to listen to the sounds around them. Their body hair grew more like fur instead of hair, with slightly sharper nails, but they looked quite human otherwise. "Greeting Talisan, sir!" The twins spoke in unison, "The demon was spotted around the north of the village. We have begun evacuation to the southern part of the village where Toshiko is ready to deploy the emergency tunnels should we be unable to contain the threat." Report being delivered, the pair hurried off to continue the evacuation. Smaller and less sturdy than humans, they were better suited to support or stealth work as opposed to the heat of combat.

Yurith stepped through the portal, and the rest of the guild funneled through and hurried off, knowing where to be and how to contain the fire. This was the town closest to them and was under their direct protection. Countless days of drills ensured when they needed to react, they could act without even needing direction.

"Any word on additional dangers?" Yurith asked as they jogged towards the northern half of town, making a straight path where the heart of the flames seemed to be. "Or is this demon alone?" He kept in stride, the only guild member who didn't wear armor. His heavy running left deep prints in the ground to keep up with his leader.

"Nothing, It seems to be alone again. Every report we have received, they have been unable to figure out if this demon is alone or not. The only description we get is it's wolf-like in nature. Guess we are finally going to see for ourselves." The pair rounded a corner which led to where the fire seemed to be at its strongest. They spotted the demon in question as they watched it tearing into a scarecrow like it was a person. Talisan glowered; such mindless rage and destruction. No wonder these beasts were confined to the prison of hell by Hilgith. Its wrath and destruction had no distinction between living or nonliving. The Silver Shields watched for only a moment before they split off to approach in two directions. Yurith kept his distance while the geared up Talisan stepped forward, sword drawn.

The fiery wolf-demon spotted Talisan first, who spun and threw the burning wooden construction towards him. Talisan made a gesture, and Yurith punched the ground, causing rock to erupt up and engulf the burning projectile, dragging loam along. Talisan immediately ducked aside, the earth and rock obscuring his view. The demon had charged right through the tide of rocks, claws outstretched. Sword in hand, he swung at the demonic creature who kept charging forward, escaping his reach.

As the werewolf turned again to face Talisan, the two locked eyes. The demon's growls ceased, and there was hesitation in its eyes before standing up enough to get a better look at its assailant.

Talisan found himself not moving, as if something was suddenly gripping his hand. Why couldn't he attack? Of all the werewolves, undead and other monstrosities he had faced, what was this strange sensation that suddenly gripped his heart? Was it the demon? What he believed to be fur was just a massive amount of hair, flowing down the back of the female creature's head like a cape. Fur wrapped around her hands, arms and legs, yet her torso was bare of anything, revealing a curvy feminine figure. Was it her beauty? Was he being bewitched? This demon acted too wild, too filled with fury to be a succubus. Finally, his eyes went back to the details of her face. He couldn't find it still, yet something prevented him from going in for the attack. He could see her eyes become softer, less feral, as if waking to reality.

Yurith, however, did not hesitate as he summoned up a wall of stone and ran through it. The rock gave, breaking into chunks which attached to his body, innate powers allowing him to mold the stone. Gauntlets of gravel wrapped around his hands as he dashed up from the side of the demon, swinging down from above. The beast leapt aside, hearing the heavy footsteps approaching and then hurried off out of the village. Yurith took a few steps forward before slowing to a stop, seeing her run off. "Sir?" he said, turning around. "It's unlike you to hesitate like that. What happened?"

Talisan breathed evenly as he let his sword dip down to the earth.

"I don't know, Yurith... I honestly do not know."

Winter came and with it, the rate of what was deemed hellhound attacks slowed, giving the guilds a desperately needed break. The other guilds had been feeding the Silver Shields information regarding every attack that occurred. Everyone agreed that the demon Talisan encountered was alone, some kind of hellish werewolf fused with a succubus. No reports have carried any information about anything being drained from the victims, yet there was a small cult forming, saying this demon was an angry goddess of flame. The cultists were persecuted by the Minerva's Blood Blades guild under the direct order of their patron goddess.

Talisan could never shake the feeling he experienced when he stared down this adversary for the first time. Her face seemed so human, but from the reports he had, it was to be expected. She was a succubus and a fire demon, yet even the wizards he spoke with would claim her behavior was more along the lines of a war demon, or a spirit of wrath. There were also very few reports of the hellhound ever hesitating, though Talisan couldn't help shake the feeling it was due to the typical fear people would naturally have when encountering such a creature. There was also the question of how it seemed to simply vanish entirely at times. Many hunters have tracked the flames and burning path after its reign of blood and destruction, only to find no trace of a demon anywhere.

Yurith knocked on the door to his office, making Talisan look up from the reports on his desk. "Come in!" he called out.

The hinges creaked as Yurith walked into the room, bundled up in layers upon layers of cotton and wool. While draconians typically hailed from mountain tops, they were still warm blooded creatures and didn't handle the cold very well, especially red draconians.

"Still going over those reports? There hasn't been an incident for a few weeks... it's kind of nice to know the Hellhound has finally gone quiet. If we're lucky, perhaps it has finally been removed from these lands," Yurith said as he sat near the desk. "Though I do regret missing the chance to have brought her down myself. Would have been quite the trophy to keep here. The Silver Shields, slayers of the Hellhound."

Talisan shook his head at his companions' words.

"Every time you speak like that, I'd swear you were meant to be born red, not yellow."

"I was the only yellow in my family of red scales. Of course I'm going to have a stronger sense of warrior pride," Yurith replied with a laugh.

"Thankfully balanced by your spirituality," Talisan remarked with a grin. They both knew red draconians were usually far more ferocious.

"I brought over some gem apple brandy to share. Felt like you probably needed a drink." Yurith said as he produced a flask from the inside of his clothes. "Might be a little warm, given all the layers I got."

"Brandy is usually better warm, especially during winter." Reaching beneath his desk, Talisan opened a drawer and pulled out two mugs, which Yurith happily filled up. "I've been studying the hellhounds behavior, yes, finding consistencies and trying to see if we can find a weakness. So far, the traits of a demon are rather evident. There are reports she is weak to silver, though holy water doesn't seem to do much physical harm aside from scarring and stinging her. This leads me to believe what we are dealing with isn't a full demon, but a hybrid of some kind." Yurith looked up from his mug and blinked. "I say hybrid because if she were a full demon, holy water would be near lethal. She reacts to it as if it burns, but reports state they don't see any physical harm to her body. Silver is able to cut through her tough fur and pierce her skin, but only as much as a normal blade would to a werewolf, though its harm does seem to last longer as it should for a demon or werewolf."

Speaking the facts aloud, Talisan felt a sense of progress. This creature had been one of the most puzzling to deal with. There were never any consistent behavior patterns. Grabbing his mug, he closed his eyes to sip the brandy, letting its warmth fill him.

"So what you're telling me is this hellhound is part demon and part something, or someone else? If so, it couldn't be a Draconian, Duram or mole... erm, Fukai Chikyu" Yurith corrected himself. "Those reports paint her physical features as human... or Huldra. She's been compared to a succubus, so perhaps she is a Huldra?"

Talisan considered the possibility for a moment, remembering the features of the creature's body.

"I doubt it. Huldra are very nature focused. Sure, the wolf-like traits would make sense, yet the fire and destruction? Plus she's far too wild to be a being that grows up in harmony with the forest. Yet there is certainly a minor sense of intelligence behind it. It recognizes threats, knows when to flee. One thing I have noticed, as these reports carry on, is there seems to be less bloodshed. Look at the first report. Look how many casualties there were."

Taking a sip from his mug, Talisan passed over the review. Yurith looked it over and winced. "Nearly an entire village was slaughtered... men... women, children... Don't know if it's any sign of intelligence."

"No, however, as more reports come in, the death toll gets smaller and smaller, as if it's learning that by killing, it's drawing in more attention," Talisan clarified as he passed over a more recent report. "The only casualties in these recent reports are those who specifically tried to kill the hellhound... it acted in self-defense, despite this report trying to say otherwise."

"That's kind of a jump in logic there, self-defense only? The report claims she attacked them" countered Yurith.

"Normally, I would agree at face value, but take a look at what the report is covering. See any official seal?" Yurith poured the page over before he put it back down, shaking his head. "That's a grey mercenary report, unaffiliated. Could have been bandits or rogues doing who knows what and making the report to try and cover themselves. Granted, the evidence of the attack itself is proven and they have seen her. I wouldn't doubt them to muddle facts to protect themselves," Talisan explained, putting the report away.

The more he discussed this, the more fear manifested in him. It felt like such an unlikely prospect, yet only two possible suspects of a demonic werewolf could come to mind. When they had caught and questioned the pack of werewolves responsible for Lethia's disappearance, they confirmed the hunter that chased her was male. There was no mistaking the hellhound was a woman.

"Alright, alright, I'll believe you there. Do you have a theory about who it could be?" Yurith asked before emptying his mug of brandy. When he didn't receive an immediate answer, he took a long look at his leader and leaned forward. "Sir... you don't possibly think..."

"I don't want to!" came a lashing response. "The idea that it's her... it makes too much sense." He pulled out a few scrolls of maps he had been using to trace movements of the Hellhound. "Look... this is the pathing I have managed to come up with using all the reports we have received. There is no discernible pattern, plus people say all traces of a demon have been disappearing. If we were to assume this demon is some kind of... afflicted werewolf... people are looking for signs of a flaming demon, not a human. If we take it into consideration..."

"Then of course she would disappear, and people wouldn't be looking for a human. If she transformed back, she would have collapsed. Those first few attacks would have been at such a scale, even if she were a new werewolf, there would be too much to take care of in those villages. We would have to send a proper military force after a beast who could do that much damage. By the time we had task forces ready to go, she would have changed back... but then someone should have found her body unconscious somewhere. It would also explain why holy water isn't lethal. She would still be mortal."

"Normally yes, but if we really are to assume it's... 'Her', how long ago was her disappearance, and the first attack?" Talisan pressed onward, and Yurith counted on his hand.

"Four... months minimum... four full moons. She would be at the stage where she would be awake when she turns back..." Yurith supplied as he leaned back into his chair. "There couldn't be any other... no wait, didn't you and Autu find that a werewolf fell in with her? What if it-"

"The pack we hunted down said the hunter who went after her was a male. If it really was him, then he could have been trying to find his way back to his pack. He would also have better control of himself in these situations. It was his first hunt on his own, which meant a werewolf coming of age. Already a few months in. The behavior pattern we are seeing is one that hasn't been around as long." Looking down at the paperwork, Talisan felt far older than his age. He looked up to see his mug refilled with the gem apple brandy while Yurith stood.

"I feel like you're going to need some more of this. I pray to your gods it really isn't her, and Hilgith has collected her soul from the pits of hell. If this really is your niece..." Silence filled the room while Talisan took the brandy into his hands.

"Thank you for the drink," he said softly before vanishing into the mug. Yurith took this as the sign he should take his leave. Standing, he gave a polite bow before leaving the office to begin drilling the other members of the Silver Shields.

The rest of winter passed easily with fewer attacks. However, this only served to make Talisan more uneasy. Time seemed to be against him. He never admitted to the fear building up inside his heart. This monster, his guild's priority, was his niece, but the evidence gathered pointed towards the seemingly impossible. He did not hesitate, however, to ensure his task force would have equipment and a battle plan to hunt her down.

After receiving months of information about the characteristics of the hellhound, and even managing to secure a few samples of her fur, Talisan confirmed silver was probably the best weapon they could use against her. It was the only material that could cut through it without the raw strength of a Draconian behind it. Talisan, Autu and Ember would be the team to hunt down the demon and finally put an end to her terror.

The hunt for her was not easy, knowing they were effectively tracking an unknown human. As winter turned into spring, the snow made the grounds damp and marshy, which would create better conditions. As the weather warmed up, the hellhounds' activity increased, though the rate of attacks seemed to have diminished. The only reports of Hellhound attacks were from armed or military personnel. Talisan was relieved to know it wasn't actively hunting innocents anymore, yet the need to slay this creature remained constant all the same.

The longer they tracked the creature, the more they began to learn its habits and patterns, tightening the circle around their quarry. The hunting party had a few encounters, but nothing resulted in pinning the demon down yet. Their hunt would last them from spring into the early stages of fall where Autu had finally become proficient enough to trace the hellhound, even when she was in her human state.

Autu was scouting ahead as they had laid a trap for the demon. Getting the aid of the Minerva Blood Blades, they were going to try and force the hellhound to run down towards Ember who would be able to grapple her enough for either Autu or Talisan to finally kill her. Ember was enchanted with water magic which kept her perpetually wet, aided by the falling rain. Talisan remained nearby beneath the underbrush, clutching a silver blade and his custom shield. He would only bring the shield, Night Bane, on the more dangerous tasks. While he was trained to use any weapon, he crafted a fighting style based on using a shield aggresively. Talisan believed a shield should be used just as much for offense as it's intended function as extra defense.

Rain pattered around the hunting party, providing the only sounds, drowning out the cautious footsteps for anyone but those with the sharpest of senses. Unfortunately for Autu, his quarry had such senses. This time, he would use it to his advantage as his job was to flush her out, not to pin her down. Pausing, he could see the familiar shadow of the monster they had been hunting for nearly two years. Nearly a full year of constant stalking, hunting and studying this singular beast lead up to this moment.

Without warning, the beast took off, sprinting in a seemingly random direction. Ready for action, Autu took his shot, aiming not only to harm his mark, but also to draw her towards the trap. A cry of pain rang from the demon as it faltered for only long enough to pull the arrow out and keep sprinting. Spears tipped with silver flew into her face, forcing her to turn a different direction while Autu fired another arrow. A solid thunk told the ranger his mark slipped out from his aim. It didn't deter him though, as he chased after the beast, knocking one more arrow to his bow before taking aim. When he realized the direction of his shot, he pulled on the bow as the arrow loosened, needing to throw it off by changing his angle quickly, making the arrow fly away.

Ember leapt out of her hiding place, a flying frenzy of loam, snake, leaves and water, throwing herself forward towards the demon. Talisan watched from hiding as the hellhound tried to dig her claws into the ground and change direction. The muddy terrain gave her no aid as she slid straight into the coils of the powerful lamia. Trap sprung, the Blood Blade mercenaries closed the circle as fur and scale shifted and moved in chaotic fashion, both fighting for dominance over one another.

Talisan, sword pointed forward and shield up, was at the front of the encroaching circle. He watched, nervous for the powerful ally. Even a race as physically dominant as lamia would have a difficult time against magical creatures. Demons particularly as their strength frequently were beyond that of mortal limits.

In the end, Ember won, tail wrapped around the demon's legs, pressing into her back. Both of the demon's arms grabbed and pulled back, she held her up, presenting the quarry towards Talisan. The guild leader walked forward, sword and shield in hand as he mentally prepared himself to put the beast down. But nothing could prepare him for the words to escape her mouth.

"U-uncle?!"

Talisan froze only for a moment before finding his voice again. "Silence... demon. I'm not going to stay my hand this time..." He brought up his sword, ready to bring it down on her neck. He locked eyes with her again, and this time, he could see it. His knuckles grew white on the sword hilt as he stood there, breathing heavily. This was a succubus. It had to be. It was playing mind games with him, trying to force him to show a sign of weakness.

"Uncle... it's... it's me... please.... I'm scared uncle, please..." she begged, unable to pull herself free while watching the blade rise. The rain continued to pour down around the group as the other mercenaries watched on, wondering why he was hesitating. Talisan continued to stand there, poised to kill, time having frozen still around him as he stared down at those eyes. Those fire red and pitch black eyes shook with fear and confusion. They reminded him of his niece from two years ago, before she vanished. Memories swam of him visiting the little flower girl, so happy yet with the spark of what might have one day been a 'devil may care' attitude. A kind of emotional freedom he would have loved to see mature into a confident young woman.

He hadn't even realized his arms had numbed from the weight of his weapon held over his head for so long. Neither did he realize Ember had shifted closer. Everyone was staring in general confusion, and Talisan suddenly became keenly aware of it. Finally, his arms dropped down to his sides; not because of want, but his arms could no longer stay above his head. There were no sounds, except for the quiet pitter-patter of rain water striking the leaves on the tree's. The hellhound, still bound in the coils of Ember, hadn't been struggling for a while. Finally, the man said the words which he feared the most. "What... is your name?"

"Le... Lethia... A-Azalea..."

"...Your mother's name..."

"Amelia... My mother is Amelia, Uncl-"

"What's your father's name!"

"What?"

"WHAT IS YOUR FATHERS NAME!"

"I don't know!"

"Yes, you do!"

"No, I never met my father, he died when I was very li-"

"WHAT IS YOUR FATHERS NAME!"

"I DON'T KNOW, TALISAN!"

Sounds of the rainfall filled the air again. The man glared at the demon, who began to cry.

He could not mistake her voice for anyone else.

His niece was crying in front of him.

He made his own niece cry.

"I don't... I don't know... what's happening... what's going on... I'm scared... I've been running scared... for so long... for... for I don't know how long... being hunted... attacked... hurt... turning into this... this thing. Not even at night, just... I don't know, I thought it was at random... but I learned it's... just when I feel... when I'm scared... angry... upset... happy... anything... everything. I... I wanted to find you... but then... I got scared... and you attacked me... of course you would attack me... I'm a monster now..."

Talisan couldn't tell if it was the rain or hearing what Lethia had been struggling with for these last two years. Everything had just suddenly felt so cold, and the weight of his years never seemed to feel heavier, or was it his body? He didn't know anymore. All his stoicism and confidence fled him, and he never felt as vulnerable to anything as now. "Minerva, forgive me... I can't do this one task," he finally muttered as he fell onto his knees. The Blood Blade mercenaries closed in around him as the captain stepped forward.

"If you can't, Talisan, then we shall. This demon clearly has been stalking you and has found a way to attack you where you can't protect yourself." With those words, the mercenary held up a spear, poised to strike. Talisan couldn't watch, eyes closed tight as he fought to keep his breath even. A gentle light caused him to blink, and he looked up for a moment to the captain. All the Blood Blade mercenaries were glowing. The captain lowered his spear and stared at Talisan, his eyes covered over with an ethereal glow.

"Guild Leader Talisan Azalea... it's been a long time." A feminine voice echoed, like clanging metal, breathing that sounded of hissing steam from a forge.

Talisan's eyes widened as he recognized the voice of Minerva. Ember and Autu both eased back while the captive Lethia shrank away from the holy energies radiating in the clearing.

"This is an interesting situation you find yourself in, isn't it? Certainly, enough of a situation to garner the attention of my mother and sister. Since you hired my blade, they had requested I do their work this one time. Father, of course, isn't happy with us meddling in what should be a simple affair." The possessed captain approached Lethia, the hellhound shrinking more and more within Ember's grasp. "I'm here as a messenger... and a warning. While I would cut you down myself as you are a demon, the others see the plight of you and your family. I was asked to... remove my swords from this situation." The captain turned and walked back to Talisan. "I don't do this for you, for the demon or any mortal, only for my mother and sister. I will require you to atone for this favor. Knowing you well enough, Talisan... I suppose I wouldn't need to wait long. My respect for you is the only thing that allowed me to humor the idea in the first place."

With the words of a goddess fresh in their ears, the four of them watched as the Blood Blades began to march home. Talisan stood and turned to his niece. Ember gave him a questioning look. "So what now, Talisan? What are we going to do with her?"

"We'll take her back... and we will stick to the wilderness. We can't let people see her as the werewolf... and we cannot risk altercations, not right now, anyway." His voice shook with those words as he struggled to stay on his feet. Autu gave him an arm so he could steady himself before the Huldra took the sword and shield for him. "My niece... needs a place to stay... so she can learn how to finally control herself... so she can be given a chance to have... what semblance of a life we can put together for her. For the time being, we will claim we have captured her in order to study the demon, so we may better handle any potential demon incursion in the future."

Chapter 3

The journey to the headquarters of the Silver Shields was not a pleasant experience for Lethia. She had to be moved as if she were a captive, locked inside a cage. The cage itself was made of steel instead of silver so it wouldn't be more painful to her, but she could feel the chill suck her strength away.

She wanted to be warm, and she disliked the fact that she couldn't handle the cold anymore. Memories of running outside in the snow, watching it hang off the forest trees with ice forming into crystals making the sunlight dance and glitter caused her to sigh longingly for her past life.

"Hey... Uncle..." Lethia started softly when the group was traveling in relative privacy. "What... what's going to happen to me, do you think?" She had yet to turn back into her human form since she had been captured. Sheer discomfort, cold and settling malnutrition made her demonic powers take the brunt of keeping her relatively healthy. Talisan gave her a weary look. It had been a few days of relatively silent travel. The wheels of the wagon creaked beneath Lethia's cage, and silence hung between them as Talisan contemplated an appropriate answer.

"To be completely honest with you, I don't know. If you claimed to be anyone else, you would be executed and studied... In fact, if you were captured by anyone else, you would have died."

Lethia was shocked to hear such a response and hung her head, but she quickly put together the reasoning for his answer and sighed, nodding. After all, he had not seen her human form yet. What reason had she given him to truly trust him? She needed to earn his trust, to show him that she wasn't trying anything.

"Then, tell me what you plan to do when I prove I am your niece?" she asked, trying to find hope she might have a future of some kind. Talisan stared at her for a moment, judging her words carefully as the wheels complained about the weight of the cage incessantly.

"At this point in time, Lethia, I don't have any real reason to doubt you anymore. This whole predicament feels far beyond anything I'm even remotely familiar with," he replied at last, giving Lethia a sense of some comfort. "My plans going forward, however, is to teach you to be a mercenary... with this kind of curse, you wouldn't be able to live any other life. Though, the first thing you would need to do is prove to me your humanity for me to even truly consider you as salvageable."

"You KNOW I'm your niece uncle, othe-"

"The idea that you're sane is the fancy of an old man who has lost his entire family!" he shouted back at her, and Lethia's eyes lit up, stubborn to prove herself.

"Then why am I being so compliant, Uncle? Would any other demon sit in a steel cage, something that I could break out of easily enough? I could... bend the bars, melt through the floor or the roof. Fire, heat... they mean nothing to me anymore. Well... aside from comfort..." she trailed off, hugging herself for some warmth.

"Then why don't you? Show me you could do those things right now," Talisan challenged Lethia.

With a huff, the hellhound stood up and walked to the bars, rubbing her hands together and gripping them. With effort, she pulled at the bars, twisting her arms, jerking at the steel rods again and again. They flexed and twitched, but refused to bend completely. She let go and stared at the bars for a moment before looking at her hands.

She had vague memories of her time running feral, which became more clear with every transformation she had gone through. Lethia knew she could breathe fire, but it wasn't magic that caused it. She didn't even understand the basics of magic, she only knew the function. From her memories, she recalled a broiling heat swelling deep inside her chest. Her feral half reacted as her internal body temper sky-rocketed to a point the oxygen in her lungs began to combust. Her fire-proof body contained all the heat until she chose to release it.

Taking a deep breath, she blew flames into her hands, and they lit up. She looked forward towards the bars again. Gripping the bars and sliding her hands up and down them, heating them up bit by bit, she knew they would be easier to work with. Her uncle watched, the other members of the Silver Shield on stand by and ready to jump in when needed.

Finally, Lethia stopped trying to heat up the steel bars, gripped them again and pulled. Letting out a grunt of frustration and effort, she began to finally bend the bars outward to create a wide enough gap for her to fit through. She let go of the bar and stepped back to admire her handiwork before exhaustion hit her, and she collapsed onto her seat. Slumped against the opposite bars, she panted.

"That... took far more... out of me than I thought it would..." she admitted. "But I did it... I still... bent the bars Uncle, like I said I could." She breathed out with a grin of victory, keeping her eyes on him. Her uncle's expression hadn't changed, though it didn't dour her mood. She had a victory, and she enjoyed it. "Though um ... you have any... extra rations or... something? Just realized how... hungry I am."

"You nearly break the cage and then ask for food?" Talisan remarks, raising a brow.

"Making those bars bend was exhausting, Uncle. You made me push myself in a way I'm not used to, and it made me hungry!" She laughs. "Like when I was younger and you insisted I learned staff fighting to protect myself. I would trip over the butt of my own weapon more times than I could even strike your stick."

Her laughter faded when she noticed Talisan glaring at her, but she soon noticed why. Another group was passing by, and she had to keep her identity a secret. She hushed up as they passed by a Huldra caravan, normally loud and unashamedly happy, bursting with music. As they passed, all Lethia could feel from the people was fear, distrust and anger; people who were normally so friendly.

Isolation hit her hard, and she shuddered, folding into herself. She wanted to see her mother again and be in her warm arms. Ride with Gunther, visiting all the regulars she enjoyed talking to back in Huntersden. The fact that she could feel fear from people looking at her made her scared and upset.

Hunting instincts honed on such feelings, making her uncomfortable with the feral nature she knew that was just beneath the surface of her mind.

The groups passed by in silence and Lethia watched them vanish into the distance. As they were about to disappear from view, she could see them resume their festivities. She turned around, breathed out and sat against the cage in silence before hearing a thwap of something near her. Opening her eyes, she could see a package of dried meat and some fruit. She had to will herself not to leap and tear into the packaging, though her motions were still quick and nearly rabid as she helped herself to the food.

"Stupid of you to risk exposing your identity when you knew that caravan was coming," Talisan chided while looking down the road again. Lethia swallowed a mouthful of food.

"I'm not used to being myself in this form. All the sounds and smells, it's overwhelming. I can't tell 'everything' apart," she replied softly. "It's just too much for me right now. Sorry if I caused trouble."

"Fixing those prison bars is enough of an apology," he replied sternly, with the hellhound obeying, pulling the warped bars back inwards. Lethia wanted to prove she would listen and behave. He was all she had right now, and her best hope.

The rest of the journey was not much different. Any caravan or travelers they passed by, Lethia would be judged and feared. It made her feel more like she was a thing, reduced to a beast every time, yet she argued with herself that it was only in passing. She would prove to them she wasn't a heartless monster. Yet deep down, she knew she had been sowing chaos and destruction, wrapped in her own fear and confusion. Proving to the world she wasn't something to be scared of would be monumental at minimum. Possibly godly at best.

The journey gave her time to look at herself. How much of her had changed since she became a werewolf? When she asked herself the question, she suddenly realized: she didn't know. To her, the memory of the boar hunt celebration still felt like weeks ago. That's when she realized that she had no idea how long she had even been like this. Time had lost meaning, having gone unconscious so often when she transformed.

The bloodshed, however, felt too real, days and nights where she woke up in buildings filled with slaughtered people. That was a werewolf's hunting instinct: anything was prey. She didn't fear its power, she feared its hunger. Her own hunger and fury that could consume her. A separate fire woke in her chest, a desire to tame herself.

Finally, at long last, they came to the headquarters of the Silver Shields, and with it more faces and people who would be silently judging her. The walls looked strangely ramshackle, like ancient ruins had been overtaken by nature. But the walls of the fortress were designed specifically by both architects and druids. The roots of the trees embedded in the walls flexed and gripped the stones to keep them in place. The top of the trees were fashioned into towers to look over the surrounding area while providing camouflage against enemy archers. Inside, the tall walls made of wood and stone was a fortress with a large open field.

The inside of the walls had fruit vines and berry bushes growing along them to provide sustainable food against a siege. A barn stood near the center of the headquarters, flanked by the different military structures that made up the base itself. A library was located to the south of the base as well as a cook house near it, knowledge was held in equally high regard as martial prowess. She saw the open training field where people practiced their archery and weapon craft as the Silver Shields kept a weapon master of different talents there. Swords, axes, spears, gauntlets, disciplines of all kinds could be seen practiced in the fields, some of pure martial talent, others a mix of magic and might.

Their wagon passed by the barracks, and she looked as a few of the newer recruits stared back. The Silver Shields were notorious for being extremely finicky with recruits. They only accepted the best of the best, and even among them, they selected people of a specific mindset. They were a commando operation, so they needed people who could keep a level head in any situation and not be overly emotional.

The wagon came to a halt at Ember's living quarters. "Come on out, you're going to be with me for your stay here." Ember said, stern and commanding despite the motherly tone she held. Lethia blinked in confusion and looked towards her uncle who was walking away with Yurith, discussing logistics. He did not notice her, so she followed Ember.

The room inside was humble. Pillows were piled up in the far end to act as a bed for a lamia as well as a fireplace for when winter came so she could keep herself warm. "This is going to be your home with me," Ember said as she slithered inside behind the werewolf, closing the door. "I've been put in charge of you, both for your well-being and your security." Seeing Lethia's confusion, she continued.

"We are going to be training you, Lethia. Your uncle seems to be holding onto the thinnest glimmer of hope that you are genuinely who you say you are. However, for that to be proven, you need to learn to control yourself, control your emotion and control this demon which is a part of you. The reason I'm in charge is because, unlike the others, I am strong enough to overpower you, and fire doesn't scare my kin as much as others. I would be best suited to be your..."

"Guardian?" Lethia suggested as she looked at her pillows. "May I?" she asked softly, and Ember nodded. Lethia dove into the pillows without hesitation and sighed with pleasure, finally getting to be on something soft after the days of travel stuck inside of a cage. Ember was about to speak up when she noticed Lethia's skin was beginning to change color. It was becoming lighter, and her body was growing smaller. The tufts of fur on her body began to fall off, shedding rapidly onto the pillows and down onto the floor.

Lethia turned her head towards a shocked looking Ember, who was staring at a naked Lethia with fiery red hair, as human as she ever was. "So you're going to help train me how to control myself? I guess I'm not allowed to leave the base. Also, I suddenly feel far hungrier than I remember, so maybe we could start with some food or something? Why are you staring at me, Ember?" she asked before looking down at herself. She couldn't stop her head from falling down further with her gaze until it hit the pillows and she was fast asleep.

After confirming it was truly his niece sleeping on the pile of pillows, and placing a blanket over top of her so she could be more comfortable, Talisan set his mind. She was going to be trained as a member of the Silver Shields, a mercenary. It would only be a matter of time before others would put the pieces together and figure out that Lethia is the hellhound. When that time came, he would be forced to exile her from the guild, and she would truly be on her own.

However, he would need to swear his guild to secrecy. Such an act would be seen as greedy and selfish, and he knew. A being like Lethia should be eradicated for the better of everyone, and if it were anyone else aside from himself who found her, she would have been. For a man whose only family left was his now insane sister and his literal beast of a niece, he could not justify himself being able to do it. Instead, he would do the next best thing he could think of and teach her, train her to be a mercenary in the vein of his own guild. That had been his goal since they captured her, right? Or had he been saying it to try and escape what he didn't want to accept as reality? His niece was nothing more than a beast? "No mortal man should ever need to handle a dilemma like this." He shook his head in defeat. "How is one meant to slay one's own family, especially the last hope of our line... Gods show mercy for my decision... and I've already asked them for so much."

As Talisan entered his office, a Fukai Chikyu stood over him. The tall, slender mole person wore thick, billowing robes overlapping themselves many times, ornate and seemingly otherworldly designs flowing from his waist. He kept his arms folded in front of his chest, obscuring the central motif of his white and blue outfit.

Talisan wondered how this individual got inside without anyone noticing and let out a sigh as he stared into the man's mask-covered face. "I don't remember having much to do with the Shadow's Ally guild today, unless there is something urgent that needs my attention. Of course, your people have a tendency to come and go without much word." The guilds were obligated to work together, never crossing one another unless legal action was required. His first fear was that someone else had already figured out who Lethia was.

"Hmm..." came a raspy response from behind the mask, oxygen filters messing with the sound of his voice. "While your assessment of business is accurate, your assumption of my allegiance isn't." He lowered his arms, revealing a sickle, the insignia of the goddess of death, Hilgith. Talisan's face flushed, but his expression did not change. "I have come with a message about Lethia for you and you alone, Talisan Azalea."

After a few days of nursing Lethia back to full health and giving her some proper meals, her training began. With Ember as her caretaker and guardian, she was in charge of helping Lethia control her transformations and her emotions. Talisan and the other lieutenants trained her in the art of martial combat, and what it meant to be a mercenary. Lethia didn't take very kindly to the idea of being taught to fight, yet she took the lessons to heart.

Her days started with Ember, as she regularly had nightmares, resulting in her waking up transformed, and a number of pillows needing to be replaced. The first thing Lethia needed to practice was to make her transformations far less explosive and fiery so she didn't burn the place down. "Hey, Ember, not to doubt you teaching me this, but... if this is something more tied to magic, shouldn't we have a magic user teach me?" Lethia offered.

"If the guild had a demonologist, or a proper mage comfortable with dealing with a demon, then we would have them take care of you. Expectantly, no one else is volunteering, plus all our magic users are druids. I'm helping you because I respect Talisan's wishes to give his only niece a potential future. We also want you to control your transformation quickly. We can't keep buying new pillows over and over, let alone having to replace the armor you will be outfitted with."

Lethia blushed, rubbing the side of her stomach, in doing so she discovered the burned-in scars of the bite she had been given. "At least, you have a very appealing figure, Lethia. I think those two years kind of helped in a way."

"Two... two years?!" Lethia cried out, face paling while her eyes erupted into tufts of flame. Only brief flames, vanishing before Ember could take notice. "I thought it had only been a few months! Are you telling me I've been running wild for two whole years?"

Ember gave a solemn nod, confirming Lethia's fear in a way she wished she hadn't. What has her mother been doing all this time?! Would anyone even remember her at this point? Remembering Ember's comment about her physical appearance, she used it as a distraction. Thinking about the ramifications now would just cause her to explode into flames again.

"Well, I suppose those two years have done... some good. Though I do wish my hair would be tamed. I noticed it has changed color due to my curse. It also returns to what it would look like before my transformation," she noted as she looked behind her shoulder to see her fire-red hair trailing down to just above her rear. "Still, I am in need of a proper haircut. Makes me look a little too wild and unkempt... yeah I know, ironic coming from me now." With a chuckle, she took a deep breath, sitting down on the floor just so she wouldn't burn another pillow. Ember coiled up her large tail and settled herself down as well.

"Focus on my words, and let them guide your thoughts and feelings. Your emotions are like water, calm and serene." As Ember described the exercise, Lethia closed her eyes to focus on an ocean of water.

Her stomach knotted up. She pushed the feeling down and focused on the turbulent water, which she tried leveling. "Are your emotions calm right now?" Ember asked, noticing the strained expression on her face.

"Not... not really... I'm doing as you say... but the more I look at the water, the more the water wants to rebel... and it makes my stomach knot for some reason," she explained as she fought the waves. Finally, Ember placed the tip of her tail in Lethia's lap, and she opened her eyes to look up.

"It's clear the image of water isn't working. Perhaps it's because of the fire demon inside of you. If so, you may have a bit of an uncontrollable distrust of water, especially larger bodies of it. Why not picture a fireplace instead?"

Lethia closed her eyes and pictured a stone hearth with a fire gently burning inside, flames licking the stones around it. She could feel her stomach calm down almost immediately as the fear gave way to a more peaceful sensation. Seeing progress, Ember carried on.

"Now, the fire is the state of your emotions. It's burning low and steady. The different emotions you carry are the fuel you can feed the fire with, which makes it react in different ways. You can make it burn lower with calm thoughts, but right now, we're going to try and find where you would transform. Let's make your emotions burn brighter."

Lethia simply nodded, thoughts focused on the flame itself. Ember didn't want to make Lethia enter into a panic or a rage, so she thought of other things she could do. "How about something... fun. Tell me, what kind of things you enjoyed growing up, what kind of games or stories?"

Lethia kept her eyes closed and pictured herself sitting in front of the fire, feeling its warmth. She noticed the flames seemed to react to her thoughts for a moment, distracting her before recognizing Ember's question.

"Well... when I was younger, I always enjoyed helping Mom sell her herbs and flowers while visiting Huntersden. Sometimes, she would allow me to play with the other kids there, and they would show me how to hunt and how to use a bow. I wasn't a good shot, but I would keep trying again and again. One time, my mom called, and I turned around right as I let go of the string and nearly hit one of the boys with an arrow." She laughed, and the fire in her mind grew bigger, warmer yet still gentle.

"Oh! The fire is bigger... I'm not actually even picturing it. I actually see my flame getting bigger... and bigger... and it's... different. It's not like when I was scared or anxious, this feels... gentle, it's hotter, but it feels warm and gentle instead of burning or hungry," she explained, blushing. "I think I'm getting more excited just by seeing this. It's like this presence enjoys my experiences. It feels very relaxing as well." Ember smiled before noting Lethia's eyes beginning to emit tufts of fire.

"Lethia, your eyes... they're on fire."

"My eyes are what?" Lethia replied and examined her body. "I don't look or feel any different. Well, I feel happy about those memories, but-" She noticed a fire reflecting in front of her. Each time she nodded, the fire moved with it. "Well, just lovely. I have a tell, warning people who I am." Her defeated sigh made the flames go out. "Oh, right wasn't supposed to do ... um..."

"I believe we had good progress for now, unless you really do want to try again." Lethia smirked at Ember in response, which made Ember chuckle. "Well I guess that answers my question. Alright, keep focusing on those emotions."

Lethia nodded and closed her eyes to let her mind wander to happier times. The flames in her eyes grew bigger until they began to encompass her being, making her skin turn darker until it was obsidian. Her body grew bigger in size, curvier as hair grew along her arms and legs. Her long hair grew out to encompass her entire back side and pooled around where she sat. Her eyes continued to burn outward as her face remained very much the same, though her hands grew thicker with claws and her feet became paws. Opening her eyes, she inspected herself and smiled. "Well, I didn't explode in a ball of fire this time."

"It seems so, but we're also in a very controlled and peaceful environment. We don't even know just how many emotions can trigger your transformation, so for now, we're still going to keep you labeled as volatile. We don't want to have you randomly transform, let alone walk around with burning eyes for the world to see." She stood and walked over to the pillows to rest.

"So I guess I transform back by just... taking a breath and calming down? Picturing a calm ocean isn't going to work obviously." Ember gave her disapproving look at her snarky response, making Lethia flinch. "Sorry for being a bit pert there... I know I can sometimes be a little-"

"Much to handle? Your uncle would tell us a lot of stories from time to time about you when you were younger. So kind hearted and helpful, yet so stubborn. Honestly, if I had joined this guild earlier, I would have loved to come and visit you. Of course I'm at the age for my kind to be a mother, though I'm not a matriarch; I'll never have children." Lethia tilted her head curiously. "Don't put too much thought into it, we're supposed to focus on your training, not my life history or my wishes. Calm your emotions, you're due to go train with your uncle soon enough."

With a smile and a nod, Lethia closed her eyes and breathed out. She tried to imagine the same fireplace and how comfortable it was. She imagined crawling inside, letting the flames hug her body. It seemed strangely relaxing. Soon enough, she felt her body beginning to shrink, all the extra hair shedding off and her skin returning to its light olive tone. Looking down at herself, she smiled as she got back onto her feet.

"At least I can say getting out of my lycan state is easier now that I know I'm safe. It was difficult before you guys found me because of all the fear and panic I was dealing with. Thankfully, I have you guys to help me learn to control myself, and I have all the faith that you will."

"You're surprisingly hopeful despite your circumstances, Lethia," Ember noted with a smile which turned into a yawn. "Mmm... I think I've been on the cold floor for too long... getting sleepy." Lethia grabbed a few blankets and draped them over Ember.

"Hopefully, these will warm you back up."

"Thank you, though you must hurry. You have weapon's practice, put on a gambeson and go meet up with Talisan." Ember ordered, lowering her head onto the pillows.

Lethia bit her lip. She didn't argue with the order, letting Ember be. While she did have a natural affinity to think on her feet, she wasn't looking forward to weapons training. Her uncle was strict with his guild, and there was no sign he would be gentle with her. If anything, Talisan would probably make her work harder.

Chapter 4

Having gotten dressed in a simple green and brown gambeson with cream cotton leggings and a pair of simple boots, Lethia ran outside towards the sparring grounds, since she was to be a mercenary, she had to dress to represent her new career. She found Talisan, wearing studded leather armor, with one of the Fukai Chikyu waiting for her. While approaching them, she slowed down, wondering if she had gotten the time of her training wrong. "Uncle? Sorry if I'm running a little late today, though if you're in the middle of something..."

Talisan shook his head, and the Fukain assassin stared down at her. Even in her werewolf form, the tightly robbed mole man would be taller. Though with the outfit on he looked incredibly thin and wispy. Dark blue fabrics tied and woven together with black linings ensured nothing could possibly drag in the wind. Lethia had to crane her neck to see his masked face, which reminded her of an alien. "So what's going on?"

"I am to be your sparring partner, Hellhound. You may call me Toshiko. I'm the assassin and escape specialist of the guild," came a wispy reply, matching his waifish appearance. Lethia strained her ears; he sounded like he was constantly whispering. She had never spoken to Fukai before, so she had no idea if he was being factual, or stern. "Your esteemed uncle has tasked me to be your partner in the martial arts as, unlike him, I have a more generalized knowledge of weapons. My people also fight with our claws, much like your wolf claws you will be wielding. We believe it would be better to embrace such abilities instead of keeping them bottled up. Such explosive passion could only lead to self-destruction if ignored and contained."

Talisan placed a hand on her shoulder. "That doesn't mean I won't be instructing you. While Toshiko knows more about weapons than I do, I am still ensuring you learn everything about what it means to be a mercenary. What it means to choose to take someone's life. At this point, you have blood on your monstrous hands, and I can only assume it's a matter of time before it's on your human ones. We need to make sure you're truly ready for the responsibility."

Lethia's face lost all color at her uncle's words. Wouldn't her 'monstrous' hands be the same as her human ones? "I'm... confused, what do you mean?"

"I mean I'm going to make sure that when you willingly take a life, without being lost in the feral rage and fury, you will be ready for it. It's no longer a matter of if, Lethia, but when, and you will kill someone regardless of your intentions."

"What, so all the lives I took in my feral mindset are different?!" She cried out, eyes igniting at the thought.

"If you were to push a boulder onto a person, is it your fault? Or the boulder's fault?" Talisan asked calmly, confusing Lethia.

"Wha..." she thought for a moment. "Mine. I pushed it on purpose."

"Good. Now say you're climbing a mountain and you knock a rock loose. That rock falls on a bigger rock, and so on, until it pushes a boulder. That boulder then kills someone. Are you still responsible?"

Lethia ran his words through her mind. She would have no idea of what had transpired, would she? "Perhaps? If it was an accident, or someone pushed me into it..."

"Something else was controlling your body. You were used as an extension of its rage and fury, its malice and hunger. Being taken as a puppet on strings to enact another's will without your conscious consent."

"Then what about other werewolves? Using the same logic, wouldn't they be innocent like me?" Lethia countered, though she shuddered at the idea. "Not that I like the idea after being targeted. Though, I suppose it was my fault for being so determined to get home."

"There have been cases of werewolves managing to retain themselves, yes. Though it's very uncommon as there are few means of keeping track of those afflicted. Then there are cases where the insane ones become pack leaders, so you could question whether the whole pack is responsible, or their leader. At the end of the day, it just leads to the morality of killing for survival, and we don't have time for that discussion right now."

Lethia nodded, the flames in her eyes dying down. She felt sick inside, her stomach wanting to rebel at the memories. Talisan gently cupped her face for a moment, and she smiled nervously before he stepped back and cleared his throat.

"You will first be using a training sword and shield, a training staff, as well as weighted clubs and axes. This is to figure out what weapon you would be most comfortable with. After all, everyone has their preferences, though few can become a true martial champion and wield all of them. Sometimes they develop a more unique fighting style. For example, I am recognized as a sword and shield expert."

He walked over to the weapon rack and drew out a wooden sword, spinning it in one hand. Lethia watched his wrist and fingers move to keep the handle of the blade within his grip as he expertly handled the practice weapon in a flurry of exaggerated movements. Finally, he grabbed the sword by the handle and slammed it point down into the soft earth below. "This, however, is not my specialty."

With those words, he kicked up a wooden buckler and grabbed it in his arm, slipping it on. "I have trained myself to fight with a shield as well. My kite shield has bladed edges I can use for surprise attacks, and I keep another shield with a chain to use it as a type of flail or projectile when needed. My instructor taught me that a strong offense is a good defense, so I decided to take it a step further."

Walking up to a nearby practice dummy, he drew the wooden blade from the earth. Taking a classic stance, legs wide, shield front and sword at his side, he readied himself. With a yell, he rushed forward, swinging the sword at the dummy before following it up with a shield bash into its face. Carrying through caused the practice dummy to fall backwards, and Talisan charged towards another where he gave the dummy a back hand with the shield, knocking off a limb before landing an upward swing with the sword. As the second dummy fell down, Talisan came down with the shield and drove its bottom section into the neck of the dummy, severing it. Standing back up, he turned to look at Lethia.

"A weapon is anything you have at your disposal: a sword, a shield, a rock... your bare hands. Never underestimate anything as a dangerous weapon." Casually, he threw the shield back towards the rack, landing short, but rolling over until it hit the wall, popped into the air and spun to land right where it was originally hanging. "Before you leave here, you will understand this concept, while also finding a weapon that suits you." Talisan walked past his pale niece and left her with her new drill instructor.

Toshiko gave her a light bow. "Let us begin with basics, stances and the like." Lethia nervously helped herself to a sword and shield. "Keep in mind, you will need to learn fast, as you won't have much time to truly learn everything, before needing to be on the front line. Normally, our guild only recruits seasoned veterans. You are the first green, untrained recruit we have ever accepted. Now stance!"

Lethia tried to imitate her uncle's stance, shield in front of her, sword at the side and legs wide. Toshiko gave her only a moment before delivering a swift and brutal kick to the shield, sending Lethia falling backwards and onto her butt.

"No good! When you take a stance, you need to be ready! You're here to fight, be ready to fight!" Toshiko's wispy words seethed out like a serpent's hiss.

With a growl of irritation, she picked herself back up and took the stance again. Another kick and a stumble, nearly losing her balance. Toshiko immediately followed with another kick before Lethia could brace herself, and the shield went flying out of her hand. A third kick, and her weapon was knocked from her hand. Bird-like talons striking like bolts of lightning, making Lethia wonder just what really are the Fukai?

"You have to keep a firm grip. Go pick up your things," Toshiko ordered, standing with his arms cross in front of her. She hated how she couldn't read anything from him. No telling what was on her trainer's mind. Her uncle once told her, Fukai Chikyu were masters of manipulating information. Seeing how she could read nothing from his body, she realized just how terrifyingly accurate that was.

With a frustrated growl, she turned her back on her instructor, who immediately grabbed her by the shoulder, spinning her around and tripping her with a leg sweep. She hit the ground with a yelp before Toshiko delivered a heel drop landing on her chest, pulling back enough so she could feel the impact on her chest, but not harm her. Air forced itself out of her lungs as the flames returned to her eyes.

"Never turn your back on your opponent, especially once you've been disarmed." He took his leg off her chest and offered her a hand, which Lethia took and she fought to prevent herself from transforming. "That was a freebie... don't expect me to pick you up again after this," he warned.

"One last thing... let your emotions flow. This is a battlefield, and you're only learning. Keeping it bottled is no good as you can only become more frustrated. Let it loose and harness it like energy. Use it to aid you, not hinder you. Hot-headedness is a dangerous trait for any warrior, but if you learn to control it, then your emotional state can be as much of a tool as anything."

Lethia couldn't figure if he was being serious or making a really bad pun at her expense. This time, however, she kept a wary eye on her teacher as she went to retrieve her practice gear. She took up the stance again and breathed out, closing her eyes as she calmed herself. Yet a moment later, she found herself on the ground again, head aching and her practice equipment on either side of her. "The hell!?"

"Closing your eyes... is always a fatal mistake," he explained coldly as Lethia got back on her feet. "I had time for one kindness. One was all you got from me." Getting more upset, Lethia took the stance one more time, eyes blazing. Another kick followed by a block. She stumbled backwards and braced for a second.

"Two..."

She muttered as she blocked another kick, each one threatening to send her guard flying off and leave her vulnerable.

"Three..."

She growled, bringing the shield down again. Finally he knocked the shield out of her grip, and Lethia lost her balance, watching her shield fly. With a gasp, she turned in time to see another straight kick coming right for her, and she barely managed to dive off to the side, crashing into the ground. Coughing, she pushed herself back up as she groaned. "Well... At least I dove away from the shield as opposed to closer to it. Why are we training with clothes on anyway? It feels so stiff and hard to move in."

"Engaging in a fight without protection is foolish. Engaging in a fight in clothes we don't know how to move in is even worse." Toshiko replied, the venom in his voice vanishing altogether. "You will have to learn how to move, how to fight, while wearing different kinds of armor, though your case may prove unique. Now, let us try a different approach. Take your shield and walk to the dummy."

With a nod, Lethia walked over to the shield and picked it up, then made her way to the training dummy.

"Strike it!" came the order which seemed to hang in the air due to the wispy nature of his voice. With a cry of anger and frustration, she swung the wooden blade against the dummy, and knocked it off its weighted stand, her eyes were burning. She was about to transform.

"I'm gonna transform unless I get a grip on things..." she informed him. "This was far easier when I was with Ember."

"Of course it is, there you're inside the comfort of a bedroom. On the battlefield, you're surrounded by death and enemies who wish to kill you, at BEST. We fight bandits, brigands, monsters and undead. They could take you and turn you into a slave, or raise you as an undead minion. The fallen Nephele might eat you alive, if they don't melt you from the inside out with acidic needles."

Lethia let go of her emotional grip, transforming in a small explosion of fire that turned her clothes to ash. The practice sword and shield smoldered in her hands from the explosion of heat. She looked down at the damaged practice dummy and drove her wooden sword through it, snapping the handle off in the process, then she turned back to Toshiko.

"Well here I am, like you wanted," she growled back as Toshiko took a fighting stance. "So what now, pick up an unbroken sword and smack another dummy?"

"Show me how you fight," he said as he dashed forward, Talon-like hands forming a spear-tip. Lethia moved out of the way, shocked at his speed, even with her heightened reflexes. She felt a jolt of pain as a knee drove into her side, followed by a swift hand chopping into her core, sending her into the ground.

Once again, Toshiko lifted up a leg for a heel drop, only this time, Lethia was able to roll out of the way and kick herself back up and onto her feet. She let her instincts take over, getting low on all fours and growling as Toshiko stood nearby, claws forward. She rushed him and swiped with both arms in a giant hug-like motion, only for Toshiko to jump over her attack and land behind her.

"Your movements are wild, easily telegraphed" he told Lethia. The area around them was flat and barren, nothing to offer protection or obstacles. This was a true one to one fight, it dawned on her how much of a disadvantage she was in.

Trying to think more than act, she charged forward again, dragging a claw through the ground and throwing earth at her trainer. He deftly ducked the handful of loam before stepping aside, going for another leg sweep. Lethia cleared his leg, landing on her hands, and spun to try and kick him while upside down, but she swung too wide.

Toshiko wasted no time, kicking her legs back up into the air, throwing her off balance. Following up, he delivered a straight punch into Lethia's stomach while she was still upside down, making her slide back a little on her head and land flat on the ground. She spun onto her stomach, keeping low as Toshiko went on the offensive, once again leading with a straight punch aiming downward. She leapt aside, pushing herself up again as her instructor kept at it, swinging a high kick at her head. Ducking the blow, she remained on the defensive, letting her instinct guide her as she weaved through punches and kicks before getting overwhelmed in a flurry of thin and blurring limbs. A punch to the jaw, a kick to the stomach, and one final kick to the shoulder and a crack of bone caused Lethia to cry out in pain. Falling flat on her back, she panted as Toshiko stood over her.

"Hmm... you're not ready for the battlefield. Those mercenaries who hunted you seemed to have lacked training. It's a wonder you survived for so long as you are now."

"Yeah, big shock. I also had the forest, trees and other geography to use to my advantage. You know, stuff I could use on the fly. This is an... agh... an open field... with nothing around."

"So you say you struggle one to one as clearly demonstrated... though I will say this, your defensive instincts are far better than your offensive ones." Toshiko leaned down to inspect her shoulder, only to recoil when Lethia growled towards him.

"Don't... it's angry at you... I'm having to fight... my anger right now. Go get Talisan... or Ember... and a medic... I think my shoulder is dislocated..."

"Surprised it isn't broken, though I suppose you should be tougher. Remember, my people can break rock with our claws. A dislocated bone is certainly far better than what you should have been walking away with." He turned to see Talisan already approaching.

"Assessment?" Talisan asked flatly.

"Raw... though has good instinct. Sword and shield isn't her style, and she can't get into a proper stance or hold onto the shield properly. Tomorrow, we'll try the staff."

"If her shoulder is healed by then. Otherwise, she's going to have to learn to wield it with one hand," he said, then dismissed Toshiko with a nod. Talisan knelt down next to Lethia. "Hey... look flower, this isn't the worst you're going to get. He was taking it easy on you. If he really wanted, he could have left you with far worse. This is something we face every day. Even during the yearly guild games, we have injuries like this, or worse. I've had some of my people get torn in half... this is a very grizzly profession you're being forced into here."

"Because people would do the same to me?" Lethia asked.

Talisan gave her a very solemn nod before offering her a hand.

"This isn't what I wanted you to have. This is something I can only do to ensure you stay alive and safe, or at least, to keep yourself safe," he explained as he pulled Lethia to her feet. "Ember will see to your wounds."

"Wait, Ember? Why not a priest or a healer?"

"Something that isn't told to most people is healing isn't straightforward. Yes, it's blood magic and it's a one to one cost: blood spilled for blood replaced. However, the more powerful someone is, be it from martial training or magic expertise, the more blood it takes to heal a person."

"I understand that, so why not have a more powerful healer? Wouldn't someone of higher authority have stronger healing magic?"

Talisan let out a soft groan of frustration "You are far more than human, Lethia. The amount of blood it would take to heal you, frankly, is far beyond what the healers could manage, even for small wounds. Guilds treat healers as a rare commodity, not as a common resource. We don't rely on them, and don't get comfortable thinking you can as well."

Lethia reached over to feel the dislocated bone and flinched from the pain.

"Are you sure you could handle doing it yourself?" Talisan asked.

Lethia gave it some consideration before she dropped her hand. "No... no I should have Ember... look at it... though I should learn to do it myself, eventually."

"Good. You are never alone. Never try to do something alone when you can do better with companions." Talisan said as he led the way back to Ember's house. "Tomorrow, we will try out a different weapon. We need to figure out what weapon you're most comfortable with so we can train you to specialize in it. From what I have seen, sword and shield are not for you, which I suspected."

"I think my bruises are telling me the same. I don't know how a club or axe is going to be any different. You know, uncle, maybe a staff or polearm of some sort?" Lethia suggested as they walked together, rubbing her aching shoulder.

"Hmm... perhaps. Still, we shall see about it tomorrow. For now, get your shoulder fixed."

As the pair arrived, Lethia smiled at him. "Thank you for trying to look after me... even though this is nothing... I wanted... I just want to go back to a normal life." Lethia managed. "But it's not gonna happen, is it?" She dropped her gaze, and Talisan pulled her into a half-hug.

"Fate is fickle. Destiny isn't determined. We don't know what the path ahead will lead, let alone if there is even a path. All we can do is continue to march forward and work hard to ensure the path we are on is the path we want, or if that fails, we do the best thing we can for ourselves. Besides, you dreamed of being an adventurer when you were younger. I remember how you would try to sneak up on me with a small staff and pretend I was a bandit." He smirked, patting her good shoulder just as Ember returned home, covered in sweat, leaving a trail beneath her tail. "Good workout I take it, Ember?"

"Yes," she breathed out, chest rising and falling between heavy gulps of air. "Yurith wanted a wrestling match. I think we went for thirty minutes before we both got tired and called it a draw. Clever Scales there would cover himself in mud, making it difficult to grip him in my tail. Still can't get me down, of course. I'm still a lot of women for any of you legged people to pin down."

"Once I'm trained and in control of myself, I bet I could take you," Lethia said with a cocky smirk. "Though right now, my shoulder kind of needs attention."

Ember lowered herself on her coils and fiddled with her shoulder, eliciting a squeak of pain from Lethia. "H-hey! Easy... it's... not in the right place..."

"Well, only one thing can be done, sweetie." Ember took the end of her tail and lifted it up to Lethia's mouth. "Bite down on this. My scales are too tough for you to actually hurt me, so it's fine. No matter what, it's going to hurt." With a nervous nod, Lethia did as instructed and braced herself for the pain.

Life at the guild was fairly routine. Mornings and nights, Lethia would meditate and learn how to better control her werewolf state and her emotions. Her focus was on learning just how flexible her emotional point of transformation was. Upon achieving that, she would learn how to better keep her sense of self during the transformations.

Only when there weren't guests or new recruits would she actually practice combat after they found out Lethia could hardly contain her transformation as the combat practice progressed. This turned out to be a blessing, as they could also teach her how to fight unarmed as a werewolf, using her claws which were as lethal as any weapon they could offer her.

Lethia and Toshiko were both taking turns drinking from a water pail after some training. He was quickly learning the unique fusion of werewolf and demonic traits had boosted Lethia's endurance far beyond his own training. The potential he could see in her was astounding. Two weeks in, and he was struggling to keep up with a relatively untrained recruit, at least as far as stamina goes. He could still beat her in a proper one to one engagement, though Lethia never stayed down for long.

"I'm beginning to fear... I don't have what is needed to train you," he admitted, his mask pulled away from his mouth to allow drinking. Lethia noticed how it opened wide with circular appendages, each one moving in sync to create a kind of funnel as he drank the water. "I'll need to speak with the Duram twins to see if we can think of some kind of... mechanism to help with your training."

"A mechanism? Like, an obstacle course or something?" Lethia asked, still in her werewolf form. They hadn't figured out a solution to Lethia's clothing dilemma, leaving her constantly naked around the guild. Thanks to the teachings of Gaia and Damien, no one thought anything of it, though it was clear her figure was drawing attention. Rumors circulated that she was a succubus that had tricked Talisan.

Deep down, the werewolf did enjoy the looks of desire she was getting, though she didn't feel like flaunting her appearance was a good idea. "I mean, I guess, though why not just have me run through the woods nearby? When I was stressed, I would run wild through them, using trees and branches as makeshift obstacle courses. Oh! Maybe Autu could hide flags or something on a race track in the woods, and I have to find them all while completing the track!"

The assassin looked towards her and Lethia once again couldn't figure out his mood. A silent mask staring towards her. After a brief moment he turns and starts heading back to the practice fields.

"Come, we still have training to do," he told her as he walked to the center of their ring. Lethia put the bucket down under a water pump before heading over to her instructor.

"Oh! Hey, Yurith!" she yells out, spotting the Yellow Draconian in his training leathers. She waved at him, and he came over.

"Lethia, focus! Now isn't the time to be disturbing the lieutenant!" Toshiko hissed, yet his words went unheeded as she directed her attention to Yurith.

"Hey Yurith, why don't you join us for training?" Lethia offered. He was one of the few people she needed to still look up towards, even in her lycan state. "I don't feel challenged enough, endurance wise anyway. No offense to Toshiko, of course, he still puts me on my ass, but I don't even feel tired. Besides, you fight with claws as well. Don't Yellow Draconians practice more hand to hand than others?"

"Well, not necessarily." Yurith begins, turning to face her properly. "Yes, we do practice hand to hand, but technically, we use the earth and stone as weapons as much as our hands. If you really wanted a draconian to train against, you want a red draconian. They are the largest and most ferocious of us, training exclusively in combat. In fact, when they are born, they are taken to be inducted as gladiators. The reds are trained to be the most elite warriors from birth." He gave Lethia a toothy grin. "Still, if you're looking for endurance training, a draconian is better than a Fukai, no offense."

"None taken, I'm aware we do lack the natural tenacity of your scaled friends. One should always be aware of one's weaknesses as well as their strengths," Toshiko admitted, still standing in the sparring circle.

"Alright, so you're gonna come see me when your done wi-"

"I want to take you both here and now!" Lethia cut in, shocking the men. "I mean, why not? The two of you make a dangerous team, so why not make this training two against one? I get pushed to my limits more, and you both get a solid workout as well, without taxing Toshiko too much."

Yurith crossed his arms, eyeing her in deep thought. "I don't think it's wise for right now. We still don't know how good your control over your wild nature is."

"Well... yeah, it's still shaky, but when it comes down to it, you two could take me down and-"

"No, Lethia, not right now," he stated firmly. "This is training. We are not going to turn this into a containment exercise because you got cocky and tried taking on two people at once." Yurith towered over Lethia as he made himself clear. The werewolf in her growled, feeling challenged before Lethia caught herself and turned her head away. Taking a slow breath, she nodded while struggling to keep the need to challenge his orders down. Out of the corner of her eye, she saw Toshiko nod in approval.

"Good," Yurith affirmed. "Doesn't mean I don't mind taking over, of course. I do see why having you train with me is a good idea. Besides, Toshiko has other tasks he needs to complete. It wouldn't do for you to take up so much of his time."

Toshiko gave a polite bow. "I shall take my leave."

Yurith nodded and took Toshiko's place in the sparring ring. He pulled off his leather armor, and she could see the lines of muscles barely hidden underneath the thick scaly hide as he lowered himself into a stance.

"Hang on, I thought everybody trained in armor." Lethia asked, confused as to why Yurith stripped naked.

"Ha, you don't remember the first time we fought? Us yellow Draconians can manipulate solid rock, it's a natural magic all of us have. When trained, we don't even need to focus on it, we just think what we need of the stone and it happens. Because of that, my kind are one of the rare people that don't need to train in armor. The leather armor is both uniform, and has weights in it, so I can move around without having boulders tearing up the compound."

Lethia looked over to the outfit that had been set aside, and marveled a little bit at it. She hadn't realized that clothing could be specialized in such a manner before.

"Before we spar, I'll teach you the basics of my martial art. Again, I'm no master compared to my red brethren, but I'm certainly better than a blue or green warrior of my kind." Lethia smiled and tried to imitate his stance. Yurith was a more calm instructor, not as harsh or driven as Toshiko, but wouldn't allow her to make mistakes either. His training, she noticed, could help with her meditation as she could practice the stances. After all, with everything now decided for her, she felt like she needed to go full force into this new way of life.

After she finished her training, she ducked back into her chamber where Ember was once again curled up by a fire with a blanket over her. The cold winter months left her unable to do much unless the sun was out and unblocked. She couldn't help but find some irony, as she was also keeping Ember from hibernation, and the poor woman was ready to sleep any minute. Hearing the door open and close, Ember turned toward her. "Is your training going well, Leth? Able to keep yourself in check?"

"Kind of. I still struggle when we get more intense in combat drills. I can feel my more wild side wanting to take control, like I don't know how to fight," she explained as she flopped onto her pile of pillows. "At least I don't have any broken or dislocated bones. I'm able to take those falls and hits better. Being tough is just as good as being nimble, I'd think."

"Being tough is good and all, but it's still a better idea to try and avoid being injured regardless. Sure, you can take a hit, but how many hits will you take before something breaks?" Ember countered, her voice soft and drowsy. "Try not to make me think too hard, Lethia, you know the cold makes me sleepy."

"So, if my uncle knew you would be too cold to do anything, then why-" Lethia found Ember's tail around her neck in a firm grip, unable to finish her sentence. She reached up and gingerly pulled it off. "Okay, okay I get it... even when sleepy, you still have fast reactions."

"It's also why I cover myself in so many blankets and stay near the fire. I do sleep as you sleep, but this keeps me from going into hibernation." She shifted to get a better view of Lethia. "Now, we should work on your meditations some more. You don't have the luxury of time or rest, and we don't know when you will be needed, or worse yet, when you will be discovered."

"I'm probably betting on being discovered first before being called into battle," she replied tartly as she took a seat nearby, looking into the fireplace. The embers crackled as the flames danced, music to the patterns which shifted and burnt at random. Lethia let out a heavy sigh. "It's kind of funny... sorry, I know I'm supposed to be meditating, but something's been on my mind."

"What might that be? Maybe it is best to simply talk it out now and clear your head than let it linger. We both know you would probably not be able to truly meditate. You seem too... energetic, even without your new state of being, you just seem to be the kind of person who would rather be doing something than doing nothing."

Lethia chuckled at her assessment. "Yeah... yeah every time I'm here meditating, I think it's time better spent just being back out there and doing something, you know? Anyway, my thoughts." Lethia shifted closer to the fire, leaning against the bricks encircling the flames. "The night I was attacked, I was at a celebration, and one of the hunters there... Gosh, I can't remember his name properly, I think it was Bret? Or Brayden? Doesn't matter, he was kind of into me. I was the flower girl though, a tomboy who likes adventure. Honestly, a lot of the hunting boys were into me, and it was fun flirting with them."

"One of them was putting the moves on me, it was clear he was trying to invite me over for sex. I was curious back then, curious now, still a virgin. I just find it a little funny though. If I had accepted the invitation, I wouldn't have been out and attacked, and also wouldn't be a virgin anymore." She paused to collect her thoughts. "The huldra go around offering sex as a service. They have so few men in their race, it's beneficial for them, from what mom taught me. She was even hit on by her teacher a few times. The men are just as promiscuous as the women. Still, I'm kind of hoping I'll get another opportunity to try and have sex one day."

"You won't get a chance to have sex anymore," came a rather blunt reply."

The words took time to settle into Lethia's mind. "Wait, what?"

"You can't have sex with anyone anymore. You transform based on your emotions. The stronger the emotion, the more explosive your transformation. Even the act of foreplay would make you transform and heat your body up too much for anyone to have sex with you. They would get burned or ignite from your body."

Silence filled the room for a brief while as Lethia let the information sink in. Memories of scorched bodies flooded her mind, causing her imagination to take over. As panic began to spiral, she stood up and started to pace the room, mumbling to try and calm herself. She wanted to experience sex, to explore her body and others, but she feared the idea of potentially harming or even KILLING a partner, or worse, a lover! Something inside of her remained insistent that she could still have sex, regardless of the risk.

She pauses at the end of the room. Was something like this worth freaking out over? Sex wasn't something that was particularly special right? She didn't know, for some it was just business, for others it was something amazing. Lethia had never gotten to explore and familiarize herself with her own desires or needs yet.

"You would burn anyone you tried to sleep with. I see this is something that isn't going to calm your mind down soon," Ember mutters, pitying Lethia.. "My people don't know how your people breed, we have a matriarch who bears children for the tribe, our queen you could say. We mate out of personal connections, not for the need of reproduction."

"So what you're saying is... you're not the kind of person who would understand my problem. I should find a huldra. Maybe I could speak with Autu!"

"Autu left his culture to get away from it, he was being suffocated from the pampering he received."

"Then... maybe there's a bunch of Huldra travelers nearby? I'm sure my uncle sometimes pays for huldra women to reward people here occasionally right? No, I'm... not allowed to see people outside the guild..." Lethia slumps into a ball against the fireplace and sighs. "I don't wanna be stuck like this. I wanna try it, I mean, what if I find someone I love? How would I be able to... you know... be intimate?"

"I'm afraid you're asking the wrong person, Lethia... I wouldn't know... now please, are you finished?" Lethia sighed out in defeat, nodding her head. "You're gonna promise you're not gonna try and do this with someone." The werewolf girl looked towards the fire.

"No promises." She replies with a grin and Ember looks up, glaring at Lethia for a moment before laying her head back down.

"I can't hold you to that promise anyway I suppose. Go outside and do what you need to clear your head, then come back in and we shall meditate some more," Ember suggested, and Lethia obeyed with a nod. With it getting late out, it would be simple to find some privacy as she walked outside into the slowly chilling night air. She could feel herself beginning to calm down after the day's events.

With nowhere to go aside from the training yard, she made her way there in the dark, casually browsing the different weapons. While nudity and the physical body is nothing to be ashamed of, the act of sex was still a personal affair. Trying to pleasure herself out in the open was not something she was comfortable doing.

Putting her mind to something other than sex felt like a better use of her time. She had been given brief instructions with many of them: sword and shield, clubs, axes, spears, whips. She knew a little bit of the long and short bows thanks to the hunters back home, so she knew how to use them well enough.

Eventually, she stopped and looked at the halberd. Of all the weapons, the halberd seemed the most interesting to her. It had a blade for chopping, a spear point for stabbing and this particular design even had a small hammer-like back end. She picked up the weapon and held it in her hands, feeling the weight. The handle was long, though she would need one that was more suited to her height. "I would have to learn to use this as both myself and in my werewolf form," she mused as she got ready to practice some stances and moves.

She remembered what she was told about the halberd. It was typically used as a general infantry weapon better suited for mounted and heavily armored opponents, or creatures bigger than a normal soldier, like Ember. It's normally not chosen due to the unwieldy nature of such a weapon inside of caves or enclosed spaces, but she felt it was not given a proper chance. Swords were very common, easy to make, maintain and also very flexible with their roles, and could easily be paired with a second sword, a shield, a dagger, or something with more weight like an axe or club. The halberd seemed to be a marriage of a few traits: the weight and power of an axe with the reach of a spear. Hefting the weapon, she tried to locate her center of balance.

Using the extra strength given to her by her current form, she held it out with one hand, palm up, and adjusted where her hand rested to find the center of weight, which was very close to the head of the weapon. "If there could maybe be some weight on the other end, like a metal, um..." she muttered to herself.

"A counter balance?" Talisan supplied, making Lethia jump in surprise at the unexpected voice. "When you hunt werewolves for a living, you learn to move far more silently."

"Yeah," Lethia replied with a nervous chuckle. "A counter balance, something to make the weight more centered. Do you think I could fight with this like it's a staff?" The idea made Talisan laugh, but he gave it a thought.

"To be frank, I don't think anyone has ever come up with such an idea, and to make a counter balance for a halberd? Why are you asking me this?"

"Well, when you told me about weapons, I remember you said Halberds are only good for combat in open areas with lots of room to move, room to maneuver the axe head, or places where cavalry would be used. What if there was a way to make this more universal? If this was counterbalanced so the weight was more center, then I could."

To demonstrate her thought process, she stepped back and made some slow motions, holding the halberd awkwardly by its center and moving it while keeping the weapon close to her body. The blade spun, and she swung it upwards in an uppercut fashion before pulling it back before the head went too high. Talisan watched and nodded.

"I think I see where you're getting with this, and maybe. We would have to make some kind of practice version of what you want to work with. I can send word to a blacksmith, see if we can't get something custom made for you." Lethia smiled, but Talisan noticed there was something behind it. "Lethia... this isn't what is on your mind is it? I can see you're trying to distract yourself from a different problem."

Lethia took a few steps away, spinning the halberd to get a feel for it, putting on a show before slowing to a stop, pushing the weapon's shaft in the ground. After a moment of silence there was a brief sob followed by a deep breath. Talisan placed a hand on her shoulder and noticed she was fighting back tears. She had never had an opportunity to process all the emotions and all the truths she was facing. When Ember confirmed she couldn't possibly have sex with anyone, it was the first and last crack needed to begin a flood of realization of what her reality now is.

"Uncle I..." She panted out before taking another breath. "What even am I? I'm not human anymore, right?" She asked, looking down at him. " I used to have to look up at you, and now you're smaller than me. I'm a monster! Mom is... I don't know what is happening with Mom. I've killed people... I know it wasn't 'me', but it was still me! Uncle, I..."

She tried to lean onto the halberd, but faltered and nearly fell to the ground. Talisan caught her and pulled her into a slow hug as Lethia cried openly into his shoulder, the only family she had that was even still mentally sound. Talisan said nothing in return, he simply held her, letting his niece cry and finally let all the bottled up emotions out freely as the night was filled with the hoot of owls.

And the tears of a transformed and lonely young woman.

Chapter 5

As promised, Talisan sent out a courier to try and find someone who could make Lethia a custom halberd, specifically someone who could maintain discretion. This person needed to know who Lethia was so when they made the weapon for her, it could be imbued with magic so her fire wouldn't ruin it.

The alchemist twins were the most mischievous in his guild. Loyal, yet loved being troublemakers and pickpockets. He normally used them for specialist tasks and information gathering, a pair of researchers as he would explain to the other guilds. The boys sported mossy green fur and two-coloured eyes of blue and yellow. The eyes were the only difference between the two, as Felky's had a yellow left eye and a blue right eye, and Telky the opposite.

They had a lab located below the base, connected to the tunnels which served as both evacuation tunnels and supply lines in the case the compound was ever besieged. All the fur Lethia had shed when she turned from her werewolf form to her human form was brought to them to study, and with how constant her changes were, they would have all the research material they ever needed. As Talisan walked into the lab, he was greeted with Felky trying with mixed results to turn Lethia's fur into yarn, whereas Telky was holding a freshly woven shirt to a burning hearth. "Master Talisan! Welcome!" they said in unison, followed by a cry of frustration from Felky.

"Any luck with the research yet?" Talisan asked as he walked over to the hearth in time to see Telky throw the shirt into the fire. With a poof of soot and smoke, the fire died. The shirt looked untarnished, black fur laying in equally black soot.

"Yes! As we have guessed, the demonic werewolf fur from your niece is entirely fireproof. No natural flame can light it on fire of which we can create," Telky explained with pride, standing tall before fetching the shirt from the smoldering hearth and burning his hands.

"Because we cannot produce magical or demon fire, we ruled out dragon fire since we are able to mimic the chemical nature of it." Felky said from the spinner as he continued to weave the fur into thread, his hands covered in bandages from the times he had cut himself on the rather powerful material.

"Well we can make a guess since neither of us have ever dissected a draconian," Telky responded with a huff.

"When you manage to kill one without ruining everything, then maybe we can!" Felky retorted.

"You're no better!"

"ENOUGH." Talisan bellowed, and the Duram twins saluted.

"Yes, of course, sorry, master Talisan. We have managed to make some basic clothing for the demon doggo," they summarize in unison.

"It will be more effective for a tailor-"

"Yet we know it is possible."

"Plus with so much fur and-"

"-a near endless source, we could make fire proof everything!"

Talisan held back a feeling of unease. The twins had a habit of speaking as if they were a single person, which made many people, including Talisan at times, rather unnerved.

"That's all well and good, but what about armor?"

"Well, her fur is very strong and nearly impossible to cut, except with silver. The only problem is that it's very thin. Might not be able to cut through it, but you're still going to feel every hit you take. It's no replacement for leather or metal," Felky explained as he handed over the shirt he was testing. "It would be great for an undershirt, if you're looking for armor for Lethia. Nothing we can do, but at least she can have clothes."

"Thank you, it's a start at least," Talisan said and he took the shirt and turned it over to examine it. It was made more as a proof of concept. "Anything else you're able to figure out from it?"

"If we were able to light the fur on fire, they would make amazing torches. They would never burn out unless Lethia herself put them out.

That's a hypothesis considering battlefield reports stating she's been a ball of flame. We surmise she can set herself on fire on command. The only way she would actually be on fire, kind of like how certain chemicals only explode with certain processes," Telky explained as he went to a bag of fur and handed it over to Talisan. "I imagine you will be going to a seamstress. If you do so, tell her the seams should be designed to be pulled apart and restitched easily. Lethia would have more than enough material to put her clothes together. She makes the fur, after all."

"Thank you, keep up the great work you two," Talisan said, and the twins both saluted before returning to work.

As the days turned to weeks, Lethia's training continued, focusing less on meditation and more on the martial prowess she would need in order to stay alive when she was finally selected for a job. Lethia knew plenty about medicine and edible plants, as well as basic hunting, so survival wouldn't be as big an issue with her. She had proven herself considering she survived as a wanted criminal for two years on her own with her werewolf powers.

The martial training also ended up helping her control her emotions as Lethia was not one who could just stay idle or empty her mind. With the werewolf curse came a primal urge to keep doing something, anything. She needed to keep herself busy so she could keep her mind focused.

Her martial training finally began to see her take on both of her trainers at once. It was becoming common for people to see both Yurith and Toshiko fighting her at the same time, with Lethia's ramshackle custom training halberd, which was nothing more than two chunks of rocks tied to a stick to simulate the weight, with one end marked as the head with burn marks.

Lethia had been working on learning to fight without allowing herself to transform, just so when she was in the field with people not in the guild, she would be able to maintain her own hidden identity. When she was human, the training was more of a free for all instead of a two on one, just because Lethia wasn't quite as strong in her human form, though she regularly surprised the two.

"Well, credit for ingenuity, I suppose. She's really dedicated to learning the halberd," Talisan noted to himself, watching her train before the three decided to take a break and split off. Lethia splashed a bucket of water on her head to rinse the sweat off her body, then noticed her uncle standing over her.

"I see you finally managed to convince them both to fight you at once," Talisan chimed, taking a hold of the pump handle and cranking it for his niece.

"Yeah... it's... those two are... a fierce pair to deal with," she panted as she put the bucket beneath the water pump to refill it. "I knew I wanted more of a challenge... I'm thinking I'm biting off more than I can chew..." They both laughed. "It's weird. normally I wouldn't enjoy this, I never liked feeling overwhelmed or under pressure... but now it fills me with some kind of... thrill."

"So long as you don't let the lust for the thrill drag you into something you can't handle or you're not ready for. Especially since you're going to be sent into the field soon."

Talisan's revelation made Lethia choke on her water. "What!? Uncle I've been training for... two months? At most? How could I be ready for field work!? I don't even have a proper weapon yet!"

"Against other people or trained opponents, no... against undead, you're ready. Don't forget, we are the *Silver* Shields, Lethia. We specialize in monsters, undead and unholy creatures, as well as protecting people. I've sent for a blacksmith to build you a halberd, something a bit more to your fancy, though I requested they come here to do so. Besides, undead are also one of the only creatures you can kill without needing to worry about the morality of such a choice."

"What do you mean by the choice? Isn't mercenary work normally to kill or be killed?" Lethia asked, confused.

"When you kill someone, you are ending their existence in this world. Anyone tied to them, family, friends, business partners... they will all suddenly and irreversibly lose a person in their lives. To kill someone is effectively causing misery and sorrow for someone. Maybe a person is a villain, and more people will be happier than not, but it's still something you need to choose to do. Killing itself isn't morally right or wrong, it's based on circumstance. But when it becomes a choice... make the choice wisely."

Lethia was caught off guard by the sudden seriousness of her uncle. The topic of the morality of killing left her feeling sickly inside. She didn't believe she was ready for it.

"You need to remind yourself," Talisan continued, "that being a mercenary isn't as fantastical as the bards and singers make it out to be. They make songs of triumphs, poems of the failures... but they do so to put on an act, a show. Never for the full detail. After all... murder is murder." He took a pause to let the information sink in. "You also want to make sure you put yourself in a position where you can make choices where it counts... because subduing a person is far more difficult than killing them. Now finish up, your sparring partners are waiting for you." Turning her head, Lethia saw the Draconian and the Fukai waving her down. With a nod, she ran off to continue her training.

"She seems rather spirited," a voice said, making Talisan spin around. Before him stood an ebony girl wearing an eye patch over her left eye and raven hair flowing freely down behind her shoulders. Her outfit was of several flowing fabrics which would serve better in a desert environment, though a few alterations would ensure the ensemble would keep her warm in the more temperate climate. Leather gauntlets traveled up from beneath her sleeves, ending in the palms of her hands, fingers exposed to the air. On her hip, she had a tool belt complete with hammers, pliers, some spikes, rope, and a few other odds and ends on her left. On her opposite side was a crossbow, but there was no sign of any quiver or bolts on her person. "Talisan, I assume? My name is Milly. My father said you have work for me. If it's magical weapons or tools you need, then you called for the right smith," she said, a mild accent in her voice reminding Talisan of those who lived in the far southern desert. He noted how her eye seemed to be youthful and wide, as if she was eager to see the world itself for the first time.

"Well you'll have to forgive me if I have a hard time taking the merit of a blacksmith who lost her eye," Talisan said bluntly, making Milly pull a face.

"That's quite a fair assumption you're making there, losing my eye. I didn't lose my eye practicing my craft. I have a bit of a light sensitivity condition. Since I was born, I have had to keep something over my left eye, otherwise it hurts."

"Certainly something you don't hear about every day. I have done plenty of dealings with your father, however I feel like this task required a younger, more flexible mind. The person you're making the halberd for just so happens to be the same type of spirited young woman," he replied, pointing towards Lethia, but he remembered she couldn't entirely keep her form hidden and quickly turned back. "I'll take you to the work station. I would assume you need to make yourself at home before you begin," he offered, guiding her away to the far end of the encampment. Milly took a second look towards Lethia, her one eye squinting before a flash of red streaked across it.

She followed Talisan to the smiths workshop, where the guild members would normally take care of their own equipment. They had never really found a blacksmith willing to work directly with them, as the nature of the guild made too many enemies. Furthermore, the quality of work the Silver Shields demanded required blacksmiths who were too famous to be mandated to work for a single guild.

The smithy itself was still in good quality with a proper anvil, hearth, tools and even raw metal on the side ready to be worked. After Milly inspected the tools before her, smiling and running her fingers over the expertly made equipment, she looked back up at Talisan. "So if I remember correctly, this is for a halberd imbued with fire." He gave her a slight nod. "Imbued with fire, from blade to tip, and balanced as if it's a quarter staff."

"Lethia has been wanting to try and use the halberd similar to a quarterstaff, yes," he replied, stepping over to a steel rod and pulling it out, looking at it thoughtfully.

"That's already a bit of a tall order... and I'm going to assume -"

"-that you are in fact imbued with a demonic soul exactly like my niece?"

"How did you know... wait, your niece as well?" Milly gasped.

"Don't act surprised, Milly. It's clear he knows about us already, otherwise I don't think he would have sent a letter to our father asking for us specifically," a third voice echoed from nearby, and from seemingly the air itself, a demon appeared, her body coming into view as if the wind was blowing off the illusion, yet her form remained translucent.

"So I guess this is where I'm supposed to say it's a pleasure to meet the most esteemed guild captain in all of the Northern Commonwealth?" she asked nonchalantly, clearly unimpressed with celebrities. Her body was a light purple tone, with darker purple stripes running along, similar to how a dancer would wear fabrics to highlight her curves and bust. Her nipples were the same dark hue, confirming the color on her body was perfectly natural for the demon spirit. Bright red hair, far brighter than Lethia's, cascaded down in free flowing locks over her shoulders accented with raven black strands like her twin. Her eyes and expression however were hard and defensive as opposed to her seductive form. "After all, who else would think of calling a demon to craft a weapon for another demon than one who made his name hunting creatures like us."

"I just wanted to make sure we were somewhere private first so we could get the delicate info out safely. Your father requested I help keep your secret" The demoness nodded in response as Milly looked a little embarrassed. She lifted the eye patch to show that her eye was the same coloration as Lilith's eyes.

"This is my twin sister, Lilith," Milly introduced them, though Talisan was having difficulty finding similarities. "Yes, we're siblings... it's complicated."

"Mom made a pact with a demon, had sex with dad, had us both," Lilith said flatly.

"Lilith!" Milly exclaimed, blushing while her sister shrugged.

"I don't... need the details, all I need to know is, can you do the job?" Talisan asked, bringing the conversation back on point. The pair looked back at him for a moment as Lilith vanished from view.

"We should be able to handle the job. You certainly seem well stocked here, after all. The thing is, I don't know if steel would be the best metal for the job. It would have to be a metal both flexible and strong enough for what Lethia intends to do."

"Strong enough for a demonic werewolf? Yes," Talisan replied before walking past Milly to a storage locker. Pulling out a key ring from a satchel on his hip, he unlocked it and opened up the locker to reveal several different kinds of metals. Milly's eyes widened at the sight.

"These metals! These are all precious metals a blacksmith would lose a leg for! This is Mithril! And Tungsten! Adamantium! How... how in the world did you get all of these!?"

"Rewards from the guild tournament games. Winning first place does come with a number of fine rewards, as well as a number of merchants eager to do business with me. Plenty of posterity to claim when you supply the best guild in the nation," Talisan explained.

Milly couldn't stop herself from running her hands over the metals, excited to be working with such rare and foreign material. "You're really sparing no expense for this, are you?" she asked, turning to face Talisan again. "I mean, some of these metals are just, they are extremely rare. Why so much for a single person? I would expect someone like you to use these for your own ends."

"She's my niece, and the only descendant left of our family. I need to make sure she has something that will stay with her for as long as she's alive," Talisan said solemnly before leaving to get Lethia so they could take her measurements.

"Well... fine, I'll admit, I had him pegged the wrong way. A little pretentious still, but I have less issues with this job now," Lilith stated before turning to look at the metals. "At least these are easier to imbue with magic. What do you think... Mithril head, Adamantite core?" she proposed while Milly continued to inspect the different metals.

"Not sure really... I don't know if we should make this into separate pieces, or mold it all into a single piece. However, it wouldn't really work with different metals. I think this is probably going to be something made inside of one another, like a composite piece." Milly replied as the siblings pondered over ideas.

"Well how about we talk with Lethia about how she wants to use this. If I remember correctly, the practice weapon she had seemed to be a little bit of a custom design." Lilith remarked, trying to remain practical about the job at hand. "Besides, I have a strange feeling she isn't going to be using the halberd like a normal foot soldier would, if the reputation of this guild is anything to go by."

"What do you think Lethia would do with this kind of weapon?" Milly asked curiously, taking out a Mithril brick to feel its weight.

"I don't know, maybe pole-vault with it? We're in a guild which uses equipment in ways not originally intended. Talisan uses his shield as a secondary blade. Hell rumor is it's the sword that holds him back, which sounds like garbage if you ask me."

"Oh yeah, dad did mention that. It's also why this guild tends to pay the most for the best quality. The Silver Shields really push their gear to its limit." Milly remarks, already trying to piece together what kind of strain Lethia would put onto her weapon.

"We really need to speak with Lethia first before looking at more of these. We have a job and to make sure we do our job right we need to figure out what she is going to do with it." Lilith reminded Milly to help keep her wayward sister from gawking at all the rare metals.

"Okay, I'll get the furnace going." Before getting to work, Milly began to strip off the large ensemble of dresses and skirts that she was wearing. As each fabric was carefully placed on a nearby table, she was left in only a pair of thigh high cotton leggings and boots.

Milly's bust was smaller, the fat on her body being burned regularly from her daily work. Her arms were shapely, muscles crafted from a lifetime of working the forge, with a steady set of abs. They flexed as she reached back to her hair, pulling it into a long ponytail, before braiding it all together using string she kept on the belt still on her hips. After ensuring her hair wouldn't get caught on anything, Milly took two strips of browned cloth, tying them over her breasts. Even with a smaller bust, they had to be restrained to help prevent them from throwing her off balance. She grabbed a Leather smiths apron, tying it on herself. She didn't even need to watch her hands, daily repetition allowing her to put it on without so much as an active thought.

After filling the furnace with fuel, she used her sister's magic to conjure a flame and ignite it. With the furnace alight, she checked to make sure everything was ready for her customer's arrival.

As usual Lethia, was in the training yards sparring with Yurith and Toshiko. Yurith noticed Talisan approaching and called a pause for the trio. "Lethia, take a break and head to the smithery," Talisan ordered before heading over to speak with the other lieutenants. She bid her companions a brief farewell and did as told.

When she arrived, she could see Milly wearing the apron, working the billows to ensure the flame was at the proper temperature. It allowed her to admire the muscles Milly had along her arms. Milly noticed Lethia approaching and turned to greet her properly.

"You're Lethia, I take it?" Milly asked before offering a hand. "My name is Milly. I've been given a contract by your uncle." Lethia took her hand, silently staring at her. "What? Something the matter?"

"Um... just, wondering why you feel different," Lethia managed.

"Oh? I have command of some dark spirit magic myself, so I'm the perfect person to make you the halberd you need! Which is also why Talisan sent you here. I need your measurements for the halberd, both as a human and a werewolf." Lethia paled at being called out. "Oh, it was explained in the letter. Plus I can sense the demonic presence inside you, and even if you said you aren't a werewolf, it feels feral, and... young?" Milly blinked for a moment as suddenly her eye shifted from her human to demonic, causing Lethia to flinch, eyes igniting.

"She's... so young... practically an infant in terms of demonic years... older than you are for sure, yet still so naive. Where did you find such a young demon? Normally they are kept guarded with the utmost greed and care. How did you fuse it to yourself?! And the curse!" The questions came pouring, and Lethia felt too overwhelmed to realize the tone of voice was much more harsh coming from Milly. Shortly after, her eye returned to normal as she leaned back. "Sorry, just... so many questions about your powers. Could you explain how?"

"To be totally honest, if I did know how all this," Lethia gestured to her whole body, "happened, I don't think I would really tell anyone. All I know is I fell through a portal, and then I was on fire. Like a different fire, you know, not burning in agony. Which I guess I'll never experience now, yay?" Lethia said with confused enthusiasm.

"Aside from that, I'm still learning how to even use it. I mean, when I was feral, I was breathing fire, but now that I'm more myself, I don't know how to do it. Like, I can, but it feels weird. My human mind can't process the beast's mind of how to breathe fire. As well as a few other things."

"Don't you think you might have perhaps other kinds of magic? Like elemental magic or some other kind of demonic magic? Kind of like this..."

Milly reached to her hip to pull up her crossbow and aimed it at a nearby shield. Astral energies began to pool in the arrow track, forming a bolt before being blasted towards the target. Upon impact, the bolt of magic exploded in a small, concussive blast, causing the shield and some other hanging implements to fly in random directions. Milly and Lethia flinched as a few of them flew at them before Lethia looked back towards the blacksmith.

"I have absolutely nothing like that!" she exclaimed. "Best I could do, I think, is light arrows on fire."

"Well then maybe sometime later, I could help you out. We could figure out maybe what kind of magic you have. Granted, I'm not an expert, I've simply studied and experimented with my own powers," Milly explained as she put the crossbow away. "I'm gonna have to clean it all up." She huffed, her tone having a hint of sternness. Milly walked over to start picking up the weapons and tools she had blasted all over the place. "So how about you tell me what you would be doing with this halberd and we can go from there?"

"Well I was thinking I could probably use it for more than just poking and slashing at people," Lethia started as she sat on top of the furnace, the flames roaring below her. "Like, what if I could put some kind of spike or blunt object on the back end of it, then both sides could be lethal. At least it was before my Uncle said I shouldn't always be killing when hunting down bounties. So instead, I want it balanced in a way which makes the handle as viable a weapon as the head. I also want to use it to vault through the air." Milly finished cleaning up the tools and noticed Lethia sitting on a glowing red piece of equipment. "Perhaps some intricate handle design where I can spin it fast enough to create tornadoes. It's possible to accomplish that with magic, right? I don't know magic very well, but you seem to."

"Slow down!" Milly held up her arms. "Also why are you sitting on the furnace?"

"Well, when I said I don't burn anymore, I meant literally. In fact, fire is comfortable for me, the heat is cozy, and it feels nice for my muscles after a heavy workout," Lethia replied with a shrug.

"This woman is already driving me insane," Lilith silently remarked towards her sister, staying invisible.

"First of all, you can't have a weapon capable of doing ALL of that, plus you wouldn't have anywhere to actually grip the halberd if it can create any kind of wind current," Milly explained. "This does tell me I need to make a weapon that is very, very durable."

Lethia blushed at the remark.

"I've never actually seen how a smith makes tools or how magic affects it," she said, making the twins sigh collectively. Milly shooed Lethia off of the furnace and proceeded to take both human and demonic measurements. Shortly after, Felky arrived with a large basket filled with clothing that had been delivered for Lethia. All of it was made of her demonic fur so it could survive the heat given off from her transformations. Eagerly, she slipped on a red and blue shirt. The seams sewn into it were loose enough so when she transformed, they would pop without destroying the fabric, though since it was made of the tough demon fur, the odds of it tearing were minimal at best. She completed the outfit with a set of tan breeches and a pair of boots padded with her fur.

"These feel so comfy... plus, how in the world were they able to dye my fur like this? It's amazing! Thank you!" she exclaims happily, her hands running over her body, feeling the soft yet strong fabric against her skin.

Felky gave a salute before sprinting off, leaving the basket of clothes behind. Lethia knelt down and scooped it all up to look through the different outfits. A good amount were duplicates, there were a few outfits of varying colors and purposes, but not much more as other types of clothes would require leather or different fabrics. They were all also designed to be either easy to fall apart, or just relatively loose enough for Lethia to grow into. "Some of these look like they were made for nobles or very rich merchants."

"I'd love to wear something like these to a ball or when meeting with a high class client." Milly commented with a smile, pulling out some lacey hosiery. "I like how colourful they all are."

"Beats having it all be black. I'm not a maiden of Hilgith after all. Though there is something strangely alluring with an all-black attire."

"Some people just look really good in black," Milly replied with a bit of a shrug. "Anyway, I've got some work to do. You have to get back to training." She turned to start making notes and calculations on some nearby parchment. Lethia looked over at the parchment to see what she was writing, but she couldn't make sense of it so she headed off to continue her training in her new clothes.

"So why didn't you let her know about me?" Lilith asked her sister as they worked on the calculations together.

"I dunno, I guess I'm not used to revealing you to others still? I mean, even if we are technically sanctioned through our father's connections, it doesn't make people comfortable around demonic entities."

"Even if someone is equally possessed by one?" came the sassy response, causing Milly to sigh.

"I just... look, I don't know, okay? It's too confusing to worry about right now. We have a job. Let's focus on the job itself."

"Think we should do something for her armor as well?" Lilith offered. "That girl is gonna have a problem getting anything to go over all her fur. If it's made from her own demonic fur, I'm sure it can hold up to most blades, but eventually, something is gonna be too strong, or she's gonna get smacked with something blunt."

"When did you become conscious of other people, Lilith?" Milly replied sarcastically.

"I'm not, I'm thinking practically." She sighed, rubbing the bridge of her nose. "If we're building a weapon like this, don't you think you would rather make sure the bearer of said weapon survives?" Milly paused for a moment, thinking about what could happen if a bandit or something worse got a hold of what they were making.

"Well then, what kind of metal do you think would handle constant molding and heat at the same time?"

"I wasn't thinking about metal," Lilith replied. "I'm thinking studded leather imbued with some of her magic. If they have as much fur as they say, I might be able to use the material as an alchemical base to corrupt the leather, attune it to her. With any luck, not only would it gain the same resistance to fire as she does, but might even take on some of her curse and transform when she does. Granted, something like this is..."

"Difficult? Especially when working with leather? We make weapons, not leather armors. That's something we haven't worked with." Milly paused in thought. "When did I become you? Why are we trading places like this?"

"I guess it's because the demon possessing Lethia is a child in terms of demon years. Yes, I am considered a child in the same span, but I grew up here. Her demon grew up in hell, so is far older and grown, but isn't educated, young essentially. At least, that's the feel I'm getting. I guess I just wanna make sure the child inside of the red head is kept safe."

Milly paused for a moment before smiling.

"Two things to protect, got it. Though I would imagine that Lethia and the other silver shields would want to find a way to reverse such a curse."

"Talisan would know this best," Lilith said as she used her magic to adjust the heat of the forge. "Lethia's condition might be permanent now, just from the amount of time alone. Not only that, but I could feel that Lethia's soul and the demon are linked, almost a singular entity now. Besides, you think any greedy or self-righteous clergyman here would think of restoring such a 'creature' as her?" Milly's face softened, looking down at the metal she had selected, a deep breath, then a powerful huff through her nostrils as she grabbed the metal to begin her work.

The project took the twins the better half of a month, learning about the metals they were given to work with on top of the side project they judiciously agreed upon. Smelting the metals and then casting them required fire they couldn't make, so they ended up pulling Lethia aside, who was only too eager to help with the project. They were able to confirm Lethia's demonic flames were indeed capable of reaching temperatures hot enough to melt the adamantium into the molds. They instructed her on how to keep the metals at a steady heat. The process also taught Lethia how to maintain the weapon herself should it ever be needed.

Taking the weapon outside to the training yard, Lethia held the halberd in her hand. The head was a wide axe blade with an extended spear tip, and a beak-like hammer opposite of the blade, good for hooking or blunt strikes. It was made with mithril that was fashioned onto an adamantium core, to ensure both perfect balance and durability that not even Draconians could break. She tested the grip she had on the weapon, spinning it a few times.

"It feels so... light," she said with a smile, becoming a bit more experimental. She spun it from hand to hand, bringing it around her body, very aware of the bladed tip. After a bit more flourish, she stepped forward and swung the blade at the minimum distance she could. The axe head cleaved through a training dummy no different than the air around her. Not expecting how easily the blade was able to cut through the target, she over-extended and lost her balance before laughing. "Whoa! This is...it's... wow this is sharp."

"Thank your uncle. He's the one footing the bill for everything, and supplying the material," Milly said, feeling pride well up inside. "I also decided to take up a bit of a task as a sort of gift, for you and your uncle, as a thank you for letting us work with such exotic materials." Milly held up a finger and ran back to the forge, leaving Lethia to ponder what in the world the gift was. A short time later, the dark-skinned blacksmith returned and presented Lethia with a set of studded leather armor with some shoulder pads. Lethia chuckled nervously.

"Wow it's armor, which might last me a single fight," She joked.

"Actually, it's more than normal leather. Hearing about your clothing predicament, we realized you'd also have no real armor to wear. I mean, sure, your clothes could resist blades the same way your fur would, but what about silver? Or blunt weapons? That in mind, I tried my hand at a bit of magic. This leather is lined with your fur on the inside, and bathed in a special alchemical mixture to try and impart the properties of your werewolf form into the armor. We had a little help from the twins in the project since they study alchemy more than I do."

Now intrigued, and knowing very well the excitement of having her own weapon was a good point to make herself transform, Lethia slipped on the leather armor. She wasted no time fitting it over her head, onto her shoulders and buttoning it up along the side, using a special fixture to lock in place. With everything on, Lethia took a breath and let herself hope. Her eyes erupted in flame more and more until she began to transform into her lycan state. As she transformed, the leather armor glowed and began to morph alongside her, turning from full studded leather armor into something akin to a leather chest piece and shorts, as unlike Lethia, the material couldn't gain or lose mass magically. When she looked down at herself, her eyes only erupted more as she was overjoyed.

"I have armor! And weapons! I actually have clothes I can wear and not worry about them breaking!" Forgetting herself, she jumped at Milly to give her a tight hug, giving the blacksmith barely enough time to ward herself from Lethia's more than excited fire.

"Hot, HOT, HOT! Lethia, I'm not fireproof!" She screamed, and Lethia backed off with a massive blush.

"Sorry, I'm just...how could I... this, this is something I never thought I could have," she said before finally realizing her clothes were on the floor, having fallen apart as they were designed. "Even the clothes work as intended... I didn't know how far my uncle would go for me..." She started sobbing, unable to keep herself from crying in joy from the kindness she had been shown after two years of tribulation. Milly smiled and picked up her clothes.

"You truly have a wonderful family. Come on, why don't you call it a day now and go through your clothing? Now you have everything proper for a mercenary, I'm sure your uncle is going to have you working out in the field. I think I'll stick around a bit more, see if your uncle has a few more jobs I can do around here."

"Sooner than you think," Talisan spoke up as he approached the two women. "I just received an S.O.S call from the Northern Pride, they have a team cornered by undead. Lethia, you're going to be part of the rescue team."

Chapter 6

The clouds simmered below a low window sill of an imperial tower overlooking the ocean of fluff. The emperor yawned and stretched, watching the sun climb high enough to crest over its own blanket, as if to wake up at the same time. Light spilled into the room, reflecting off his wise, piercing yellow eyes. His scales were a deep, rich blue, though they were showing signs of faded color that came with aging Draconians. His physique, however, was still the epitome of his kind. Broad shouldered and rippling muscles beneath a clean and unbreaking sheet of scales glittering dimly in the light, polished daily. Wings stretched lazily behind him, spanning the room when fully extended. The top of his head sported very short frills which hardly moved, the only trait not immediately idealized in his culture.

With a grim nod, the Draconian began to dress in his customary regalia. A flowing morning gown of royal blue, white and gold silks intricately woven with the royal emblem on the chest. A golden dragon's head, noble and thoughtful, to show the imperial intelligence and wisdom the bearer chose to lead his people with, for as long as the people chose to listen. While dressing, a letter from Talisan fell off a nearby dresser. Sparing the moment to kneel down to pick it up, he remembered the contents. He had requested the guild leader to inform him how well Yurith was doing. He took great care to know about the incredible feats of his kin from beyond his borders.

Stepping out from his quarters, two guards, covered in enough armor to look more like machines, saluted in unison the instant he came into vision. "Morning, your grace," echoed from below the helmets of both guards while the emperor nodded in recognition. Both guards fell back behind him in a simple procession leading to the main banquet hall. As he arrived, a smile crested his lips to see he had beaten the higher nobles here for once, a rather rare occasion, and he may eat his meal in relative peace. Walking towards a hearty morning banquet laid out at the same time every morning, he helped himself to a small variety of foods. His decree was that breakfast was not to be treated with any formal affair; it was too early in the day for all the gravitas.

That did not stop him from eating rich, of course, sliced candied apples, Fresh baked bread with cinnamon, fruit and other such treats baked within. Fresh cheese, and meats hunted from across the known world. Fruits of all kinds: grapes, strawberries, pears, peaches. Even a hearty porridge made with dried goods diced into a rich aroma of savoury sweetness. The emperor helped himself before turning back towards his two guardsmen. A simple nod, and the two soldiers took it as permission to relax enough to help themselves to the food. His two personal guards were also nobles, so they had the right to eat at the lords hall.

Shortly after, another door opened into the large banquet hall, and two more Draconians walked inside, one of similar height to the emperor and the same piercing yellow eyes. While only an inch or two shorter than him, he bore similar traits to the emperor. Frills lining either side of the back of his head, forming a pseudo crown, typically ran flat down the back of his head unless he wished to make a statement or draw attention, unlike his father. Blue scales running along his body with only a few, if any, signs of the more delicate problem their race was having. Seeing the emperor was first to arrive, both boys paused and bowed at the same time, though the little one, who had similar eyes yet his frills did not form a crown, needed a slight prompt from his brother.

"Good morning, Lord Father," the older brother spoke with a tone of humbled authority, prompting his father to shake his head. With a raise of his hand, he signaled them to be at ease, and the smaller one smiled and ran forward.

"Good morning, Father!" cried the youngest and gave the Emperor a hug, making the emperor chuckle and place a hand on his head. He had only put on a set of silk pants and stockings, wanting to try and catch his father before he was too busy. "Are you going to get to eat with us today?"

"It appears I may get the chance to do so this morning, yes," he spoke, the authority and wisdom in his voice inadvertently making everyone within earshot pause and turn towards him. A deep, reverberating tone, even when speaking humbly, had a tendency to echo in the halls around him. An intentional design of the construction around him so he had a simpler time speaking over the crowd. "Come, help yourself to the food this morning." With the open invitation, both sons took their own plates and began to help themselves to breakfast.

"I'm surprised the nobles have not come here already begging for your guidance, or for permission to execute the tunnel workers again for lack of progress. No spies or alerts, or emergency morning meetings. Is the world finally at peace?" the older sibling commented while helping himself to the food, already wearing his day wear which consisted of a plate hauberk bearing the royal emblem and padded leggings with a set of boots. "Or maybe the dragons have returned to our world and all the nobles are in too much awe to be aware of the spectacle before them."

"You talk like you've met dragons yourself, Faffy," replied the youngest as he jogged towards a table with his plate of food, jostling as he did so. His father normally would remind his son not to run in such a way, but he was still young enough to enjoy being a child, plus on such a rare occasion, there was no harm in letting his energy show. Fafnir rolled his eyes at the comment and at the childishness of his younger brother before looking at his father, who merely smiled and gave a light shrug. The elder son shook his head, wordlessly saying he didn't approve of the behavior, but he smiled all the same. Eventually, the three sat down, having breakfast together in a rare opportunity to simply eat as a family.

The main banquet doors opened, and a few lords and ladies walked in, ruining the atmosphere that had been presiding in the room as they chatted about the day ahead of them. Upon seeing the emperor, a few immediately began to approach him, asking about the daily plans, the potential renovations to the castles, economics and other such affairs typically the emperor's duty. Knowing his time with his family was at an end, he let his children continue to eat in peace while guiding the flock of nobles away. Fafnir shook his head as he drained a goblet of wine.

The youngest noble looked up to his brother before asking in a rather nervous tone, "Fafnir, are you going to become busy as well?"

"Yes, and so will you, Ladon. As the children of the emperor, we must live up to his name and responsibility." He replied, lowering his face to hide his grimace as he saw a painful reminder of his people's ailing needs. Even their royal bloodline was affected as he saw how few scales were on his little brother's back. A grim reminder Draconians were losing the very thing which was their race's namesake, their very tie to the legendary dragons themselves.

They didn't worship the gods as the rest of Celosia did, though they recognized their very clear existence. They worshiped their ancestors, the dragons. The gods had made the dragons extinct generations ago, long before his father was even born. It made the young prince furious that they have yet to find a cure for him and his people. Eventually, Fafnir stood up, leaving a little of his breakfast on his plate. "I have work I must attend, I'll see you later in the day," he told Ladon, his voice a slight hiss, though well hidden under his brotherly tone as he walked down the hall to the throne room where his father was carried off, leaving his young brother alone with the guards.

Fafnir walked the halls in thought, looking over the architecture of their noble estate on the top of the mountain. He paused, noting how the clouds had parted, allowing the sun to gleam down a carpet of gold upon the large capital of the Draconian empire. The castle was built into the very mountain itself, peaking over the lands and allowing them to see far beyond the borders of their nation. Though his gaze was locked upon the golden shimmer of the noble and common estate below, draconians going about their daily lavishings and drills. They were a powerful, noble and rich land, filled with pride and prosperity. Knowing how the rest of the world was like, how misguided the commonwealth and the three kings were, he pondered. Why have they not marched their superior might and wisdom over the lands?

Glaurung sat in his throne at the head of the table filled with the delegates representing the differing aspects of his council. Military, economics, diplomacy and lesser representations of the people, land and slaves. The normal morning routine as the emperor listened to the lords' express concerns of minute details regarding issues, many of which were nothing to truly require his direct attention, but were to merely serve the nobles' own agendas of raising their stature above one another. Fafnir walked into the hall and silently took his seat at his father's right, listening in on all the rants and arguments of what shall be done. In hushed tones, the pair spoke to one another. "Breakfast was nice for once..."

"For once it was, yes..." came a solemn response from his father. "So what of your estate? What do you need for my endless wisdom and guidance?"

"I've come to direct this conversation towards a more pressing issue." Fafnir spoke up deliberately to catch the attention of the nobles. A few glares came from them for being interrupted, though none dared speak back to the emperor's son. Having everyone's attention, including his father, Fafnir continued. "You are all aware of it, so are the lower nobles and commoners. We are losing what makes us proud dragon people. We are losing our scales and our heritage with each successful generation. Only our emperor remains the pure symbol of what our proud people once were. I ask our emperor simply, what plans do you have to fix this problem, something of which is in dire need of correction now instead of later." He paused for a moment to allow someone else to make a comment or remark, but when no one spoke up, he pressed on. "I for once believe we should abolish the idea of allowing people to mate or take on Huldra as wives or husban-"

"We shall not impede on the tradition or the agreement our two races have," Glaurung's voice rang like a bell striking without warning. The following silence was deafening. "We will respect the only people who give us the connections we have to our hollowed ancestors. Anything less than cohabitation would be an insult to the people who give us the chance to speak with them."

"I have no intention of speaking down or disrespecting them, fa... your grace. I speak of this only as a means of preserving that exact heritage." A few nobles nodded, though Glaurung could sense the hollowness of the statement. He also knew why the nobles were agreeing: his people had grown fat, proud and arrogant. They had been prosperous for years, and his people aged slowly. While the other races lived fleeting, rapid lives, it made them flexible and strive to improve what little they ever had.

"Regardless, the stance we have with them shall not change, or would you rather deal with the split families and being rejected to speak with our hallowed ancestors. We cannot force them into our service, their gods would not allow us to subjugate them. We would be wise not to risk the wrath of those who were able to wipe clean the living breath of our hallowed ones,"

Glaurung spoke, and a grim silence fell through the crowd, followed by a subtle aura of malice, many of them knowing the history of the extinction of the dragons. They were spared because they were loved by Minerva herself, the mortal icons of her strength and diligence, the only god they truly respected. Fafnir opened his mouth to speak again, but hesitated enough to realize the topic was finished. "Stay here after the meeting is finished," his father ordered beneath his breath. His son nodded.

After the rest of the morning delegations turned the hands of time into the early noon, they began to disperse to take care of their respective manors and estates. A very select few remained behind, namely Fafnir, the General-commander and the head of foreign affairs. Silence drifted between them as the door shut for the last time, and they finally all stood in unison headed towards the back of the hall behind the emperor's throne. There, Glaurung muttered an incantation, and an illusion faded to reveal an iron door sealed with heavy metal bars. Two men took a side each and pulled, requiring their combined strength to pry the bars open so they could help themselves inside, a necessary precaution. The chamber opened and led into a small den with a portal residing inside. Stepping inside, the emperor turned and pulled the doors shut, the bars sliding back into place with an echoing clang. A lever on the other side of the door was the only mechanical way to open it from within.

Stepping through the swirling portal of blue and green, the four men appeared in a laboratory hidden away in an undisclosed location. Around them, potions, glass and oddities marked the shelves, and the sickly hue of green draconians scrambled about in a seemingly chaotic fashion. Though what looked like a cluttered mess of vials and ingredients of which were looking to be haphazardly placed was actually an intricate dance, of which alchemical scaled scientists had nearly memorized as they reached for vials or ingredients without looking, or moved past one another wordlessly, slithering in a uniform dance of venom and disease. Eventually, one of them paused his macabre dance to approach the party and gave a deep bow, kissing the very feet of the Emperor. "Your lordships, welcome back to the royal labs," the head scientist greeted them, his voice a sickly wisp, requiring a bit of strain to hear properly with his face so low to the ground. "I'm to know you are here to discuss the progress of our project?"

"That is correct, Hisshire. Have you managed to make any leads into what we are searching for?" Glaurung inquired, his voice a more gentle tone to avoid having it echo and bounce off the delicate glass. Too many times, he had allowed his voice to boom and ruin many an experiment, something even he needed to respect, lest he destroy everyone within the tower. With a flourishing sweep, the alchemist stepped backwards, and the other scientists began to clear a path to allow the four to walk without disturbing the many experiments and the delicate, confusing dance of the macabre around them. Fafnir swallowed his feelings of disgust; Unlike his father or his two trusted delegates, the prince found green Draconians repulsive.

Pushing a door open, the four were finally granted a reprieve from the snaking crowd as they came into a grand hall. Moldy tomes and books lined the walls around them, knowledge copied, pilfered or left behind around the world. A library of experiments and wisdom, both forgotten and forbidden. At the center of the large hall was an intricately drawn diagram made in blood, chalk and dust in an arcane pattern of which only the original artist would know what symbols were actually embedded into the stone itself. Six cages were positioned equal distances from one another around the outermost circle, with a throne in the very center of the diagram, many sizes too large for even the emperor, and on the seat, a single dagger.

"This is where our research has brought us, a duplication of what we believe is the correct spell to enact the magic that can resurrect the dragons of old," Hisshire croaked out in pride, stepping gingerly over the bloodied carvings in the floor, trailing clawed fingers over the stone work. "This of course is not charged with the appropriate magics for it to work here. The royal labs here are far too small for the dragon to be able to even leave this room, let alone even stand to his mighty height. We would have to replicate this all on the highest point of the royal castle, sadly where the gods could see from their high thrones."

"Such a place is higher than any god's throne. What would make you assume they could see it so easily?" Fafnir asked in a curt tone. A cough from his father silenced him, though a cursory glare told the emperor this conversation wasn't over.

"We have had to place many, many seals and spells to hide this very room from the eternal watch of the five gods, especially the one who has gifted us with his wisdom and cursed us with sickness. The father of invention and knowledge has always a keen eye for those of his ilk after all. Though we worship the dragons as superior as all others of our kind, we know more than well enough, should he learn of our dealings, he would be one of the first to smite us all with the hollowed curse which ravages my brothers and sisters." The response made Fafnir wince at the idea of becoming as sickly and weak as the green scaled draconians before him, the other delegates replicating his reaction.

"There is still too much up in the air upon the more... delicate intricacies of such a powerful spell. What we do know is, to bring a dragon back from death itself, from the black goddess after holding them prisoner for so long, is sadly impossible. Such a spell would require the blood of two entire worlds which simply cannot be gathered. So we have surmised a compromise. We believe we can find a way to instead transform your grace into a dragon himself, to become a lord of all living beings. Instead of resurrection, polymerization."

Fafnir walked around the circle, looking at the six cages and noting the dagger on the throne, getting an idea of what the spell would entail. This was the first time he was brought into this chamber, clearly being entrusted with something kept a top secret. A secret he would die keeping indeed. Such a powerful spell would of course require very powerful catalysts. It was clear why the only two delegates allowed inside were the head of all military and the head of foreign affairs.

"I see, so I am to assume you're seeking permission to use the viewing platforms on the top of the castle for this experiment?" Glaurung asked, and even with strain to control his voice, it echoed around the room. "I'll see that it is done and the room be made only accessible to those with the privilege to be there. Minister, see what you can do to find what catalysts will be needed." The Minister bowed respectfully, one of the very few draconians who, due to his position, was not blinded by pride, yet was fiercely loyal to his lord and country above all else. The general looked onward at the cages, already considering what might need to be done.

"Anything else, my liege?" The science mage asked eagerly, standing tall with anticipation.

"No... I believe our duty is done here for now... let's return to the castle. Keep us updated on any findings regarding this experiment, or anything else of particular note."

"Of course, your highness." Both the minister and head scientist echoed at the same time, before the group of four returned to the castle. Fafnir hesitated, looking back at the room, and at the dagger, most of all. He finally noted the blade itself was vamprilite, a rare demonic metal that could leech life. It became very clear in his mind what was to come, and of the conversation he certainly had in mind to speak of with his father.

As the group returned to the meeting room, Glaurung and his General stood together for a moment. "It might perhaps be time to visit the Commonwealth and pay respects to the notables there, specifically Hicoth and the lieutenant Yurith." The General suggested while reaching for what few documents he brought with him on the table. Glaurung looked towards him thoughtfully. "We still have friends. Not all of our kind who defect from the empire think of us as cruel slavers. Those who actually know what you are like, anyway."

"You would hardly think they would consider helping with such a scheme, do you?" Glaurung replied, a little surprised, though this only resulted in a laugh from his childhood friend.

"Absolutely not, but we're not looking for co-conspirators. They would more than bat an eye if we came down to ask people to join in a political plot putting leaders and notables at risk. Besides, you know it does relations well for the other kingdoms to see you in person, as you enjoy doing. Those loam breathers still recognize how dangerous a foe you are and wouldn't dare risk coming after you. Nobody would, or else risk a tide of enraged draconians washing over the lands."

"Assuming they lived long enough to even reach me through you and your elite," Glaurung replied with a nod. "Very well, it would be nice to be out and about in the green and lush, and away from the lazy incompetence of my lords." He rubbed the bridge of his nose in distaste. "When did our people become so-"

"Spoiled, your grace? As glorious as your rule has been, perhaps it has been too successful. Our golden age seems to have no true end, not so long as you rule over us. The other kingdoms are terrified of the notion of attacking us, plus the Commonwealth and Three Kings have never been able to see eye to eye long enough to consider wanting to regulate us. We have been growing unchecked, and it shows. I mean, look at what we're plotting now. We are literally plotting against the gods themselves, which, even I'll admit, feels foolish."

"I agree, it does. Yet if the gods refuse to cure us of our ailment, then we will take the matter into our own hands, as they have clearly told us by their inaction. Though I cannot truly blame them. If ruling as emperor is as tiresome as this, I could scarcely imagine the tribulations a god deals with on their day to day. Still, we should suspend this conversation now, this room is hardly a safe enough place for it. I'll set things in motion so I will be free to journey with you, friend."

Fafnir had retired to his room, locking the door behind him as he looked around. His room contained books of all kinds, scrolls and parchments of military strategy, economic theory and many other scholastic necessities for ruling an empire. Running a hand along his chin, he paced the room for a moment before stopping in front of a window curtain. "Did you hear enough?" Silence filled the room as the curtain flowed gracefully in a breeze. "Good... I was just shown something... interesting. Details I cannot surrender yet, but certainly knowledge you would murder your own master for. I need you to go and find me power. Not items or relics, people. Give me a list of names of people who stand out, of people who have a unique strength about them. People whose blood would make for an offering even Minerva would have to be equal." The curtains billowed lazily as if the prince was speaking to only the wind itself. Then the curtain went still.

Chapter 7

Nervousness was a constant emotion Lethia was dealing with during the march to the frontier lands which bordered the Grave of the Gods. Swamp land normally too hostile to colonize, the country offered monetary rewards for people to try and reclaim the land and make it into fertile living land. While the swamps were deemed to be Hilgith's territory, the goddess of death, her disciples had informed officials the goddess was okay with this development. Zealots, blind in their religious fervor to the black goddess, contested such expansions into their hallowed lands. The guilds would take turns patrolling the borders of the grave swamps as well to ensure nothing too dangerous could slip into the country.

The Silver shields had been contracted by one of their fellow guilds, the Northern Pride, in the rescue and reclamation of a frontier village that had been overrun with zombies. The implications being that, if the town fell, there would be no security checkpoint between the village and the farmlands that the swamps were being converted into. Years of terraforming and reclamation was at risk of being devoured by the seemingly living swamp land, and the heretical fanatics who opposed the expansions. Having been from a frontier town herself, Lethia understood such dangers of the town falling.

However, it wasn't the swamps, the undead, or the fact this was her first mission and her uncle would not be present to watch her which made her nervous.

Lethia was nervous because the only person who knew and trusted her was Yurith, the lieutenant who was chosen to lead this job. The other members of the team only knew Lethia as the Hellhound, and they were suspicious of her. The only reason they did not attempt to simply kill Lethia was because their loyalty to Talisan was strong enough to go along with it, but they questioned the authenticity of Lethia being safe enough to travel with. It was only made worse as the tension Lethia was feeling made it far too easy for her to transform and reveal herself, forcing the party to avoid major roads and any other town along the way.

Lethia offered to go hunt for game, wild fruits and vegetables for the band of mercenaries, since her heightened senses made such a task very easy for her. It also helped the young mercenary to train her senses and make logic of all the sensory information she received. She was bringing back two bucks she had hunted down, coming into the camp as a number of the guild members were talking with Yurith.

"I still don't think having this demon in our midst is a good idea," came a mild, growling voice. Lethia paused and kept out of sight as she watched and listened. The same man continued on, "Fine, so she's Talisan's niece and the only living family left outside of his now insane sister. We get it, but it don't clear her name. She's still a demon, a monster! What if this is a ploy of some kind? Some greater demon brainwashed her as a sleeper agent, sent to try and kill us off one by one. Perhaps she hasn't mastered her werewolf powers and she goes insane and just slaughters everyone. We know how werewolves work: they either go insane or take their own lives. How could she be any different!?"

"I hear your complaints, and having worked with her personally, I can assure you she has control over herself." Yurith replied to a mature looking man, his features scarred, not aged yet reaching the tail end of his youth. He had been a warrior for quite some time and has garnered a reputation of being level headed in the most extreme cases. However, Talisan refused his requests to become a lieutenant because of his short sighted nature, having problems picking up small details when viewing the larger scope of things. "You're missing the fact that if Lethia were to have difficulties containing herself, Mason, then Ember would've needed to be visiting the healers far more often."

"She DOES visit the healers regularly, for burns. Don't think I haven't noticed, Yurith. She had burns on her body that need to be treated every month or so. That's easily once a full moon," Mason replied, arms crossed as he stared right at Yurith.

Lethia hung her head. Those nights were indeed full moons, but the burns were because of nightmares and the fact her transformation caused her body to heat up. Ember's selfless embrace helped her calm down and regain herself after such horrible nightmares, even if she endangered herself in doing so.

"I'll keep following orders, but know this isn't just my own stance, this is all of us. If she does anything to you, the rest of us will bring her down. We easily have the equipment needed to do so."

Two heavy thuds caused the group to jump as Lethia threw the bucks near the campfire. She walked over and took an empty seat by the flames, still in her werewolf form while taking a moment to look over the group. The conversation hurt, but she knew it was relatively justified. "So..." She began, taking a slow breath as she pulled out a knife from a nearby bag.

"Who wants the first piece!" she shouted with a big smile, acting like she never heard a thing. The rest of the group stared at her, confusion written clearly across their faces. "Oh come on, someone tell me, otherwise I'm just gonna chomp down on these guys. I'm hungry!"

"I'll take a leg since you're offering," Yurith said, giving a smile before looking over to Mason. He gave Yurith a solemn look before relenting as the rest of the soldiers began to make requests, softening up a little. They didn't like working with her, but they knew well enough they may as well deal with it. They were professionals, after all. They voiced their concerns and complaints, so there was not much they could do unless they were given a reason to out the werewolf. Lethia meanwhile carved up the catches and handed them out for the soldiers to roast them over the fire.

As the night waned, Lethia got ready to take over for watch. She was in her human form again as she walked over to Mason, who sat on a stump, axe in hand and a buckler on his arm. "Hey, my turn to watch. Go get what rest you can."

Hefting his axe and gripping it, he stood up and faced her. Before he could say anything, Lethia spoke up, "Yes, I get it, you don't trust me." Her voice stayed flat, her eyes alight, but her expression was calm. "If I were you, I wouldn't trust myself either, an emotional demonic beast. All this mistrust isn't helping me relax either, and I'm scared of turning on people. You wanna try and kill me, there isn't much stopping you right now, so if you really dare try, then do it." Mason stared at her for a good long minute, silence stretching between them.

"My respect for your uncle is what's stopping me. Even if you weren't a monster, you're still an unbloodied rooky who is being given a chance simply because you have power and lots of it. You hardly know how to control or wield it, let alone what it means to actually be a mercenary, a warrior," he replied, his voice harsh. "You're just some girl corrupted into a monster, one who should be put out of her misery."

"Do I seem miserable to you?" she asked. "Do I look like someone who is suffering? Crying, begging 'why did this happen to me?'" She chuckled, but it turned into a sigh. "Well, you're not wrong, but you're not correct either. Yeah, I don't like what happened to me. I hate what I did during those two years. However, like Talisan was helping to teach me, I shouldn't be bottling it all up inside, letting it all sit and fester. Seeing only the negative and letting it swallow me up would make things worse." Walking past him, she looked up to the moon as it was descending over the swamp lands.

"So I choose to be happy. I choose to look at what I've become as more of a left-handed gift. Oh I did horrible things I'm not proud of, but I have something that can give me a chance to make up for it. To atone, and to atone for it I have to live with it. So I choose to be happy, I choose to try and keep a healthy emotional state. It's hard, but it's better than being miserable all the time." Mason gave her a look of distrust. Hearing it and saying it was always easy. "Go rest, we still have a lot of traveling to do." Having heard her piece, Mason hefted his gear and turned away before looking over his shoulder.

"You know I don't sleep with you on guard."

"Only Yurith does," she replied, looking out towards the sky.

The following days' travels were very much the same, the rest of the soldiers keeping a wary eye on their demonic companion. Lethia being on edge was a boon as she was ready for when they finally arrived near the frontier town. The swamp land had regrown unnaturally forward and had engulfed half the town, indicating someone was pushing the swamp lands back into reclaimed territory. There were also a number of undead wandering the fields beyond the village outskirts, making any approach difficult.

Yurith had Lethia scout the surrounding area, giving her explicit instructions not to get involved with heroics. She could engage stragglers while the rest of the soldiers started clearing the outskirts. Running off, Lethia transformed so she could make better use of her supernatural speed to get in and find out what she could.

Lethia had been told about the undead, though seeing, let alone smelling them, made her suddenly wish she was anywhere else. With her heightened sense of smell, the necrotic scent of long dead corpses left her blind at first. To help combat this, she tried breathing fire through her nose. The flames helped burn off much of the smell, allowing her to see.

She regretted looking at the face of a rotting husk as it shambled towards her. Without even thinking, her halberd flashed through the air and cleaved the face in half. The undead body crumpled in front of her into a pile, unmoving. "Huh... they arn't... all that scary, disgusting for sure, but pretty frail."

Getting to the walls of the village wasn't much of a task. Much of the undead were simple zombies with no direct control or guidance, merely following sounds from where they last heard them. They would bump into one another or trip over the most simple of hurdles, filling Lethia with confidence as she approached the village.

Claws digging into wood, she scaled the palisade walls and peaked into the village. The village itself was overrun with undead, many of them zombies, but she noted skeletons, acting much like legionary soldiers. Sporting spears and towering shields, they seemed surprisingly more collected than the wandering and mindless dead flesh. Their bones were also black, as if charred by flames. They were few, but wearing relatively impressive equipment. Staying on the walls, she crawled along the horizontal surface like a spider, moving sideways to get a better view where she could.

After a few minutes of searching, she spotted the Northern Pride, indicated by a banner waving off the town hall which they fortified. Skeletons had blockaded the structure, preventing those inside from escaping, but refused to press the advantage of numbers. "Looks like the undead are trying to starve them out..." Lethia muttered to herself. She could not figure out what was happening but felt confident they would be able to help. Dropping down, she made her way back to the war camp.

Mercenaries kept the perimeter clear, cutting down any undead that stumbled into range. They knew from experience that ranged weapons were hardly efficient against undead, so they relied on blade and axe. A few soldiers sported clubs and morning stars as secondary weapons, expecting skeletons at some point.

Lethia cleared the horde, going wide around the group and entered the camp from behind. There, she found Yurith taking stock of other reports the other scouts had brought him. "Your report?" Yurith asked, covered in stone and ichor.

"Sir, the inside of the village is overrun, zombies running amok within. But I noticed the skeletons in there are different."

"Different? How so?" Yurith asked while clearing off the gunk from the boulders on his body.

"They seem professional, like a legion. They are wearing heavy armor with tower shields and spears. I think I saw some crossbows as well, but I didn't risk getting any closer than the village wall. They were also charcoal black, like they were burned."

"Well then, this is certainly a development. We're dealing with a rather infamous necromancer," Yurith replied, pulling out a map from a nearby satchel. "Malik 'Black Bones'. He was exiled into the swamp land a long time ago for malicious practices. Not necessarily in the art of necromancy, but what he had accomplished. Supposedly, when he finished his classes, he had killed not only his teacher, but every single one of his peers. He summons skeletons with charred bones, supposedly because of a mishap during his classes. Though zombies normally aren't his thing. Apparently, he doesn't like the smell of dead flesh. That tells me either he's not alone, or these are plague zombies, which is far more dangerous."

"Plague zombies? Wait, those are the ones that transmit the virus once they bite someone, right?" Lethia asked.

Yurith nodded gravely, then turned around. "Mason! We have vital information. These are likely plague zombies. Ensure everyone is prepared and properly armored. One bite will spell the end for any of us. Our objective hasn't changed, but we have knowledge of a necromancer in the area. Do not engage the necromancer on your own, and be sure everyone is kept in groups of three. You and Lethia will be with me."

"Sir!" Mason saluted before running off to pass the word along to the others.

"This is your first mission, you need to be with us. As powerful as you are, we're fighting against numbers that can overwhelm us if we're not cautious. Therefore, I'm going to be keeping a close eye on you."

"What? Why?" Lethia protested. "I'm more than strong enough to handle a bunch of dumb unde-"

"That's the exact attitude that will get you or another killed, Lethia, so shut up and fall in line," Yurith ordered. With a nervous gulp, she nodded, suddenly feeling the tension more than ever. The thought she was going to be stuck in her wolf form for this entire endeavor crossed her mind. With a resigned sigh, she grabbed her halberd and prepared herself for what seemed like a long and grueling campaign.

"Just double checking, but the plague, it can't be cured, right?" Before Yurith could give an answer, Mason returned.

"Sir! Orders are given, but we have spotted a patrol of skeletons headed our way. I think they mean to intercept us before we're able to get into the town. Looks like a small squad of them, five or six."

"Two teams will engage the skeletons, the rest will provide cover around the flanks. If this is really Malik's goons were facing, they are no mere brainless undead. They will be drawing the attention of the zombies." Yurith turned to Lethia and nodded, then led the trio towards the fight itself.

Lethia didn't know how to feel between the anxiety and the sick feeling in her stomach and lungs from the undead. The harshness of Yurith's orders, a side of him she had never really seen. She hadn't been on a proper mission with him, and up until now, she thought he was the most relaxed. This change in personality shook her. To top all of this off, any mistake could be fatal. This wasn't a moment where she could get stabbed and walked it off. Any kind of bite or piercing of her skin by a zombie, she would die. She was so swamped in the emotion, she never realized how automatic her body was acting. The halberd slicing and piercing the decaying, soft flesh without as much as a second thought. She had become a machine working on raw instinct, not paying attention yet focused all the same.

Lethia didn't realize just how scared Yurith actually was for his team, especially her.

The skeletons proved to be harrowing opponents. While the Silver Shields specialized in fighting undead, these ones were quite skilled. Yurith guided his team to the flank where Lethia could focus on easier opponents as opposed to the elite skeleton guard. Her pride felt hurt. Even after training with the lieutenants for so long, she wasn't being trusted to fight against more dangerous opponents.

Her halberd proved to be quite helpful in keeping the shambling numbers at bay. With the skeletons shattered by her allies, the elite squad pushed forward, cutting through the undead to make their way into the village proper. They needed to link up with the Northern Pride members quickly to ensure they were okay.

Once they reached the walls, Yurith displayed the true strength a draconian could wield. Summoning a number of loose rocks from around the battlefield, he created a boulder made of pebbles, stones and other debris, throwing it all at the door. A thunderous crash rattled the gate as the stones scattered, paused, then rapidly returned to his fist. Another throw, and the gates snapped and bent inward, mostly broken, but still in the way. One last gathering of stone, and the gates were sent scattered into splinters, the rocks and pebbles flying through the air and maiming many of the undead. A huff of annoyance escaped his mouth as he saw skeletons come out of hiding, having known about the threat.

"Our goal is to break into the town center. Clear the path, Shields!" Yurith commanded, and they took up formation, a large V charging through the main roads. As if knowing they were outclassed, the skeletons took up skirmish tactics, trying to flank and strike at the mercenaries from unprotected sides. It made the fight messy for both sides, but eventually, the mercenaries pushed their way into the town hall where the survivors and other guild members were holed up.

The first objective complete, and momentarily protected by the walls of the fortified building, the Silver Shields as well as the Northern Pride began to take stock of the situation. Lethia had scurried onto the roof top, hidden behind decorative croppings, and sighed. There would be panic and questions if she had gone inside with the others, so she kept hidden. All she could do was sit and watch, waiting for the signal for her to jump down and rejoin her comrades. "First mission and I can't be seen by anyone not of the guild... I'm so nervous I can't stop being in my wolf form," she mused, hugging her legs. "Yurith demands I don't go out on my own, even though I could handle zombies so easily. I know I can't just burn them, I'd set the whole village on fire. I'm so much stronger though, why couldn't I just hunt these undead down on my own?"

"Why not indeed, my peculiar adversary?" a voice echoed around her, causing her to jump, fire swirling around her body and leaving scorch marks on the roof. "When I saw you, I thought the swamps had finally begun to claim my sanity, but no! Here you are, a demon werewolf, working alongside the Silver Shields, a guild sworn to slaying your very kind!" the voice continued, and Lethia's heart sank. "Oh no no, don't worry, the others below cannot hear me through the roof. Your secret is safe. After all, I've already heard enough of your rampages and yet, how do you exist, I wonder?" The voice had a sinister yet scholarly tone, like a man who would dissect living creatures just to see how they work and discard them without a care. He was also strangely collected for someone she was told was a madman. Almost honest, in a strange sense. "I promise you, this little conversation is quite private."

A man in black robes hovered above the roof, landing nearby. Lethia brought up her halberd, ready for a fight, but the man simply tutted. "Such rude manners. Why don't we introduce ourselves? My name is Malik. If you're to blame me for this current outbreak, then I'm afraid you misjudged. This outbreak is from zealots of death who unleashed the plague. I just happened to be in the area and decided to... do some shopping. I left gold in the stores where needed, it's so rare I'm given an opportunity to come into any town. More so, it's half reclaimed by swamp land, so I'm by definition, not breaking any of my conditions of banishment."

Lethia's annoyance at being snuck upon showed through her mannerism and voice. "Well, forgive me if I trust you about as much as a draconian trusts a Fukai. I'll also have to apologize for being unable to share my name."

"Unable to share your name? Why? Do you suffer from amnesia? Poor, poor thing, no wonder the Silver Shields were able to recruit you," he mocked, turning his head enough for Lethia to get a good look. She guessed him to be between his forties and fifties, certainly aging yet toned and rugged. He didn't seem scrawny or malnourished. The necromancer looked to be rather methodical, but held himself like he could hold his own in a fight. He summoned a cane to his side and pulled the hood down, and she could see what looked to be armor fashioned into the shape of bones beneath.

"Actually, I don't believe you. No, you seem far too collected to be suffering from amnesia, especially since you've been around for, nearing four years now? If I were to guess your age from your bone structure, even in this form, I'd estimate you at early twenties, twenty one if I may be so bold." Her fire sparked at the uncanny guess, and Malik simply smiled. "It's simple, my dear. I study bodies, corpses. I could tell your age, your favorite food, what you enjoy spending your time doing and your specialty. That being said, you're a fresh recruit."

She felt a sickening sense of awe at his intelligence, though she refused to lower her guard. "Alright, alright, I get it, you're super intelligent and have a fetish for corpses."

"That just hurts," he pouted.

"Well I don't see it being remotely healthy spending all of your time around corpses and turning them into undead soldiers like this," Lethia challenged, her tail waving behind her to indicate the lands below.

"Poor little girl, you don't understand. It's about information! The dead know such secrets! Secrets which were meant to be taken to the grave, but I can dig them back up. Control the soul, the body long enough to extract juicy bits of information. After all, gold and strength of arms may lay the foundation of empires. Secrets are what tear it all down with. Yet you, you have me curious how you function, how you even exist. If you humor me with a question, I promise you I'll make things easier for you and your friends." Having heard him be so honest and straightforward, Lethia slightly lowered her halberd.

"I was bitten the same time I fell into a summoning circle. It was at an abandoned hut, I don't know anything beyond that," She explained, her hands twisting on the halberd nervously. "I'm guessing based on the magic, hell messed with the werewolf curse."

"It's a touch more complicated, dear Lycanthrope," he said, staring at her for a long moment. "You tell the truth, it seems, so I'll tell you this. It wasn't the energies of the demon realm alone, though I imagine they had to have some involvement. No, there is another soul inside of you, a demonic one. I'm not as well versed in demonology, but if I had to guess, a succubus." Lethia's eyes widened at the revelation that he could guess it. Who else would be able to simply feel her presence?

Without a word, the skeletons laying siege to the house suddenly began abandoning the village, leaving only the mindless hordes of the zombies, still quite numerous.

Lethia watched them leave with relief, unaware of Malik's subtle hand gestures. "Good. This means the rest of my team can clean up the horde a bit more easily."

"You're clearly still very new to all this, otherwise you would know more about who I am." Before Lethia could react, she found herself without anything below her. Turning to look back towards the necromancer, there was a faint shimmering distortion, muddling her vision of him. Flames crept into her vision, and she felt panic rise sharply from within, hot air rushing past her. A scream ripped from her lungs which drew the attention of everyone inside of the building.

Mercenaries turned to the windows, seeing a furry ball of fire falling past and striking the ground below.

Yurith got up and hurried outside to check on Lethia, shoving the door open, and the other Silver Shields followed after him. They noticed the skeletons had all left, but with the commotion, the zombies were now heading towards the town hall in force. "Shields! Hold them back!" he shouted out as the mercenaries split off to try and keep the massive horde off the perimeter. Yurith turned to go see how the young recruit was doing.

Malik was hovering over the roof, dark energy pooled in his hands ready. "Lieutenant, I'm surprised the head hasn't made himself available for this job. Still, I suppose delegation is pretty key in making sure one does not overburden themselves. She and I made an agreement. She told me something I wished to hear, and in return, I pulled back my forces. Now if you excuse me, I intend to take the hellhound with me. There is so much I could learn from studying her." Lethia gave a half groan, half growl, the impact from the fall having cracked a few bones. Yurith stomped on the ground and rocks burst from the earth, making the ground unstable. The encroaching undead would fall into pit traps, making it easy for them to be picked off.

"I'm afraid I cannot allow that. The powers of a hellhound would be far worse in hands such as your own, Malik," he countered, creating a small barrier around Lethia before Malik could get to her.

"Well, resourceful indeed," Malik noted as he fired bolts of black energy towards the Draconian. Stone intercepted the blasts, and Yurith watched them rot and melt away. Shedding the stone armor, he smashed a number of boulders together in order to ensure he had plenty of ammunition and resources for the fight ahead. "I'm beginning to see why you're the lieutenant... Your ability to assess the situation is impressive. However, I do not think I will leave here without her."

Yurith fired a number of rocks at Malik, who dropped down onto the ground. Energies coalesced into orbs of black, dripping masses of deathly fluid, and the two began to have a magic shootout, rock and acid flying back and forth. Yurith used the rock available to create shifting walls and barricades, his stance firm while Malik focused half of his magic on offense, the other making a barrier pop up to melt the rocks that came his way. Zombies began to climb the wooden walls, and the opponents had to split their attention between each other and the undead. Few stragglers would shamble over towards them, making the entire showdown only more complicated for the pair. Yurith's powerful martial prowess would crush or dismember a threat while keeping the rock and stone focused on Malik. The necromancer would summon bone implements, ripping them out of the walking corpses only to slice open others, giving him valuable tools to throw at the draconian in return. Such effort caused some holes in his magical defense, and rocks pelted against his sides and limbs.

Lethia could hear the fight from within, her head having stopped spinning from the fall and impact. She was hurting all over, though the pain was rapidly going away. As she assessed her situation, she realized her fire was still billowing underneath the stone dome, making it into a deadly furnace. Remembering how the heat of the smith's furnace acted, she got an idea. "Yurith! Can you hear me! Weaponize my fire!"

The draconian took one look at the dome, saw it was glowing bright from heat, and he clued in immediately. He made his way over to the dome, using stone to create a barrel and removed the rock from where it was placed. Heat and fire roared from within, spitting out in waves of vicious, hungry flames. Yurith directed the flames towards the undead who were incinerated in moments, ash and melting bone all that remained of those struck by the hell fire. Recognizing the danger of such potent fire, Malik retreated and watched as the makeshift flamethrower melted the encroaching hordes.

Eventually, the stone couldn't handle the raw temperature and began to melt into a more deadly fluid. Lethia stood up completely, her lycan body managing to regenerate enough of her broken bones so she could handle herself. Magma dripped off her body as she brandished her halberd, staring down the necromancer who chuckled. "My, my, such healing prowess. Of course, you're a werewolf, I shouldn't be surprised. Anything that isn't silver or holy is hardly permanent," he said, backing up from the pair in front of him. With Lethia healed up, he knew he was at a disadvantage. "Seems like my chances of winning have dramatically decreased, but Yurith, you're all out of stone."

Lethia turned in surprise. Yurith was only in a set of leggings and leathers. On top of that, despite her flames having cleared a large chunk of the zombies, many more were still coming. Lethia looked at Malik, then back to the zombies still clambering over the walls around them. Many of the defenders had retreated back into the town hall with the Silver Shields keeping the entrance clear. Remembering Malik claimed they weren't his, Lethia decided to rush the horde.

"Yurith, get back inside the town hall, I'll deal with the horde!" Lethia cried out as she ran over to them, halberd in hand. Yurith reached out to try and stop her, but his hand was burned from the heat coming off her body.

"Lethia, stop!" he yelled, but she was already off. Malik laughed as he refocused his magic to make himself invisible to the hordes. No point in spending more energy when everything was about to be overrun by the ravenous dead. What did it matter to him when he could enslave all their souls once they were all dead, or rather, undead.

Lethia launched herself at the undead as the beast she was, her halberd now super-heated and cleaving through the shambling corpses. Red steam hissed through the air as the fluids inside of the undead were vaporizing off the blade itself, making the grim duty far easier to handle. Realizing they had no sense of self preservation, Lethia began spinning the halberd in a horizontal circle, a deadly, flaming, spinning blade. However, each cold, long dead body was cooling the blade, and the numbers hardly seemed to dent. For each zombie cleaved, another one shambled in its place just as quickly. The flame on the halberd was getting cooler and cooler, but the inexperienced werewolf didn't pick up on it as the fire on her body roared with intensity. So much so it was drawing the undead away from the members of the Silver Shields who were holding the entrance.

The blade was slowly becoming gunked with flesh, making it harder and harder to cleave and cut through the seemingly endless hordes. Her blade finally caught in a zombie, forcing her momentum to a halt. She ripped the blade out, but the second it took was enough for a zombie to grab her arm. She quickly slashed it away with her claws, and batted another zombie away. They were within arm's reach now, and while grasping her body would burn off their limbs, the undead cared not unless they were able to get the bite of flesh they so desperately craved.

Yurith finally rushed into the crowd, having gathered what few rocks were left to form a battering ram and running over a fair amount of the horde, firing the rocks like a cannon blast. "Lethia, move!" he shouted as the werewolf looked towards him. Taking it as an order, she began to retreat. An unlucky grab caught her hair and yanked her backwards, catching her off balance. The horde descended on her in a moment, and Yurith followed suit. Fists, claws, scales, fur and flesh tangled, meshed and fought until the pair managed to get back up and stumble out of the fray and towards the safety of their team. The other Silver Shields were still occupied with the few zombies who were more interested in closer prey than Lethia. Once everyone was finally inside, the doors slammed shut, and the only sounds in the hall were gasps of shock, the rasping of breaths, and the pounding of the tireless horde outside.

Lethia felt exhausted and found her body turning human again. As her skin went from black to white, there were clear signs of a few bite marks on her shoulder and arms. Yurith sported a bite mark on his thigh from when a zombie caught him from below. Their eyes met, both panting heavily as the Silver Shields and the Northern Pride looked warily toward them. "Well Lethia... I'd scold you for being an idiot and rushing into a horde like that, but it hardly seems appropriate now." Yurith panted, looking down at his leg. Lethia grit her teeth and shook her head, forcing herself to stand up. Her leather armor was all she had on, her clothes still back at the camp.

Running over towards the Northern Pride's supply of medicines, she grabbed a number of them. The mercenaries and survivors refused to get anywhere near the woman as she hurried back to Yurith and began to try and bandage his leg, leaning down to even try and drink the diseased blood out from his wound. Yurith watched silently and Mason walked over, seeing how desperately Lethia worked to try and save the lieutenant. The scales and flesh around Yurith's wound slowly turn more pale and sickly, the disease spreading despite Lethia's best efforts, but he noticed her own bite marks refused to grow more infected. Yurith saw Mason's expression change to confusion, and noticed Lethia's wounds were healing despite the goddess's plague.

"Sir, Lethia's wounds, aren't they infected anymore?" Mason noted, placing a hand where her wounds were. "Her skin isn't becoming necrotic. She's even healing from it!"

"That isn't possible!" Malik shouted from a window. Crossbows immediately aimed at the necromancer as phantoms carried him through the window. "If you take a shot at me, I will break the doors down and allow the hordes inside," the necromancer threatened, and the mercenaries restrained themselves, though they kept their weapons trained on him. Malik walked over to Lethia and Yurith. Mason stood up and placed a hand on his axe. The pair stare at one another darkly before Malik spoke again. "If you let me inspect her, I'll do nothing more. I just wish to see what is happening."

"If you make one wrong move, I won't care what dark magic you curse me with, I'll be sure to have your head rolling on the floor," Mason warned. Silence stretched between them, and Malik finally knelt down. Lethia had finished doing everything she could to Yurith's leg, though the necrosis continued to spread. She turned and stared at Malik, who placed a hand over the shrinking bite marks. The moment his hand touched her skin, he recoiled in shock.

"Your body, it's burning up! Your body is so hot, you're actively purging the plague from your blood, something that is meant to be impossible to cure!" he exclaimed, shock overtaking his expression. "This is a disease born from the magic of the goddess of death, yet you're able to deny it any permanent hold on your body from the sheer heat," he explained, stepping back. Lethia looked at him, then looked at Yurith, then her own hands. Yurith chuckled and shook his head.

"Seems like you would have been fine, after all. Though I don't think we would have ever thought of seeing if you could be made sick through disease" Yurith said. "Still, you shouldn't have rushed into the horde like that. That's exactly what makes them so dangerous and powerful. They have no sense of self preservation, and they will come at you tirelessly, without mercy, until you're nothing left but bleached bone. Still, up until now, you've been doing a good job. Though now, I have one more order for you."

With that, he took a small breath and sat up properly, crossing his legs. "Take my head off. I'm going to die, and that's the end of it. To stop me from becoming undead, my head needs to be removed." Lethia's face paled upon hearing the request, yet Yurith sat there calmly, eyes closed and in meditation. The Lieutenant knew if Lethia couldn't do it, Mason would have no problem following through. Malik had walked over to a corner to watch in silence, one hand on his chin to think about what had transpired.

Lethia looked at the silent draconian, the necrosis spreading through more of his body rapidly. It would be minutes before he died and turned. Mason hefted his axe after seeing Lethia's hesitation, but she stopped him and shook her head. "I caused it... I'll... I'll do it." She muttered and flexed her hands. Mason handed her his axe, and she clasped it, looking down at Yurith. With a clean strike that would make her teachers proud, she cleaved through the draconians neck, the axe blade passing through without resistance. Before Yurith's head could fly off, she placed her other hand on top and used her fire to quickly cauterize the neck, sealing his head on his shoulders, despite being separated. No one who wasn't a witness to the mercy execution would even know Yurith Loamscale was now in permanent rest, his body locked in a pose of meditation.

"Such admirable strength of character," Malik murmured, stepping forward. "Actually managing to follow through with his wish and end his life before he could turn. I have seen this scenario play out countless times, and it always ends in hesitation and tragedy immediately after." Mason and the rest of the Silver Shields brought up their weapons, facing the necromancer.

"You know full well that any breach of your exile means your life." Mason stated, taking his axe back from Lethia. "You are in a frontier town on the lands of the northern commonwealth. You are hereby-"

"Listen to yourself, rambling fool." Malik cut in with an exhausted groan. "Look around you! This is all swamp land, and the northern commonwealth does not recognize the swamp lands as its own. By all legal rights and standings, I am in no breach of my agreed upon exile. Besides, the resources it would take you to kill me would leave you vulnerable to the encroaching hordes." Lethia stood up to face him, her own eyes still alight. "I will leave. Do not put his death in my hands, he made his choice. Lethia here would be far too difficult for me to even contain, let alone capture." Straightening himself, he pulled his hood back over his head. "You are still very naive of your own nature, though you have earned my respect. Something I seldom give." With his piece said, he turned back and walked away from the group. "Unseen one," he said, and Malik suddenly lifted into the air, as if the winds themselves carried him off and back out of the window where he had come through. The survivors watched, the hall silent from relief, and in remembrance.

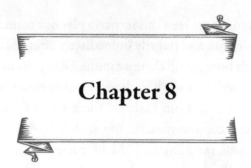

Chapter 8

The Northern Pride members and the survivors learned Lethia was quite in control of herself. While they did not trust her, they did agree to keep quiet about her secret as a thanks for helping rescue them. The rest of the mission went without further incident. The initial skirmish which broke out due to Malik's interference had cleared out far more of the zombies than they had anticipated. Lethia was much more conservative in helping to clear them out, and Mason took over as the leader of the operation. They did take advantage of Lethia's powers, but they knew she had learned her lesson and would only engage controlled numbers of undead at a time.

Within a week, the town had been completely cleared of the undead, and the survivors were free to pick up the pieces of their lives. The Silver Shields were paid for their duty, and the Northern Pride would aid in the villages recovery, sending out couriers that the village had been rescued successfully. With few survivors remaining, they would have to redevelop the land and build anew, even deciding to rename the village Gravelodge in honor of Yurith.

The mercenaries carried Yurith's body back home in a small casket that was offered to them by the villagers. As a security measure, they had nailed it shut just in case he might still rise again from the plague.

Lethia was trying her best to be positive with the group, helping them celebrate the good memories of their fallen comrade. While Mason and the others still had reservations about the werewolf, they had grown to have respect for her, and helped with the levity they would share in Yurith's memory.

Things didn't stay that way for too long as when they returned to the headquarters of the Silver Shields, the air among the crew became heavy as they had to report Yurith's passing. Mason and Lethia walked into Talisan's office, both wearing solemn faces as they greeted their leader. Talisan himself was writing a letter on an embroidered piece of parchment in response to a message from the draconian emperor himself. "Welcome back. From the look of your faces, and the lack of your lieutenant," he looked up from his writing, leaning back in his seat, "am I to assume he fell in active duty?"

"I'm afraid so, sir. We went up against plague zombies as well as Malik Black Bones, who was taking advantage of the situation. Things got complicated, and he was bitten. We couldn't stop the spread in time as it turned out to be a major artery. Even if he had been brought to safety, he was finished," Mason explained while Lethia was silent. She couldn't hide the guilt on her expression.

"Anything to add to this statement?" Talisan asked Lethia. She looked up at her uncle, suddenly very tense with emotion. Her eyes were burning fiercely, though she held her posture enough to maintain her human form.

"Yes, sir, he... Yurith. He had sacrificed himself in an effort to rescue me when I wasn't truly in need of rescue. Turns out that due to my condition, my body temperature is hot enough to purge out the plague. That still doesn't excuse my carelessness; I rushed into a fight not thinking. I thought my power could be enough to deal with them all and-"

"Those who believe power is everything will eventually be crushed by it," Talisan said firmly, interrupting her. "Your rash actions have caused the death of my lieutenant, but worse still, you have failed to protect your own comrades." He stood up from behind his desk and walked over. "Considering the circumstances, as well as having such a threat as Malik in the area, I don't think I am too surprised. Was he apprehended?"

"No, sir," Mason responded swiftly. "The town had been reclaimed by the swamp, and the villagers claimed the attack was from death acolyte extremists. For all intents and purposes, Malik had not broken the rules of his exile, and the zombies were not of his making. In the end, he left without causing more of an issue. He had a keen interest in Lethia's condition, but learned that it was more risky than it was worth to keep her captive against her will." Talisan nodded and looked back to Lethia, seeing tears running down her eyes despite her best efforts to maintain her posture.

"In response to this, Lethia, you will be responsible for building Yurith's grave and memorial on your own." He took a slow breath. "On top of that, you will have to be the one to tell the emperor the news."

"The emperor? Wait, you mean the draconian emperor? He's visiting?!" Lethia stammered in shock "But my condition! I'll... I'll transform! How could I-"

"This is a test, Lethia. You need to learn to control your emotions, as well as know discipline. It was both a lack of discipline as well as a lack of knowledge that caused this."

"In Lethia's defense," Mason interjected, "if she hadn't run into a horde of zombies the way she did, our position would have been overrun and things would have probably been worse off. If we had known she was immune, I'm sure Yurith would have found some other means of assisting her, or the rest of us would have." Stepping forward, he placed a hand on her shoulder. "Reckless, sure, but given the choice of fighting Malik and fighting the horde, Yurith was more suited to dealing with the necromancer at the time. She made the right call from a tactical standpoint. It was her recklessness and overconfidence that made her go too deep into the horde." Talisan leaned back in his seat and thought about it. Lethia smiled softly towards Mason. He gave her a stern look, which made her drop her gaze. "I still have reservations about working with a demon, but from what I've seen, I think she has hope."

"Fine, but it still doesn't change my decision," replied the guild leader. "Now, the Emperor is going to be arriving in three weeks. You have to build a memorial for Yurith as well as get your emotions under control. Dismissed." Talisan vanished back into the documentation at his desk, pulling out a list of people who would make strong candidates to replace his lieutenant. Lethia felt a knot in her throat, wishing for some kind of comfort from her uncle, but kept herself in check. Mason opened the office door behind them and let out a small grunt. Lethia stepped back, bowed, and left the room, her eyes still burning fiercely.

She made her way back to her room, hugging her arms, fighting to keep herself from transforming. Ember took one look at her, and it was clear she was in agony. Before she could comfort her, Lethia held up a hand and shook her head. Her eyes were on the brink of tears, fire and water mingling in a way that shouldn't be possible. But a steel resolution was in her eyes. Nails digging into her skin, almost ready to break flesh as she was internalizing and letting her feelings boil. Ember watched with concern as Lethia walked to the fireplace, shakily unbuckling her armor. Stripping naked, she knelt down on the cold stone floor. Realizing Lethia was going to try and meditate to tame the whirlwind of fiery emotions, Ember left to let a few of the mercenaries know, and to be on standby with water just in case.

A lot of people felt a change in mood in the base without Yurith there. To them, he was a big brother: level headed, wise yet still relaxed. With him gone, it felt like people had to try just a little harder to bring some humor and fun into the guild. With the pending arrival of the emperor, they were busy making sure they had a welcome presentation fit for the emperor and for the name of their guild. Lethia worked hard, though she started to apply herself differently. What used to be a common sight for a werewolf to be in the sparring yards changed. She could still be seen sparring against Toshiko, but she kept a collection of books, tomes, scrolls and manuscripts that were always nearby. She also started wrestling against Ember to make up for being unable to spar against Yurith, though it was far more difficult for her. Both of them were even, starting to make her memorize different creatures and different traits in mid spar. She was determined to prevent making the same mistake twice.

Milly watched as Lethia was sent flying and crashed on the ground nearby. She hurried over to help her onto her feet. "What the hell was that!?" came an uncharacteristically sharp comment from the young blacksmith. Lethia stood up shakily, one arm gripping Milly, the other holding the wall as Ember came running over.

"Lethia! Are you okay?"

"I'm fine." she panted "I'm, I'm fine. Let's keep going."

"No, we're finished for today," Ember replied, concerned for Lethia. As she reached forward to check on her, Lethia growled, but relented. Milly looked between them.

"How hard is she pushing herself?" she asked, and Ember placed a hand on Lethia's arm briefly. With no reaction, she began to gently check her for wounds or broken bones.

"Too hard, I think, at this point, though I'm not helping matters I suppose, agreeing to be doing this. Gods, Lethia, why are you still punishing yourself over Yurith?"

"I'm not." She replied, swallowing saliva as she let Ember feel her body with her hands. The firm digits sliding from her arm to her chest, pressing upon her breasts to try and feel if her ribs were in one piece. Her hands then slid down as Lethia continued speaking. "I need to fight to keep myself in human form even with my emotions raging. I'm not beating myself up over Yurith, I'm just..."

"You're forcing yourself to be emotionally unbalanced," Milly interjected, still supporting Lethia's weight.

"Yeah," Lethia confessed. Ember stood back up, satisfied Lethia hadn't broken anything, or at the very least she had already healed it. "I've got two weeks until the emperor shows up. I can't let myself be exposed so easily. Besides, draconians are masters of magic, right? What if they are able to just sense me outright like how Malik did? If the Emperor learns about me, he will have authority to have me captured! Maybe worse, he'd find a reason to declare war!" The other two women exchange glances, and Milly knew what Lethia needed.

"First of all," Milly began, her voice once again changing tone, "the Emperor isn't from this country, which strips him of any authority to arrest anyone, unless such a person attacks him or his company directly. Secondly, declaring war over a single person is an incredibly rash and foolish decision. No leader would... should, make such a move. The worst they could do is demand Talisan to act... which he would be forced to or risk being labeled a criminal himself. Him and everyone here."

Lethia bit her lip. She still felt paranoid all the same.

"Here, come with me, Lethia. I can help you," Milly said, and Ember tilted her head curiously. "I know a thing or two about hiding a demonic presence." Easing herself off of Milly's shoulders, Lethia followed her to the forge where they could talk in private.

At the forge, Lethia got to work trying to build a memorial for Yurith. She figured one made out of marble would be fitting considering the draconian used rock and stone to great effect. Milly had gone and grabbed a few scrolls from her private quarters. "Alright, so Lethia, how much do you know about magic?"

"Can't say much, if anything," she admitted as she worked the marble with a chisel. With her enhanced strength, shaping the stone was easy enough; the difficult part was not using too much strength where it wasn't needed. "I haven't really tried to learn any magic. Trying to memorize so many different traits of creatures, species. How to fight, meditation, basically everything since I got here. That's already so much to deal with."

"I guess it makes sense. Well, first I need to be honest with something. You see, Lethia, there's a source of my magic. I'm possessed by a demon as well."

Lethia froze. "You're... wait, what?"

"Yeah, it's why Talisan trusted us to build your halberd over anyone else, actually." A purple figure slowly materialized beside Milly, looking quite impatient.

"This isn't the first time we met, mutt. Though this is the first time you are seeing me," she said roughly, crossing her arms beneath her bust. "My name is Lilith. I'm Milly's twin sister. Yes, twins."

"How, I, but what!?" Lethia stammered, unsure how to really respond to what she was seeing.

"Long story short, mom made a deal with a demon for magic. First born daughter was to be a demon, myself. Mom instead had twins, and since us demons are spirits, the two of us were born sharing the same body." As Lilith explained, Milly pulled off the eye patch she had been wearing. Lethia could see the demonic red and black eye, the same kind of eye that was on Lilith's features. "Milly wears the eye patch to hide the fact, since it's the only tell of our nature."

"Yup, plus Lilith is the one who actually studies magic, though I'm able to call on her magic whenever I need it. It flows through the same body in the end anyway." Milly placed the eye patch on a nearby table. "That is also how we are able to hide Lilith's presence. The magic is in my body, so instead of hiding the magic, we just bury it so the source is too deep for anyone to detect without actively searching for it. It's like trying to find a piece of glass in a lake. You can't find it without something specific, and you know what you're looking for."

"Alright, so, basically I need to invert my magic to fill my body?" Lethia pondered, not having even the slightest idea of where to start. "How would I go about even finding my magic?"

"Well, first thing you need to do is know how to sense and feel your own magic. It's like learning how to walk, in a sense, only you're an adult. When you're born with magic, you gain a sense of it naturally. Gaining magic through other means usually leaves people unsure or unable to actually access it."

"Though no one is born without magic." Lilith interjected, floating over to Lethia and placing a finger over the center of her body. "Everyone is tied to magic in some way. The kind of magic is usually determined by where you place your faith most. Do you place faith in yourself? In the gods? Or in nature? This is the key difference between astral, spiritual and nature magic."

"Well, I'm not certain, to be honest. I know Minerva has turned me away, and only aided me because it was a direct request of her mother and sister. I would imagine Gaia then has some acceptance of me, and Hilgith, I don't know. What would it tell you when lady death steps in to spare your life?"

"That's not the focus right now." Lilith stressed before either of them could speculate further on the significance of it. "So, spiritual isn't a pick, and you're certainly not much of a nature lover. Your magic at this point would be astral. The more you believe in yourself, the more potential it has, but potential and wielding it are two different things. You can have the confidence of a zealot, but can only have the tools to access hardly even a fraction of it."

"Okay, how would I wield it? What tools?" Lethia asked.

Lilith sat in the air, legs crossed. "First, you need to recognize it and know what it is. As of right now, the central source of your magic is the succubus residing inside of you. It's why people can detect you; they can sense the source of it. We need to bring those energies forward." Lethia felt nervous; she never had any kind of training like this. Sure, her mother was a druid, but she was in no position to teach Lethia about magic either.

"Take a seat," Lilith ordered. "You've been practicing meditation with the snake, right? Sit and meditate, envision your magic like it's fire. On that note, sit in the furnace." With a bit of an undignified look at the demon, Lethia stood up and started to strip naked. She didn't want her clothes to be caked in soot and ash. It was far more difficult to wash it out of her clothes than her skin. She crawled onto the hot coals, turned, and sat cross legged.

"Alright, so, envision my magic like it's fire, right?" She asked from within, and Lilith nodded. Closing her eyes, Lethia started to try and meditate. The heat and fire inside the furnace was a major distraction, and she just felt hot all around. The heat of course was a comfort, but it didn't help her distinguish any different kind of flame. "You sure doing this inside a furnace is a good idea? All I feel is heat."

"Your own fire will feel different. It would feel unnatural yet familiar. It would feel like it's your own essence." Lethia closed her eyes and focused more, searching inside herself. She remembered a flame when she would meditate with Ember, and looked inside herself for it. Eventually, she found the flame, and she could tell it was different from everything else. Whenever she embraced it before, it made her transform.

"You sure this is a good idea, Lilith? What if the demon inside of her is asleep and this wakes it up?" Milly asked, looking into the furnace through a face shield.

"It's basically an infant spirit, for demons. Arguably, it's more Lethia than its own identity at this point, so it's more of a catalyst. Best comparison I could think of is how different fuel for a furnace produces different flames. The flame is alive of course, but it's at this point not entirely intelligent, conscious or aware of itself." Milly didn't entirely accept the idea of another soul being more of a thing than a being, but she put faith in her sibling's words.

The fire inside of the furnace swayed and danced around Lethia, who focused on separating the fire she felt, and the flames she could see inside of her. Eventually, she began to tell them apart. The feeling of the fire around her was wild, consuming. It wanted to grow large, powerful and furious with the amount of heat it was generating. The flame inside her felt like it wanted to be free. It seemed to behave when she mentally waved her hand through the flame. It followed her hand, like an obedient puppy thinking it was going to be pet. She began to mentally colour the flames blue, and it stuck out against the raging, mindless inferno around her. "Okay, let it fill me," she whispered to herself. Opening her eyes, she could see she had turned into her werewolf form inside of the furnace, but with a bit of time, she turned back into her human form and tried again.

This time, she didn't want the blue fire to flow past her skin. The beating heart of young, blue fire spread within her eagerly. As it did, Lethia took her time to visually fill one part of her body at a time, starting with her arms. Once she felt like the magic was underneath the skin in her arms, she did the same with the rest of her torso, down to her hips and thighs and along her legs. The twins watched as Lethia's body shifted and changed colour, like she was a piece of charcoal herself, tanned skin turned charcoal black then back to white seemingly at random. A few minutes later, Lethia crawled out of the furnace with a deep yawn. "All this meditating in fire is making me sleepy. Never thought I'd say this, but it's actually very cosy in there, even if I'm sitting on a bunch of rocks."

"You did alright, but you still need a lot of practice," Lilith noted as she drifted over to Lethia and placed a finger on her head. The image passed through as if she was reaching into her brain. "Keep in mind this is something you will need to do as second nature if you're to disguise yourself properly."

"I don't think I'd be able to get that good with magic, but I haven't given up on any kind of training yet," Lethia said with a yawn, her voice drowsy. "Wow... okay, yeah, the furnace really put me to sleep. I need to go wake myself up somehow..." She grabbed her clothes and started to get dressed.

"Hey Lethia?" Milly came near her.

"Yeah?" Lethia yawned a reply, grabbing her pants and stepping into them.

"Have you always had that?"

"Had wha-" mid statement, she pulled her pants up sharply, not paying attention. She caught a new set of balls conspicuously hanging between her legs. The fabric, being as strong as it was, and Lethia pulling as hard as she did, smacked and pulled on the pair of orbs without warning and without mercy. All wind left her lungs and her body's muscles seized up as the next thing Lethia found herself doing was laying on the floor, her hands cupping the freshly made and freshly bruised pair of testicles between her legs. Milly and Lilith both cringed seeing how quickly the werewolf collapsed from the shock of the pain. After the initial shock passed, Lethia squeaked out a whimpering "Why?"

"Well, if we had any doubt Lethia is possessed by a succubus, it's gone now." Lilith stated, kneeling down, looking at Lethia's ass and new set of tools between her thighs. "Succubi and incubi are able to swap genders at will when it suits them," she explained, yet noticed the feminine sex was still present underneath the set of orbs. "Though it seems Lethia can't do it completely."

"Hey Lilith, how about giving Lethia some space for a moment?" Milly said softly as her demon sibling simply faded from vision. Eventually the now hermaphrodite got back up onto her feet, still shaky. Milly walked over and helped fix Lethia's pants, pulling them up properly, though they were definitely not designed to have room for extra baggage. Lethia squirmed, the bulge and tightness making her uncomfortable.

"God this feels so awkward. I'm gonna need to see my uncle about this, or some guy to ask how the heck they live with a dick." She groaned, pulling at the groin of her pants to try and get some levity with the tight fabric.

"Probably going to need all your outfits hemmed as well." Milly noted and Lethia looked at her pants. Without hesitation she slipped them off and breathed a sigh of relief.

"Yeah, I'll stop by the twins and let them know. Gods they are so sensitive, how do men live with this!?" She exclaims, looking back down between her legs. "They're so awkward and sensitive, and they keep slapping my thighs even when I'm just shifting my weight!" Milly could only giggle, shaking her head.

"Stop shaking your junk at my sister and get your ass moving." Lilith's voice rang through the air. Lethia laughed before heading off to get her stuff organized, as well as get some new sex ed from her uncle, or someone may have time to teach her.

Trying to walk through the guild with a new set of tools was a very awkward experience. People were not used to seeing someone suddenly change gender, though thankfully nobody would make a comment. Besides, it was common knowledge Lethia was trying to learn about her demon magic, some weird things were bound to happen eventually. She knocked on the door to her uncle's office, having turned into a werewolf again. She looked down at herself, and mentally tried to suppress the blue flame inside her body. As Talisan opened the door, he was greeted with the sight of his niece, pantless, shedding and growing fur and her skin in a constant flux of white and black tones. "Hey, you have a minute?" Lethia asked and the bewildered guild leader just looked on for a moment. Finally he stepped aside, holding his door open and Lethia walked inside. He then noticed she was also sporting more tools than normal between her legs.

"Are you sick?" He asked, trying to piece together in his mind why she was looking so chaotic. "I have never seen any werewolf in all my time being in such a state of flux. Restraint yes, however this looks exhausting." Lethia yawned as if agreeing, nodding her head.

"Milly and-" Lethia caught herself before Talisan gave her a nod, indicating he knew. "-her sister Lilith are teaching me a way to hide the succubus possessing me. It's difficult, but it's not why I'm here. I kind of need to know how to manage having a dick." She says bluntly, yawning again. Talisan considered her words for a moment before walking over to a bookstand.

"Well I hope your mother at least taught you the basics. I'm more than happy to answer questions, but how to live with one. Well that's just something you learn with experience." He replied before pulling down a book on demonology. "Here, this won't give you all the answers, but it should help you understand your succubus passenger more." Talisan hands her the book. Lethia scooped up fur that was piling around her and used it as a cloth to hold the book and avoid burning it.

"Thanks, this should help some." She replied, looking at the bindings. Talisan nodded his head before grabbing a broom nearby.

"Good, now please leave my office before you drown me in your fur." Talisan orders while watching the mounting piles of fur grow higher and higher. "I'll be sure to get more fitted pants for you in the meantime, we have more than enough material for it now." With a deep blush, Lethia bowed and quickly left the room. "Bit tactless, but at least she asked me and no one else." He sighs and starts to sweep up all the fur, looking around at the mess left behind.

Lethia returned to her quarters and stopped managing the magic inside of her. She returned to her normal appearance and sat down to read the book. After a moment of reading, she noticed the sun was setting and tried to remember what state the moon was in.

"It's going to be a full moon tonight. I think perhaps I'll go for a run." She noted to herself as she pulled off her shirt and put it aside. Looking down, she realised somehow she had returned to her original female gender.

"Well, I'm not a herm anymore, how do I?" She placed a hand between her legs curiously. Closing her eyes, she once again filled her body with fire. Opening one eye, she saw this time, nothing was changing. "Wait, then why did I change earlier? Was it because I was looking at Lilith? Does me being horny have anything to do with it?" She pondered to herself. Shortly after a tingling ran over her skin and she looked out the window. "Aaah, worry about it later. Tonight let's go on a run." Still naked she stepped outside, no point getting dressed when her transformation would just render her naked. As the door opened, two of the mercenaries gave her a polite wave as they were doing evening rounds.

Lethia waved back "Evening, full moon tonight, so doing my midnight run, wanna let the next patrol know?"

"Lethia, it's your patrol tonight, remember?" The one guard answered, making her blush.

"Right, right, I was so focused on studying and projects I forgot to check the patrol list." She fumbled through her excuse and nodded "Change is in three hours right?"

"Four" They replied in unison "Be back by then, don't think you can afford another report on your name." The original guard replied. No one had really outwardly expressed their dissatisfaction with the hellhound. Lethia smiled gently, feeling like there was a hint of a backhanded statement. It's been more notable the past few days after her return without Yurith. Her eyes ignited as she returned a salute.

"I'll be sure to be back before your shift ends. Take care of yourselves!" She replies, trying her best to sound upbeat about it. In the end it only made her feel more isolated. Sure Ember was a sweetheart who took care of her emotionally, yet to her there seemed to be something disingenuous to a degree. Like a fear or something unspoken between them. Ember was very good at hiding it, but it still just felt like something was off.

Shaking her head, she pushed those feelings and notions aside. She was going for a run, to feel wild, free and untamed for tonight. The moon peeked over the horizon filling Lethia's body with energy. Having grown so accustomed to her changing body, she lifted her arms up and stretched as they grew longer, angling her body so the lengthening of her bones and muscles wouldn't crack, snap or cause pain. She would exaggerate her walking stride as well, her legs growing longer with each step. She had been transforming so often, it was becoming a far more casual action for her, and the transformation itself much smoother.

Skin a dark, coal black, hair flowing freely in the night breeze as she looked out at the woods beyond the wall. Flexing her claws, she sprinted forward and scaled the inner structure quickly, grabbing the edge of the battlement and flipping over it. Landing on the top, she jumped forward and into open air. Something she had wanted to experiment with was how high could she fall in her wolf form and not suffer injuries. The walls of the guild base were a solid twelve or thirteen feet tall in her judgement. A fall that could be quite fatal for a normal human at the right angle.

Air rushed past her with a leap and a sense of vertigo filled her head as gravity began to throw her earthward. Keeping her legs stretched, she leaned forward a little as she watched the ground quickly approaching. The moment she touched earth, she flexed her muscles and tucked forward. Rolling along the ground, her wolf body was able to withstand and deflect enough of the impact to keep going. Maybe a bruise at worst, yet able to transition from a roll to a run, and with a cry of exuberance, she ran off, freedom and energy coursing through her veins as well as the desire to feel like her own person. No one kept her caged or held her against her will, yet there was always a sense of liberation anytime she left society behind for a night to be a wolf and just prowl. The silver disc in the sky guided her, following her. It was a comforting sight for her, letting her believe everything would be fine in the end.

Chapter 9

Lethia and Milly stood atop the perimeter walls watching the dawn over the front gates. Milly, who got a full night's sleep, was helping herself to a fruit scone for breakfast as Lethia sat on a small ledge to take a break from the hours of standing and pacing. "So, how is my aura looking?" she asked with a nervous smile. "The Emperor is reported to arrive sometime today."

"You're doing well. A casual glance over you will just have you look like any other magic user," Lilith answered, materialising below the walls so she wasn't spotted by anyone. "It's still a little shaky. You're nervous, and it shows visibly and spiritually." Milly nodded in agreement with her sibling, munching away.

"I just pray and hope one of the gods will still listen, maybe even help. Gaia or Hilgith might still have a little favour for me." With a gentle sigh, she stood straight. "I actually favoured Minerva back then. Doubt she would appreciate me praying for her protection when I'm the cause of so much death." The siblings look towards one another for a moment.

"Don't worry about them. Besides, they would rather we stand on our own feet for a challenge like this," Milly encouraged, walking up to place a hand on Lethia's shoulder. "You haven't backed away from a challenge yet, it's actually one of your charms. You have this bravado about you, and it's inspiring."

Lethia chuckled and gave her friend a hug. "Thank you, Milly, it's nice to have a friend who doesn't see me as just a monster." Milly grinned and rubbed Lethia's shoulder affectionately before looking over the perimeter walls again. Lethia paused for a moment as she could see a small dust cloud in the distance. She reached for a nearby spyglass and looked through it to confirm what she was seeing.

In the distance, the draconians were marching down the road on foot in military procession. Emperor in front, Fafnir directly behind him and both flanked by eight generals. Every one of them clad in armour so thick, it made them look like golems. Lethia spun around and shouted towards the compound at the top of her lungs. "The Emperor is arriving down the road!"

The words acted like a firing mechanism, and the grounds below exploded into a frenzy of activity. Mercenaries were getting the best military dress they had, from silver and gold trimmed armors to sleek uniforms. Flag poles were stuck into the ground to form a designation for the marching procession to follow, bearing the Silver Shield insignia on one side, and the colours of the Northern Commonwealth opposite. At the end of the row, three flags were placed, the Northern Commonwealth and the Silver Shield banners flanking a flag of the Draconian Empire.

Lethia found herself being placed in the line meant to receive the Emperor directly, standing near her uncle. Her eyes were burning with intensity, so much so it was obscuring her vision. Talisan noticed her anxiety and placed a hand on her shoulder, causing her to flinch. "Breathe." Lethia took an exaggerated breath after a moment. Her muscles relaxed, and the fire in her eyes eased up. She blinked in confusion. Had she not been breathing? She took another deep breath before standing properly to attention. Ember, Autu and Mason stood in line with Talisan as well.

"Where's Toshiko?" she asked after seeing everyone but him.

"Draconians and Fukai Chikyu don't get along. While the Emperor himself is patient towards them, the rest of the Imperial Draconians despise them. It's actually considered disrespectful to greet them with one in your ranks," Talisan explained briefly not having the time to elaborate.

Glaurung approached the large gates, hewn of wood and stone and lined with steel. The gate opened outwards, greeting the Emperor along with the vision of the retinue standing in preparation. As the Emperor walked forward, soldiers brandished weapons in the air in a military salute towards the Emperor. Glaurung's gaze enveloped all before him. Humans, Duram, the occasional Draconian and some Huldra. Certainly a healthy mix of recruits and veterans from all walks of life and professions. He spotted Milly in the distance, watching from the smithy, noting she wasn't part of the military entourage. A guest, he deduced, perhaps here for work.

Talisan stepped forward as Glaurung and his generals came within a few feet to greet them properly. "Greetings your majesty, welcome to the Northern Commonwealth, and to the guild of the Silver Shields. What grants us the honour of your presence today?" he asked, giving a polite half bow. A few of the lesser generals in Glaurung's group growled quietly, while those who knew the emperor better kept silent.

"I came to visit the guild which houses one of the more recognized of our kind, as well as a request of information. My visit must be short, we have places to be, but perhaps there may be some time for pleasantries," he started before taking another look at the procession around him. "Yet, I find myself asking, where is Yurith Loamscale, your right hand? In his place you have one of your other Lieutenants. A Huldra stands there, Autu if I recall?" The Hunter nodded in silence.

"It's with regret to say he had given his life on duty to protect someone." With that, he turned towards Lethia, her eyes alight. "He gave his life to protect my niece who, due to circumstances beyond her control, has joined me here."

With a hum, Glaurung stepped past Talisan and approached Lethia, who stood still. Her body felt rigid as the rock and earth she stood on, yet her knees trembled. "It's typically polite to bow to an Emperor," he said patiently, giving her a soft smile. Lethia bowed low, dipping a knee before breathing out.

"Forgive me, it's... I'm a little star struck, your majesty. I never thought I would meet someone of such royal standing so soon, let alone at all! I don't think I could have ever been ready for it." This produced a hearty laugh from the Emperor before patting her shoulder.

"It's bold to be so bluntly honest to a draconian, as well as reckless." His grip flexed lightly, making Lethia wince as she could feel his mood shift. "Was Yurith throwing his life away for someone who would do the same so casually?"

"NO!" she practically screamed back. The generals stepped forward before the Emperor raised a hand. "Um, I'm sorry. No, I don't intend to do so... not anymore perhaps..." she stumbled over her words. Taking a breath, she fought to calm herself. "He died protecting me because of my rashness."

"Where does such recklessness stem from? Being the niece of the greatest guild leader in our current time? Or perhaps whatever the source of this is?" He gestured to the flames coming from her eyes.

"Ah... it... it was..." She gulped. Lilith and Milly had prepared her for this question while she trained to hide her demonic presence. "I got caught up in an alchemy experiment" she started, voice still shaking. "Now I'm... fireproof, and also produce fire. I can't control it, yet. Though my body burns when I want it to, even my insides." She pulled the top of her red and blue top down, exposing a still healing scar from a zombie. "They were plague zombies, they pinned me down. He gave his life saving me when... a result of my fusion makes my blood too hot for any disease to take hold, it burns off. His intentions were noble... but we never knew until it was too late."

Glaurung listened, his eyes boring into hers. He could practically taste a lie. "I feel as if you're telling me only what I wish to hear... and not the whole story," he murmured under his breath, enough for her to hear. "Still, I suppose what personal details you have are not of my direct concern."

"I had built him a gravestone, a monument, to celebrate him," she added, reaching behind Ember, she presented the marble slab in the shape of a shield with silver lining. Yurith's name was written in polished obsidian, making it shine against the gleaming marble and silver.

"What an insult!" a younger general spoke up, stepping out of line. "It should have been carved into the dragon of our ancestors! He will be rolling in his grave because of this outrage!"

Talisan stepped forward and leaned into the general. "Are you insinuating you know my guild members more than me, their own leader? You believe you know what my childhood friend would want to have as a memorial?" He growled as the general met his gaze. After a moment of intensity, the younger general eased off.

"This is not your place, Fumerage. Yurith pledged allegiance to the Silver Shields first and us second. We will honour this tribute," Glaurung said, glaring at his general.

"Your excellency, we need to ensure people respect our ancestry lest they are fo-"

"This is not our empire," he growled, fumes escaping his clenched teeth. "Do not enforce something where it doesn't belong. Now get back in line before you lose your place in it." Fumerage flinched, hesitating before silently lowering his head, giving a quick glare, then looking away. Glaurung let out a breath and looked back to Talisan. "Shall we speak in your quarters?" he asked. Talisan simply nodded in agreement. The rest of the procession was led off towards accommodations while Glaurung, along with his own right hand general Glaurin, went to Talisan's office to speak with him and Autu.

The moment all four were inside the office and the door closed, Talisan, Glaurung and Glaurin all took a deep breath. Autu looks between his leader and the guests. "You're new to this, Autu, so you're probably going to be seeing and hearing a few things you might not consider familiar with the public image of who the Emperor is."

"You say that as if I disguise myself in front of everyone," the Emperor replied in exhausted mockery. "It's not like my subjects are so proud of themselves that they are blind." Glaurin cleared his throat, making the Emperor nod. "Yes, right, I'm rambling. So rare I get to make such a comment without judgement."

"As always, Your Majesty, while I do enjoy letting you relax here, we are still someplace with ears," Talisan pointed out as he took a seat "Still, may I offer you a drink? Water, ale, perhaps some tea?"

"Water will do just fine, actually, thank you," Glaurung replied.

"I'll have some ale, actually. Something to dull the headache our younger generals cause on a daily basis." Autu nodded and quickly got two ornate mugs, filling them with water and ale and handing them to the draconians.

"So what else brings you to my guild? Again, I apologise you are unable to have found Yurith alive, but that's the life we live. We choose to put it on the line regularly, death our eventual reward. Hilgith is now his keeper, or if you prefer, your ancestor dragons."

"The two of us hold both in equal regard. After all, it was the gods that gave life to the dragons, and consequently us. Though if you allow me a moment of curiosity." The emperor looked towards the Huldra hunter. "A Huldra male is a rare sight indeed, more so outside of the society that cherishes you. One that even chooses to risk his life and limb for others."

"I grew tired of that life." Autu said, getting to the point. "I'm not a trophy, nor just a breeding tool for political clout. Huldra women are treated almost like royalty if they have a husband of their own race. It's a more common problem than it looks, but because there are so few of us, well." He poured himself ale. "Let's just say that I avoid my own kind when I can, and I'm not the only one. You would be shocked at the extent Huldra males will go to escape a life of being objectified." The draconians shared a silent look between them.

"Strange how such news doesn't reach the ears of the public," Glaurin commented, but Autu shook his head.

"The elders are very strict with rules and regulations. I chose exile over it. Besides, I'm more at home out in the wilds than in the caverns."

"Thank you for indulging my curiosity. I'm sure men of other races would struggle to comprehend those difficulties, though I feel we have digressed enough," Glaurung said, then turned back to Talisan. "I'm here in hopes of hearing news about important figures of the land, at least your opinion on them. We have some plans of magical nature, something that is very important for us. We're looking to see if there is any news of anything major that may disrupt it. I know Nephele Mutations are still somewhat rampant, with your country's failure to keep their arrival policed properly. We don't wish to have another incident of that nature again." Talisan closed his eyes, realising the weight of what he was asking for.

"I can only offer what information I can," he replied, reaching into his desk to pull out some notebooks. He offered a few across the table and kept the rest by him. Glaurin took one and perused its contents as Talisan quoted from his own. "The mage guilds have yet to recognize the current world's lead magician after the passing of Michilar Thom. A power vacuum if there ever was one. As for the candidates, I'm afraid I cannot rightly say. Even with all of my years of service and recognition, they don't feel like giving such information is a smart idea. As if it's a weakness that the mages are undecided on who the strongest is, or the wisest, I should say. Then again, walking into what is effectively a wizarding war zone isn't the smartest thing to do either, with all those experiments."

"It seems so. Why don't the mages have some sort of democratic order to make these decisions? Seems strange they would follow a 'might is right' philosophy," Glaurung said while going through the dossier. He paused at the list of likely candidates of who could achieve the title of the Northern Commonwealth's arch mage.

"Well, a similar reason to why we have the Guild Games. We need to demonstrate to the wider world just what it is we are made of. Magic users are no different, it's just a different kind of sport."

"Hmm... well I suppose that does make some sense. A list of candidates, hmm? Quite a few here, a number of human and duram, no surprise there. Two draconian, Huldra, and Nephele... now that's interesting. No surprise the Fukai Chikyu do not pursue magic with the same vigour as the other races." The Emperor paused for a brief moment before continuing. "Wait, a harpy? A wind harpy thinks it can contend with these elite mages?" Talisan burst into laughter fired like a cannon.

"I nearly forgot about that. Yes, a harpy of all things. The wind harpy thinks his worldly knowledge makes him as much a contestant as any other mage. I won't deny he certainly sounds more intelligent than the rest of his kind, yet he clearly fails to understand the purpose of the competition." Glaurung couldn't hold back laughter himself, brief merriment shared between opposing ideologies. Eventually, Glaurung passed back the documents and leaned back in his seat, relaxing while out of view of his more radically minded followers. "I hope my answer is satisfying enough for you."

"Considering our circumstances... yes, yes it was, actually. Not something I was hoping to hear, but it's something that can help prepare myself, or rather, my own royal mages. I only wish there was an easier way to..." Glaurung paused in his thoughts, then shook his head. "No, never mind. I think I have taken enough of your time, Talisan." The Emperor stood from his seat, Glaurin mirroring his leader like a shadow.

Meanwhile, Lethia was helping keep the rest of the Emperor's entourage comfortable and entertained. She worked alongside Ember tending to the more tempered, level headed older generals as opposed to the more anxious and opinionated younger generals. This also included keeping the prince company, though unlike the generals who were fine picking a spot as mercenaries got them drinks, he was more interested in wandering around the battlements and surveying the immediate area. Wanting to keep an eye on him, the youngest mercenary followed him.

"Needing to ensure I'm not on my own now, hmm?" Fafnir commented playfully as Lethia approached. "It's funny, normally saying someone's eyes burn with the dragon's flame is a romantic gesture. For you, it's something actually relevant. I haven't seen the fire in those eyes waver even once since we set foot in your stronghold."

"Aaah." Lethia began, blushing heavily at the strange gesture. Was he flirting? Or just making an observation? "I mean, thanks, I suppose. It's just that it's hardly been a year since I joined the Silver Shields, and I wasn't expecting such honoured guests so soon. I mean, the royal imperial family? I used to just be a small village girl, so I'm rather star struck." Fafnir laughed beneath a claw, politely covering his mirth.

"A year, and yet here you are being trusted enough to stand beside the prince. They must have some true faith in your character, or perhaps the powers you wield." He looked over the edge of the battlement, where the tree line was almost directly beside the structure of the walls. "Yet, I question a number of decisions of this fortress of yours. This tree line should be cleared a couple hundred yards, just to ensure proper line of sight and avoid ambushes."

"On the contrary, the druids we have available are able to use those very trees to batter away at enemies that try to sneak through. Plus we always have scouts. There are some security measures in place to make sure we are never caught off guard, same thing with escape routes in case we find the walls breached."

"Escape routes? You don't stay to defend the fortress if the walls are breached?" Fafnir asked, rather surprised.

"No sir. Our base is important for sure, but the people make the guild, not the structure. Our central philosophy is survival first. So long as we stay alive, we have not failed our mission."

"Hmm." Fafnir pondered, a claw scratching his chin. "So the people are more important to the guild than anything. I suppose Yurith embodied that to a T when he chose to give his life for you. Certainly a very honourable Draconian." A sensation of heat flooded Lethia's body. Shame? Embarrassment? She couldn't find herself able to look up. Seeing this, Fafnir turned to face her properly and grinned. "Some of the soldiers here are nicknaming you the Hellhound because of your use of fire. Why don't you show me ?"

"Sir?" She blinked, caught off-guard. "Are you suggesting a duel with me?"

"Of course! I wanna see what the niece of the esteemed leader of the Silver Shields is capable of. After all, if everyone is already giving you a nickname as well as the life of the second in command, you must be quite formidable indeed."

Lethia suddenly became extremely nervous. She couldn't refuse him, but what if she couldn't keep her emotions in check? She hesitated a little bit before taking a deep breath. This felt like someone had just sprung a surprise test. "A-alright... if you wish to have a duel with me, I'll accept. Though I'd rather we use practice weapons as opposed to real ones. I wouldn't wish to risk injury to his majesty." Fafnir roared with laughter at the response.

"Agreed! Though you're taking this as if a red draconian was just offered a wrestling match by his crush. Don't be so shy about it. Imperial draconians love the sport of dueling. Not just our coliseum, but between one another as well. Though of course, I don't fight like a barbaric red anyhow."

The next thing Lethia knew, she was slipping on her leather armors and grabbing the practice halberd she had helped design. Milly and Ember were by her side as the news of the duel had swept through the entire fortress. All the generals and the Emperor himself had gathered around the sparring arena. Milly couldn't contain the energy from the situation as she held the practice weapon for Lethia. "Well Lethia, who knew the start of your legends was to duel the crown prince of the Draconian Empire? On his request! I heard rumours he was a little bit of a firebrand, but to see him make such a declaration so casually, and for sport!"

"I have no idea if I'm ready to face someone like him," Lethia whispered back to Milly, sweating from nerves, though her friend was sweating from the heat of the fire coming off from the flames on her eyes. "It's taking all my will power just to not transform already, and now this! I can't back out now either, or else it's a grave insult."

"You'll be fine, Lethia, it's just like training. I've seen how you do training, you get right back up and get right in there. Think of it like that, only with an actual winner and a loser." Milly patted Lethia's back, and the nervous woman stepped forward in surprise.

"Easy for you to say when your secret isn't tied to your emotions," she whispered, exasperated. Her hair flashed black for a split second. Looking over her shoulder, she was glad to see the draconian party wasn't paying attention to her. Yet having heard legends of the Emperor's tactical genius, she wondered if he really didn't notice, or was simply playing the fool. Finally, she took a deep breath and exhaled, letting the stress leave her body as she mentally secluded herself from her panicked thoughts. There was only one thing she needed to focus on now, and that was the fight. Just like any other kind of meditation training, she took a single aspect and focused on it. "Alright, I think I'm ready."

"You are ready for this, Lethia. Now go show the prince what you're capable of," Milly cheered, handing her the practice weapon. As she walked, she could see Autu and her uncle on the sidelines, watching. She wished Toshiko were here to watch, but she knew better.

Fafnir was stretching and breathing fire on his limbs to help warm up his muscles. Ensuring his body was limber, the heir stepped into the arena. As any draconian would, Fafnir was covered head to toe in plate. The armour was brushed with gold and silver to give the appearance of scales and a pattern of wings on the helmet, with fire coming down on the chest to create the image of a winged dragon carpeting the area in front of him in fire. For a draconian, only the highest of officials could have the honour of brandishing any form of dragon markings on their armour, and the crown prince was certainly one of them. Looking at the armour, the young mercenary realized she couldn't pick out a single real point of vulnerability aside from the open part of his helmet which allowed him to see. She wouldn't be aiming there unless it was to pin him.

"You're wearing very little protection. If we were dueling till first blood, I feel like I would have a significant advantage over you," Fafnir noted as the pair stood ten feet apart, just outside of weapon reach for either of them. "I wouldn't mind offering you some scout plate if you wished, just so you had some protection."

"The best protection is ensuring you're never struck in the first place." Lethia retorted almost on instinct, remembering her lessons. "So while your offer is appreciated, Your Majesty, it would only slow me down at best."

"Ha! You sound confident, or perhaps it's just the training that is drilled into you talking. Either way, I hope you keep me entertained," he replied as he drew a wooden training sword. He used a massive two handed plank of wood, one hand below the hilt, the other above. Pressing his upper hand on the weapon, he spun it around his body, the bottom grip acting as an axel to allow the blade to spin, the wooden weapon sweeping through the air. The wind generated from his swings tickled Lethia's skin, and he swung such a large and cumbersome weapon with astounding speed and grace. "Another reason this fight is in my favour is the natural behaviour of weapons. A sword versus a pole arm, I again feel at a bit of an advantage. You use a halberd, correct? All you can really do is stab and slice with a very specific part of your weapon."

"That's a very narrow vision for the son of the legendary Emperor, I'm surprised," she blurted without thinking, causing the prince to growl with disdain. Finally a horn blared, signalling the start of the dual. Fafnir lunged forward, his blade swinging through the air and poised to come down hard on Lethia's shoulder. A thunk of wood echoed as the halberd spun upwards, knocking the two handed sword off target while Lethia stepped sideways, spinning the practice weapon. The practice halberd was still of her design and balanced. It was more cumbersome and heavy, but served to be more an advantage for this particular bout.

Recovering immediately, Fafnir threw an elbow at Lethia's core, landing the blow before bringing the wooden blade to bare in an upwards slash. The air cried out as the wooden sword cut through it, missing Lethia by a hair as she side stepped, bringing her halberd up to spin it around the back of her head and deliver a punishing smack to the back of Fafnir's head. As he was stumbling forward, she swept low for the legs. She caught one, yet the prince was far more agile than he looked in full plate and managed to get his other foot on the ground and jump away to disengage. It wasn't enough for the prince to stay on his feet, however. As he hit the ground, his shoulder touched first, and he rolled through, using his weight and momentum to propel him back into a standing, combat ready position. This time, Lethia was the one to press the attack, charging forward as she started with a thrust of the head of the halberd.

Realising he had already underestimated her, Fafnir took a defensive stance, bringing the sword up to parry the blow and push it aside. Lethia used the momentum of the parry to bring the back end of the halberd around to strike what looked to be his unguarded side, yet the wooden blade was already there before she could follow through. Undeterred, the halberd began to spin back and forth, striking at opposing sides as the two paced back and forth in the ring. Fafnir's face and breathing was a stoic expression of concentration and focus, blocking and parrying the rapid strikes of a halberd from the fire-eyed warrior. Eventually, he found an opening, as Lethia over-extended a step. Parrying the halberd, he directed it down into the ground, forcing Lethia to lean forward. In a blur of movement, she found her feet suddenly in the air behind her, her weapon buried in the ground and a palm racing towards her.

There was a small burst of explosive astral energies as Lethia was sent flying, disarmed. Hitting the ground, she rolled a little ways before orienting herself and jumping back to her feet. She breathed heavily, holding her chest. "Magic? In a duel?"

"We only agreed on practice weapons, nothing more, nothing less. Unless you feel like surrendering." Surrender? Now? That word made her angry, as if the very gesture spat in the face of everything she had worked up too. She couldn't help her fiery nature as she stood up and started to rush towards him. Fafnir laughed and took a stance, ready to swing at the unarmed mercenary. When she came into range, he took a backstep, turning and gripping the edge of the handle with both hands, delivering a massive horizontal slice towards his opponent. Lethia dropped, sliding just under the swing and between his legs. Hands planted on the ground, she spun, knocking out his legs from underneath the prince. Following through, her feet landed square on his back and shoved. Lethia cried out in exertion as she hardly managed to shove the weight of a fully grown Draconian in full plate away. It ended up forcing her to roll backwards and push her body downwards in an awkward position, a rash action resulting in less than ideal consequences. Still, she got herself up on her feet and walked over to the halberd, ripping it out of the ground. Fafnir also took a less than graceful fall, so both fighters took a minute to get back onto their feet and catch their breaths, glaring at one another.

"Yeah, alright, not my brightest moment, though the word surrender only makes me angry. You don't know the work and pain I've gone through, and you never could," she said through laboured breaths. Smiling, Fafnir stepped out of his combat stance and shook his head.

"I believe I'm finished, then. I know by rules I'm surrendering, but I don't think I should risk breaking you before you have a chance to truly grow." Lethia stared at him in confusion. "I see potential in you, Lethia Azalea. You're rash, but even in a blind state, your instincts are pretty good. I would love to see you when you have fully matured as a fighter."

"Then how about I help spare your pride and consider this a draw?" Lethia offered, walking over and holding out a hand. Fafnir looked at the hand and smiled, taking it firmly and shaking it. He returned to his father, and Lethia rejoined her friend Milly, the pair hurrying off towards the smiths.

The moment they were out of sight, Lethia exploded into her werewolf form, clothes shredding off her body, and collapsed on the ground clutching her legs. "Shit, shit shit shit…"

"Whoa, Leth! What's going on?!" Milly rushed to her.

"When I threw him in the armour with my legs, I had so much adrenaline pumping through me, I didn't feel anything at first. Now it feels like I fractured my legs and sprained all the muscles in them." Her face screwed up in pain. "What the hell was I thinking!? Why would I do something I normally would only do in my werewolf form? I didn't even think things through, I just went and did it!"

"The fact that you actually managed to MOVE him at all was actually impressive. I think this curse has given your human form enhanced strength," Milly noted as she lit the forge to get the coals hot for her friend.

"Believe me, it damn well doesn't feel like anything to be proud of right now. I feel like I couldn't even stand on my legs without them breaking," she whined, her wolf form making it come out more as a whimper. The pain was rapidly going away, though it was still too much for her to stand. "You think that's why he decided to end the match? Because he knew I just did something that was going to cripple me a moment later?"

"If so, then the prince seems to certainly be a very honest man, which I won't lie, is a little surprising considering the pride of Draconians. They all seem so pompous and smug." Milly let out a sigh before her eyes lit up in a dream-like manner. "They probably guard their smithing secrets with the utmost jealousy! Did you see the prince's armour!? That gold and silver looks like it's a part of the steel plate itself, and I know for sure it's steel. Silver or gold would have absolutely dented when you struck him. Actually, even steel should have bent, so perhaps it's mithril, but then why would they make such a powerful metal look so dull? Normally, it has such a bright lustre."

"Perhaps for the same reason why I got mine coloured?" Lethia suggested before seeing the burning furnace. Wordlessly, she pointed at herself, and Milly nodded. Rolling onto her stomach, she crawled using her arms and pulled herself into the furnace for the fires to help relax her body. "You're the best, Milly!"

"It's a lot easier than prepping a hot bath for you. Now if you excuse me, I need to look at the Emperor's armour. I think it was made of platinum!"

"Milly, you're hopeless," the disembodied voice of Lilith echoed as the twins disappeared to rejoin the draconians. Left alone, Lethia lay in the burning hot coals as her leg muscles relaxed and slowly set themselves again. She breathed deeply, closing her eyes so she could nap, letting the fires lick along her body. Before she could get comfortable though, a trumpet sounded. Her eyes flew open as the trumpet sounded loud and long again. What did it mean?

Then she remembered.

"We're under siege!"

Chapter 10

On the walls, Milly looked over the roads to what was happening before them. A large number of misshapen, unrecognisable creatures were shambling towards the fortress. At the base of the fortress were random amounts of rotten food and animal carcasses, a number of it inside the fortress as well. Off in the distance, a small group of bandits hidden inside a magical field stood by a catapult, loading garbage and other noxious organics onto the large contraption. "What in the world are they doing? What is all of this!?" Milly exclaimed, confused by these bizarre tactics.

"Monsters!" Talisan exclaimed "They are throwing rotten food and other strong smelling things to ensure the monsters come right for us. Those that have a sense of smell anyway. Looks like they think they can get us killed by drawing a random assortment of monsters to attack the base. How did they manage to make so many?" the guild master wondered.

Every monster was different from the last. Discoloured, monochrome, winged, bipedal and eight legged creatures scurrying around in seemingly random directions. Each creature was a chaotic mash up of limbs and torsos, thrown together as if batter fired from cannons at itself at high speeds. No discernable rhyme or reason to any of them, many of these mutating monstrosities falling apart just on their approach towards the fortress. Those that did collapse, however, seemed to melt and were scooped up by other amorphous beasts, coalescing and fusing into them to make each creature bigger and even more intimidating. A good number resembled a collage of different animal parts, a number recognisable, but far more exotic than the known animals of the lands.

"These are the monsters that need to be hunted down and eliminated regularly. Reaching numbers like these is dangerous," Talisan said as the guild soldiers lined the walls. With the unique way the Shields handled equipment and membership, they lined the walls armed with an array of different equipment and gear, not hesitating before opening fire. Milly looked around in surprise at the intensity and speed of their defense. The monsters likewise were not wasting time in attacking, so the defenders found themselves on the back foot, trying to get everyone on the walls and the gates secured.

Milly thought she could go get Lethia, then remembered she was in her werewolf form, and the odds of her turning human again were very slim. "Lilith, we need to help."

"What!?" Lilith exclaimed in shock as she materialised beside her. "No! We need to get ourselves some place safe, we can't be risking your life!" Milly paused with confusion. "We are blacksmiths! Not warriors, this isn't the kind of fighting we can do!"

"I don't wanna sit around and do nothing!" she retorted and ran through her. "We need to do something. This isn't a long siege, this is an assault. We can't just man the smiths and maintain equipment, this is going to be a straight up brawl!"

"Then we stay out of their way, and keep you alive, healthy and uninjured. These are all professionals, they don't need someone who hasn't been in a proper fight!" Lilith argued as Milly ran towards the forge. When she arrived, she grabbed the crossbow the two had made for themselves for self-defense. The crossbow itself was fairly ordinary looking with a steel trimmed stock. It sported a spring loaded mechanism and a handle to pull back on the slider for the bolt. She never grabbed bolts as she started running her way back towards the wall. "Milly are you even listening to me! We can't be rash about this!" Finally, Milly stopped as they looked over the wall at all the mercenaries currently fighting off the invasion.

"I mean..." Milly started, panting as she gripped the crossbow in her hands. "I can't just sit down and do nothing," she said, turning around to face Lilith.

"Wait, where did Lethia go? We left her at the forge, but when we got there, she was gone." Lilith pondered. "Is she really so reckless as to come fight when stuck in her werewolf form!?" She growled, frustrated after all the work they went through. The Emperor's procession was still around, and she could be discovered easily.

"I doubt she is that reckless. She is probably trying to calm herself down. Too many prying eyes, friendly and otherwise," Milly said. "We need to do something to help. They are a man down because of it!" she argued, only to receive stalwart silence as a response. With a smirk, Milly spoke up again. "Or you can put your faith in people who can't protect me as well as you can."

"I'm not putting faith in anyone! I'm the only one who can really keep you safe, me and my magic!" Lilith replied with indignity.

"Then I'm surprised you're just arguing against something that would only be protecting me in the long run, preventing monsters from getting past those you don't have faith in," Milly replied with a playful smirk. Lilith continued to look at the battle as she processed what her sister was saying.

"You need to stop taking lessons from our mom on how to manipulate people."

"I don't, I just listen in on you two when you talk."

"You're a brat, Milly." Lilith sighed, exasperated. "But I do love you, though sometimes you're more of a pain in my ass than anything. Let's go show these guys how to really defend a fortress." Milly wasted no time as she ran towards a flight of stairs, defenders going past her up and down to ferry ammunition to the wall-walk. The smith kept down low, walking in a crouched stance as random objects flew over her head, stingers and fluids. She could swear something was literally firing hands over the walls which landed limply on the ground to twitch and melt away. "These monsters are... bizarre."

"No kidding, they make no sense!" Suddenly a section of the defensive structure up high was blasted by a beam of energy, evaporating the wood and stone behind them. Down low was a creature with its chest wide open and a half-formed crystal protruding out of it's flesh. Arcane energy was pooling around the crystal as it spun, charging up what was apparently a focused laser of magical energies. Defenders wasted no time in trying to take the creature down, but the arcane energy it was absorbing formed a defensive barrier around it.

"High value target. It's crystal produces an energy that protects it from physical attacks," Milly said as Lilith focused on the energy glowing in the crossbow. Taking aim, Milly fired, the magical blast piercing the barrier and striking the crystal, shattering it. The creature melted immediately after, only for another monster to cannibalise it and add its dying mass to its own. Milly shot at it as well, the beams of dark purple energy causing the creature to explode.

"Those are arcane bolts, aren't they!?" one of the defenders shouted from nearby. "Monsters are mutated nephele, beings of pure arcane magic. How is yours being so effective?"

"Because it's not arcane magic, you idiot," Lilith mocked while Milly focused on her task at hand, firing another blast. "I'm a demon. It's weaponized energy from my own form, my own spirit. Think of it as basically my sister firing very angry punches at a speed faster than even the heaviest crossbow. With a little bit of an explosive punch for good measure." Milly took another shot, Lilith losing just the tiniest bit of colour each time.

"Well, be careful not to drain yourself too much. Can't have you dying on us," he told her, firing his own shots at the enemy.

"I'd die to ensure my sister will live," Lilith muttered to herself, reloading the crossbow.

The battle waged on around them, the defenders focusing on keeping the enemy away from the walls as much as they could. Milly focused on trying to shoot down any of the monsters that looked to be far bigger threats than others. Yet the hordes managed to reach the base of the walls, scaling them or trying to claw through the wood and stone structure holding it together. Druids on the other side commanded the trees and vines built into the walls to lash out, piercing and whipping large wounds open. The natural magic struggled to make any lasting damage on the arcane fueled creatures as they scaled the walls. Milly focused on the monsters on the walls, firing at them to kill or at least knock them off. Lilith was quickly running out of strength, not used to using this much of her power in a short amount of time. "Don't know how much longer I can keep this up..." she growled before Talisan, who had been doing rounds on the wall, came around to her.

"We need to evacuate our VIP's before our base is overwhelmed. I want you to go with them," he ordered, placing a hand on Milly's shoulder. "You two have already done more than we should have asked, thank you. We can take it from here." Lilith nodded and faded from view as Milly holstered her crossbow and got off the walls. As she did, a few monsters leaped up from the edges of the walls at the defenders. They drew swords and cut them down in a clean slash. Milly paused, seeing them all glow with a glimmering light.

"Minerva has answered our prayers and blessed our weapons with spirit magic. We shouldn't have too much trouble cutting them down now," Talisan explained as Milly continued down towards the royal family.

Fafnir, Glaurung and their retinue were all armed and standing by the entrance to the main barracks. As Milly approached, she saw them watching the battlefield, itching to do something. Only the Emperor himself had a relaxed pose. Shortly after, Lethia and Toshiko ran out from the barracks behind the draconians, making them turn around in alarm. "We have an escape tunnel prepared to get you out of here."

"A tunnel!? You expect to drag the Emperor through the muck and dirt where your filth can-" one of the younger generals started before the Emperor turned on him. In a swift motion, his balled fist collided with his stomach, through his armour. It left an impressive dent in the solid steel frame, as well as knocking the wind out of his lungs.

"We leave through the tunnels. It's the safest route, and we do not owe the Silver Shields in the defence here. It's not our place. If they wish to have us flee, then we will swallow our pride and escape through the tunnels." The Emperor commanded, his voice a broiling tone of dominance. The cowed general looked up at the Emperor with a fiery glance for a brief moment before nodding.

Lethia was in her human form again. She shook her head, silently warning Milly and Lilith to say nothing, though her eyes were still completely on fire. "We're also escaping with precious cargo," she added, pointing to a few sacks filled with the demonic fur. "This is fur from the hellhound we keep prisoner on the compound. We are to ensure it doesn't get taken by enemy hands. I ask you to each take a bag. We don't have enough men to spare taking them all ourselves."

"Why should we do such a thing?" Fafnir demanded.

"Because this fur is stronger than steel and is completely fireproof. If you aid us in this, we have permission to give you one such bag as both compensation and a gift." That settled the debate quickly as the draconians picked up the bundles. Toshiko nodded silently towards the group before leading them through the barracks and to the escape tunnels that lead beneath the complex. Milly and Lilith brought up the rear with their crossbow, a bolt charged in the holster and ready to fire when needed.

The tunnels beneath the complex were crafted expertly, walls of stone with torches lit. As the party walked through the tunnels, the draconians noted how every ten feet, it would split into different directions, yet the path they followed was the only path with lit torches. "Why don't the other tunnels have torches?"

"Only the route I choose has torches. When not in use, these tunnels are pitch black. Should invaders ever discover and use these tunnels, they are designed to be a trap of mazes. That is all I shall say to those not of the Silver Shields," Toshiko responded in an even tone.

"Typical of the Fukai Chikyu to withhold information from outsiders." Fafnir grumbled.

"I'm surprised you said the name of my people and not the insult," Toshiko said. "I suppose there are those of your empire who can respect us, even in nobility."

"Not that you deserve it, mole," came a harsh retort from a general. Toshiko looked forward and let the silence fill the air.

"If you weren't honoured guests, lizard, I'd show you how foolish it is to insult me in my own turf."

"That's enough," Lethia barked, making all of them turn, eliciting a blush from her. "We shouldn't... we shouldn't be fighting each other right now..."

"She is right. The more time we waste arguing, the more likely we may be discovered," Toshiko remarked. Fumerage huffed in indignation as the group continued to march onward. Eventually, the tunnels turn from formed brick into rounded dirt supported by wooden columns. The torch light grew fainter the further they went along.

"This is like some of the draconian horror stories we tell the younglings," Glaurin says with a smirk. "Don't walk down an earthen tunnel with no lights, there are things even the deep earth dwellers fear. A tunneler of the soft earths, it makes tunnels just like these. They never make a noise as they burrow around you. Before you know it, you are walking in its tunnels, led astray by the disappearing torches. Then it comes for you, without warning, the earth falls beneath you, and you're swallowed by the legendary earth shark!"

"How would you know about them?" Toshiko asked, perplexed. "Though they are sand sharks, not earth. Solid earth is too difficult for them to burrow through. They prefer the softer earth that borders the great deserts in the Land of the Three Kings."

"We visit those lands from time to time, and they have attacked a few settlements on the surface," Glaurung added. "We have received requests to assist our draconian brethren who live there." Toshiko nodded, as if accepting the answer.

"Regardless, we should be at the surface soon. This tunnel leads opposite of where the attack began. Still, these are monsters, and many of them wander randomly even if given a specific target. Keep your weapons drawn and your magic ready."

Lethia and Milly were sticking to the rear, making sure nothing managed to follow them. "I don't think I needed to know that horror story," Lethia said. "This is my first time in a tunnel. Why are they even talking about such a thing so casually in the first place?"

"It's to help with our nerves," the prince spoke up, dropping back to walk with them. "We're proud people who normally have very tense relations with the Fukai Chikyu. Right now, we are wandering through tunnels made by one during a siege of monsters that can turn into anything at random. Who is to say they won't randomly come through the walls? Or worse, what if we're being led into an ambush?" The Emperor turned his head and growled lowly, warning his son of the potential harm he could cause from those words. Fafnir dropped his gaze. "They are very secretive people. You don't know what he is hiding."

Finally, they spotted light emanating from around a corner. The crew unconsciously picked up speed before Toshiko signalled for them to halt. Shadows flickered in the sunlight that filtered through. Silently, the assassin signalled them to backtrack, and the group began to turn around. A sudden crackle of electricity filled the air, making the hairs on the Humans and Chikyu stand. What followed was a flash of blinding light and a deafening crack of lightning. The only other thing which was heard immediately after was the cry of sheer panic and terror. Milly fell to the ground, crying in fear. Lethia ran over to help pick up the girl as the scream had alerted the monsters and they started charging in. Another crash of lightning, and a monster appeared above the procession.

The monster looked down at the group below, bone and sinew crackling with thunderous energy. It took note of Milly, who was so enthralled in panic that Lethia couldn't even get her to stand. Another deafening crack and the beast was flying through the air towards the two women. Lethia shifted herself to protect Milly with her body, forgetting about the risk of exposing herself.

Glaurung reacted faster than anyone. A sudden blast of purple and orange as he spat an arcane ball of fire at the creature. The moment it collided with the monster, it exploded and sent the beast hurtling towards the ground. Drawing his blade, he thrust upwards and skewered the monster on his polished steel. The blade glowed as energy flowed from hilt to blade and exploded in a bright ball of spiritual dragon fire, evaporating the creature instantly.

"Run!" Toshiko shouted and the group tried to retreat, slowed by the currently incapacitated blacksmith. Knowing they wouldn't have enough time to evacuate them, Lethia looked back at the tunnel exit. "Toshiko, get them out of here, I'll buy you all time," she said as she grabbed a number of the fur bags from the draconians.

"What are you doing!?" Toshiko shouted when he failed to catch Lethia by the shoulder.

"Collapse the tunnel behind me, Toshiko," Lethia instructed, giving him a look of finality. He saw her eyes turn demonic and got the message. Without another word, the assassin flexed his claws and tore up the support, slashing at the walls with his claws. The tunnel collapsed, separating Lethia from the rest of the group. Finally isolated, she dumped the fur around herself and threw a few bags down the tunnel. "Alright, you monstrous bastards, I'm tense, in pain, and pissed off that you terrorized my friend." With no risk of being discovered, she allowed her body to transform again with explosive results. The fur that was caught in the blast reacted to Lethia's mood and exploded as a result, causing a chain reaction of fiery napalm to envelope the tunnels, heating it up to a degree that evaporated the moisture out of the earth in seconds. The monsters coming down the tunnel were caught in the blast and burned alive. Very few of them had tolerance to heat and continued to bear down on the werewolf.

With the numbers cut down by a large margin, the werewolf took her halberd and held it forward. This was a tunnel, they could only come from one direction, and Lethia exploited that. The simple minded beasts cared not for the burning hot implement of death the demonic mercenary was carrying as she skewered them, the bodies melting away as she struck them down with lethal efficiency. It didn't take long for Lethia to emerge from the tunnel. Toshiko would be leading the Emperor and the others to an alternative exit. She raced towards the second exit, easily reaching it before the others could, and made sure the exit was clear for the entourage to emerge from.

Back at the fortress, the Silver Shields were struggling to hold the walls. Minerva's blessing only worked on melee weapons as bows and other ranged implements were deemed to be weapons of pure aggression. The goddess of protection wouldn't bless them. With their stance on member survival over holding the fortress, injured members were pulled off the front to be tended to by healers. Situations like these were the only times they justified the blood magic art of healing as they needed to keep people fighting. Still, with how cautious they were about preserving life, it ensured it was much more difficult to hold the lines.

"The enemy numbers are dwindling, but we are getting more injuries than we can keep up with," Autu reported to Talisan as he fired his bow at another mutant trying to climb the wall. Talisan struck down another that had climbed up between him and another defender. After slaying the first, he ran over to skewer the other monster that had pinned his comrade. Inspecting him, the mercenary he saved had a major hole in his shoulder.

"Medics!" He called, blocking an attack from a mutant before skewering it, protecting his comrade. Autu ran over and checked the wound while Talisan kept them covered. He made a tourniquet out of a bandage he kept on his hip and covered the wound to help slow the bleeding before standing up and continuing to fight off the hordes.

"Not gonna lie, this is looking dire, sir. We may need to order an evac," he said, firing another arrow into the back of a monster. "We are losing defenders, and we don't even know how many are injured or dead."

"You're right. Send the word before we're overwhelmed," Talisan said before turning back to knock a monster off the wall. As he did so, he looked over for a moment and chuckled. "We may not have to, after all. Look who is coming to the rescue." He says as Autu turned to look over. A trail of fire smoldered behind Lethia as she raced through the woods, cutting through the monsters from behind and drawing attention. As a giant ball of flame, half of the monstrous horde either ran towards it or panicked at the sight of the flame. The defenders on the wall had enough time to get the wounded away safely and have fresh troops mount the walls.

The bandits responsible for the siege in the first place recognized the demonic werewolf. Knowing better than to stick around with the infamous Hellhound in the area, they abandoned the catapult and ran. They had never expected the Silver Shields to hold out as long as they did, let alone to have the burning wolf demon appear from seemingly nowhere. With the hordes split and distracted, the mercenary guild was able to repel the attack and ensure not a single monster remained standing. Lethia continued to run around the outer perimeter, slaying every last monster that had been brought to the compound.

After the battle concluded, the guild went to work at tallying the injured and the dead. First priority was ensuring the wounded were taken care of as best they could. Lethia was tasked to gather medicinal herbs from the surrounding woodland. Milly and Toshiko returned after escorting the draconian entourage to a main road so they could continue onward away from the fighting. Toshiko got busy digging graves for those who had fallen, as well as a hole to mop up and dispose of the melted remains of many of the mutants. Milly got to work helping make splints for people with broken bones and limbs. When everyone was accounted for, they had lost very few members in the siege, though many more might be entering early retirement considering the extent of the injuries they had suffered. Talisan sat down on the steps leading to the top of the wall after he finished giving orders, watching the grim aftermath of the siege.

Lethia flopped down onto the ground nearby, huffing up into the air. "This is what the mercenary life is like, Lethia," Talisan said "Blood, death, conflict and graves. Toshiko told me what you did in the tunnels." He looked down at his exhausted niece. "Reckless, but smart, using your fur like tar fire. You are becoming quicker on your feet and good at improvising. Those are talents you need to continue to hone and sharpen." Lethia smiled and laughed, which made her cough.

"Ugh... thanks uncle. I'm feeling absolutely exhausted right now. Holding back the beast for so long, my brain was getting a bit fuzzy. I don't think it likes being held back like that. It's almost like trying to hold a big hound by a leash, but the more I hold it back, it grows bigger and bigger. I'm nervous it might grow too strong for me to hold back if I do that for too long." Talisan nodded solemnly, remembering what the feral side of Lethia was like back when she first reappeared in Celosia. "I'm kind of scared of becoming feral again. I don't wanna cause that kind of harm and devastation again."

"That is why I'm trying to encourage you to let it out as opposed to holding it all in," Talisan said. "At this point, it's safe to say you will not be able to keep your identity a secret for very long. Still, hide it for as long as you can. The more of a positive reputation you build upon your own name, the more faith people will have when they learn your secret. Granted, knowing the greed of our country, that faith is only going to go so far, as well as the fear. Has anyone actually told you how high the bounty on the head of the hellhound actually is?"

"No. How big is it?" She had completely forgotten about a bounty being placed on her head, and the realisation sent a cold fear through her spine.

"Fifty thousand gold pieces. Enough gold to start up your own guild on par with my own."

Emperor Glaurung heard a day later that the Silver Shields had repelled the siege and ensured every monster had been properly disposed of. Rumours about the hellhound showing up at that point in time felt rather convenient for the group as they travelled onward, their next destination being the central city that hosted the guild of the Fire Wyrms. Hicoth was once an imperial draconian himself, so they knew he would be someone they could go to for a more straightforward response to their inquiries than Talisan had given.

Right now, however, as the group travelled, the Emperor and crown prince were both puzzled over the sudden appearance of the Hellhound. The timing of it just felt far too clean and convenient, and even the older generals were putting the connections together. After all, news of the Hellhound that had razed an eighth of the northern commonwealth spread far. They knew it was an exaggeration, but the amount of damage she had caused in those two years was certainly nothing to scoff at. They hadn't seen her personally, and the rumour could only be so informative. Still, it was confirmed the Silver Shields had captured the Hellhound. "You think they are weaponizing the Hellhound?" Fafnir asked as they marched through the woods.

"It wouldn't make sense for Talisan to do such a thing. He's a man of very stalwart character. For him to employ the use of a demon would mean he is very desperate for something bigger, or there is something extremely personal that is making him keep the demon around."

"Then I suppose it would also be very difficult to keep such a thing a secret," one of the older generals said. "If you don't mind me speaking up, your graces."

"Not at all. This is a less than casual setting, so holding everyone responsible to adhere to the rules of court would be strange," Glaurung replied. "As of now, we are travelers in a caravan, and you all are my trusted generals and body guards. Such a conversation may prove to be fruitful for you all as well. I do believe, however, that Talisan's reasons for having the Hellhound are much, much closer to home than we all may guess." With those words, the other generals began to hatch their own theories of what might be happening.

"What makes you believe that?" Hisshire asked.

"I have seen Talisan climb the ranks and take ownership of that guild. He is as stalwart as he is compassionate and thorough. We also met his niece, with those burning eyes of hers. On top of that, all the shedding they have, I don't think the Hellhound is in captivity. We don't have much evidence, but I suspect Lethia is the Hellhound." The younger generals laughed, and even the older ones stifled chuckles from the idea. Glaurung simply smiled and shrugged. "The shedding would make sense. Why in the world, let alone how, could they manage to keep such a demon tame enough to trim it?" The chuckles immediately stopped as the logic settled their heads. Such a beast would certainly have many problems with being shaved regularly. What would a shaved hellhound even look like?

"What you are suggesting then," Glaurin said after a moment, "is that, somehow, Lethia is some kind of demonic werebeast?" When he said those words, the whole group paused as if the pieces all came together. "That makes way too much sense now that I have said it aloud."

"So it does..." Fafnir murmured, thinking back to his duel with Lethia. With that in mind, he now assumed Lethia was holding back. "What do you suppose her burning eyes would mean then? How much power is currently flowing through her?"

"Let's not start assuming such a thing is truly fact," Glaurung said. "At this point, we are merely speculating, nothing more. All we have is anecdotal evidence to support nothing, a guess of something impossible. First, how would a were-creature become a demon and still maintain those powers? When one dies, they lose their physical form. That would include the werewolf curse as that is a physical ailment, not a spiritual. Then there is also the fact that there should be some kind of demonic influence somewhere on her body."

"If you exclude the fire coming from her eyes, there wasn't one single clue." Hisshire said, crossing his arms. "The flames did seem to be a curious shade of green at the base, as if wafting directly from the centre of her eyes."

"If you don't mind my asking, sir, but this all feels like pointless speculation. Is there a purpose to this conversation? You said it yourself, everything there is mostly baseless. All we know is that the Silver Shields are weaponizing a Hellhound."

"That is exactly the point. The Silver Shield's, in one manner or another, are employing a demon. One that had the country issuing a nationwide alert," Glaurung said, and the group nodded. "If they have indeed discovered a way to tame them, void of how they do it, we now know we need to be more cautious than ever. Whether of a demon incursion on our borders, or the greedy upper echelon of the Commonwealth thinking they could push their borders into our mountain range."

"Then should we not act on it? Set up tariffs or some other action to pressure the Silver Shields into giving up this creature they are harbouring?"

"Perhaps..." Glaurung said pensively. "It would have to be in a way that keeps us covered. Any indication of our involvement will of course have political ramifications. However, we do have a solution for this dilemma. It just so happens to also be the same individual we are going to be visiting."

Chapter 11

The Emperor's group travelled north east along the border, heading for the trade capital of Tollarel. The city itself was a curious sight to people outside the Commonwealth, as when it came into view, it looked like a small hovel of large farm houses surrounded by an ocean of colour and fabric. The trade port was in fact a massive trade and camp city, where merchants would arrive and set up temporary stalls to sell, trade and barter with people coming and going from the port, or with other merchants from around the known world.

The outer rims of the tents were the most loosely put together, as they were merchants only just starting out, or only had few goods or little time to make trades. Tents could be seen regularly being taken down and put up, making the outer circles of Tollarel feel like a morphing mass of colours. It was important to have bright, vibrant colours in order to attract customers and stand out from the crowd, a dance of every color palette to create a constant swirling rainbow.

Further into the second circle were the more regular merchants and those who were well established. The city itself would rent out spots to merchants for a few days or weeks at a time depending on how rich they were, or how popular. Here the tents also served as homes, being large enough to accommodate people and even had a number of workers who helped run the store front while the owners went to see what goods they could take advantage of from other merchants. Streets were always packed with people and animals as they wandered and commenced in commercial war and banter.

The inner circles were where structures became permanent, towering houses and mansions with luxurious wares intended for nobles. These were the owners of the city as well as the town hall, and they were protected with a large wooden palisade. Mercenaries from the Blood Blades patrolled the walls and the city limits as black markets would pop up within the port city, hiding between legitimate business or cutting deals.

Tallorel was also home to the Emperor's destination, a large fortress overlooking the port city from the top of a cliff, the central headquarters of the Fire Wyrm mercenary guild. The port city was on the edge of a cliff overlooking a large beach. Fukai Chikyu had crafted stairwells through the cliff and stone leading towards the docks that housed thousands of merchant ships. The coast was wide and open, with a few caverns scattered which served as moors for the boats under the protection of the grand fortress above. The castle walls stood fifteen feet tall with cannons lining the walls, and towers sported Ballista, waiting to finally retire in leu of the more devastating artillery developed in recent years. A second curtain of walls stood behind it, and between them was the training grounds and barracks, as well as a number of defensive structures designed to trap, slow and maim any invaders should they break through the first set of walls. The second walls stood twenty feet high, easily towering the first set of walls and allowing defenders to fire volleys over the first stone curtain. Inside the second wall were farms, a manmade lake, tunnels leading below the castle towards an iron deposit for smithies to work their craft. The castle was a meticulous design of modern construction compared to the Silver Shields' fortress of nature blended with technology.

Glaurung and his group were welcomed with the same treatment they had received from the Silver Shields, however, the guild leader hadn't deigned to greet them. With far more guild members being draconians, they were able to treat their guests more favourably, having knowledge of typical imperial fair they enjoyed. The Emperor headed towards where the guild leader could be found.

Hicoth's personnel floor was both an office and meeting room. A human and a red draconian sat there, spending their time going through paperwork from the checkpoints they had scattered across the land. Monster sightings, mercenary requests, news and other hearsay from the country were organised by the two lieutenants. As they worked, a crash was heard from above and the red draconian started to wag his tail. The human, having caught sight of the eagerness in his companion, sighed. "Stop perving over those two, Mik."

Mik didn't respond as a few more crashes were heard overhead. He squirmed a little in his seat and his companion took on a huffy tone. "For crying out loud, you get like this every time those two go at it!"

"I'd do anything to be in either of their shoes." Mik replied as he turned from his paperwork, "You should know Sean, look at our leaders! Hicoth is easily the most accomplished Red draconian and he is just, so fierce and unrelenting! Then there is Cinder... she's just so... Mmmm... my scales just rattle imagining her throwing me across the room."

"You reds are so weird, I'll never understand." Sean replied, shaking his head as he went back to his paperwork as a grunt and smash echoed from the floor above. Suddenly the door opened up as the Emperor, along with Fumerage, walked into the office room. Both Fire Wyrm lieutenants stood immediately and saluted. "Evening your majesty! To what do we owe the pleasure sir?" they spoke in unison.

"At ease," Glaurung replied casually. "I'm just here to speak with Hicoth, are they-" A scream and a sudden smash of what sounded like glass made the four men look upwards. "Aaa, I see that I came at a bad time."

"I can go get them for you!" Mik offered hastily as he stood up, though as he turned to go, he found his feet frozen to the floor. Sean stood from his desk as chilled air left his body.

"I will go get them, Mik. You're already risking demotion from the amount of times you barge in on them." He stated as he walked past his much larger companion, leaving Mik to use his fiery breath to thaw himself free from his companion's ice magic. "You can keep the Emperor entertained."

As Sean vanished behind the door leading to Hicoth's private quarters, Fumerage crossed his arms. "Forgive me for speaking out of line your majesty, but I fail to see what aid this whelp of a draconian would give us. He was an utter disgrace in ou-"

The sudden crack of wood silenced the young general as Mik's fist collided with his desk. "Don't you dare talk ill of our leader like that! Who are you to insult the master of the house!" Flames billowed from Mik's jaws while he struggled to reign in his emotions. Fumerage strutted over until the two large males were face to face.

"No other Red Draconian has ever had a losing streak like Hicoth, not a single win to his name. It's a wonder he has made himself a guild owner, let alone enticed what many considered the most attractive woman in red society." Fumerage growled back, the eyes of the Emperor the only thing preventing the pair from breaking into a fight.

Sean climbed a stairwell that led up to the living quarters of Hicoth and his wife Cinder. As he made his way up, the sounds of huffing and heavy breathing got louder. Finally he got to the large door led into their room and opened it wide. Stepping inside, he took out his shield to block a club was thrown his way, knowing when the lovers were going at it, things were chaos.

Both red draconians were stark naked as Hicoth rushed Cinder with a broken spear, aiming to sweep her legs out from under her. Taking a step, she stomped on the wooden shaft and broke it into pieces before delivering a swift hook to Hicoth's head. She stood a full two feet over the whelp, allowing her to throw punches at his head with ease. Hicoth however rolled with the punch and delivered an elbow into her stomach, making her double over. After he grabbed her shoulders and flipped over her to land on her back, pinning her to the floor with his weight for only a moment. Cinder got an arm free and grabbed Hicoth's, pulling him off towards her side and rolled on top of him, pinning him down.

"Excuse me for interrupting your love session," Sean began. "However the Emperor has come to see you."

"Damn, I was just about ready to get a proper advantage over her." Hicoth growled and Cinder laughed.

"Hun please, look at yourself, you're pinned under me. I was about to take you all for myself." She replied and they both playfully huffed fire at one another before kissing. After the large eight foot tall woman got off her husband and stretched. Hicoth rolled back, legs in the air and jumped up onto his feet as if he had just woken up from a nap.

"I would have gotten out and made you mine, just you wait till tonight." He says as he rolls his arms.

"Already am, now common, we need to get dressed. Don't think we should greet him sweaty, naked and smelling of love."

"I'm never going to understand reds." Sean says softly "I'll let the Emperor know you two are on your way down." With that, he turned and walked back down to the meeting chamber where the ruler waited. When he showed up, Glaurung looked at him with a raised brow. "The lovers were fighting again like it was life and death. I really don't understand how that is love, but they are cleaning themselves up and will be down shortly." The Emperor gave an amused chuckle at the statement. "No, seriously, I remember one time they both came down with dislocated arms saying they needed a healer, they were both out of action for a week!"

"They must have been really passionate that time." Glaurung breathed out, noting how Mik was looking far more flustered remembering the day. "A red draconians most cherished characteristic is their fighting prowess, how well they can handle themselves. If I recall, a human slang for sex is, what was it, dirty wrestling? That is an accurate enough statement for Red draconian sex."

"To me it just looks like they are simply fighting naked, there wasn't even any intercourse."

"Then you simply miss those moments." He replied. A short time later, Hicoth appeared, the six foot two inch Draconian wearing cotton pants with a chainmail shirt. While tall for humans, he was much smaller than many of his kind. Lean and powerful muscles glistened beneath the steel chain, scales a bright red. A spike protruded out of the centre of his skull with a trail of smaller spikes leading down his neck to his back. His wingspan was equally small, with black leathery skin between the scaled frame.

Behind him, Cinder came down in a Huldra inspired green and white gown. The green was chainmail that had been painted while the white was sheer silk, allowing her muscled bodice to be visible through the fabric reaching down below her knees. It looked strange for such a flowing and immaculate dress to be on the body of a powerhouse of a draconian woman, however her movements were rather delicate to compensate for her muscled mass. Hands over top one another and resting just below her stomach, she acted far more civilised than typical red draconian fare. She also did not have wings which hinted towards her mixed lineage of having a Huldra father, as well as a more curvy and busty frame.

"Your majesty," Cinder said with a curtsy. "What can we do for you today? If we had received word you were going to be arriving now, we would have put off our love making for another time."

"You're fine. I think it's good the two of you are cherishing each other," Glaurung responded with a smile. "There isn't a minute where I don't yearn for my wife, Hilgith cherish her."

"Hilgith, your majesty? Don't you mean the ancestors?" Mik asked curiously, and the Emperor turned his head to him.

"I'm a draconian who has travelled these lands countless times and have seen much in my lifetime. While I do hold the dragon ancestors as favourably as anyone else, I know better than my people that the gods are the ones who truly run the world we live in. There is no point in blinding myself otherwise," he explains before turning back to Hicoth, "If you two don't mind, I'd like to walk and talk in private. I'll let you get dressed first before we head outside." With a nod, the four exited, leaving the two lieutenants to continue their paperwork. As the doors closed, the room regained its silence aside from the scribble of quills on parchment.

"Okay fine, I wouldn't mind spending a night making love to Cinder, she is quite attractive." Sean admitted, not even looking up. Mik simply laughed in response, looking at his companion and nodded.

"Yeah, though I don't know why she wears such frail looking clothing. She should dress more like Hicoth, armoured and rugged."

"It's because she's half Huldra," Sean replied, and Mik looked at him in doubt. "No, really, her father was a Huldra way back in the day, and she has been studying her Huldra heritage to emulate them. Why do you think she left the empire?"

"I thought there were only women in huldra society, I never saw any of the men." Mik replied, making Sean roll his eyes.

"Mik, we fight one at the-" he paused mid-sentence. "Wait, no he never shows up at the grand tournament. Still yes, male huldra exist. Besides, I like her outfit, it's rather pretty."

"I don't get how you can enjoy the pretty stuff," Mik said, and Sean merely smirked.

"Just how I don't get why fighting is the same as sex for you guys."

Cinder sat on the bed, legs crossed as she watched her husband get dressed in a plate mail set of armour and a cloak. The cloak was more for decoration for draconians as it normally interfered with flying. "Are you sure you wish to speak to him alone?" she asked softly, concerned. "I know having the emperor visit is a big thing for us, especially for you. It's still been decades since we left the empire, you don't owe them any loyalty."

"Perhaps I don't," he replied, fastening the belts on his armour. "Yet even you know how respected the Emperor is even by those not of the empire. The fact that he is treating me as a respected, even cherished draconian is something I've strived for my whole life. Fighting in the pit over and over." He laughed without humor. "Such time wasted when I could have spent it hunting real challenges out here." Cinder never argued against him, even though she knew the truth. Standing, she walked over to him and hugged him from behind.

"Yes, yes, as you've said time and time again, and even these lands can't provide a good enough challenge for you." The two shared a quick kiss. "I just worry this love of the empire and of your new found title is going to clash someday. You know the vow you made."

"If I ever break my own pride, I am not worthy to lead this guild," he replied solemnly, before grinning and giving Cinder a light elbow to one of her ribs to tickle her. She flinched, giggling. "That won't ever happen. I'm Hicoth, the fire wyrm!" With that, he ran through the nearby door and headed off to meet up with the Emperor. Cinder sighed, crossing her arms beneath her chest.

"That man, as wild as the flames in a volcano. Just as fierce as well," she muttered before turning to look out a window. "I suppose I'll go practice some dancing today."

Hicoth sent word to the mercenaries patrolling the walls to stand down so he and the Emperor could talk in privacy. Afterwards he found him standing in an archway leading to one of the many walkways on top of the walls. With a bow, Hicoth approached him and the pair began to tour the outer edges of the wall. "Living the good life I see, Hicoth," Glaurung started with a smile. "Beautiful wife, bounding success, fame and wealth. The second most prestigious guild and ranked the strongest in raw military might. For being the empire's smallest red draconian, you have made so much for yourself." Hicoth laughed boastfully in response, looking up to the Emperor.

"Please, the coliseum is nothing compared to this. I have faced every challenge this land has thrown at me and have carved my way through them with brutal ferocity," he growled, boasting of his accomplishments. "So what is it that really brings you here, your majesty? I know you have come to pay respects, yet normally that isn't enough to get you to leave the importance of your job behind. There is something you need, I imagine."

"Yes, actually. I have started a great project to revive the dragons of old." Hicoth's eyes widened in shock. "I am being serious. We are looking into the project, however, we are worried such magic is very... delicate. We are hoping to figure out who may have the power or influence to possibly disrupt it. Considering the Commonwealth seems to be a veritable breeding ground of religious fervour due to the influence of all the Gods here. Druids, merchants, machines, technology, war, death. Everything that represents the Gods in both positive and negative happens here, so it's no doubt they may have someone intervene."

"Well," Hicoth started as they continued to walk along the stony fortification, "that is an interesting question to ask me, and yes I would certainly say there are many who would probably wish to stop such a plan. Namely the very Gods themselves. That is what my wife would say, she knows far more about them than I do. I'm always focused on my next challenge and my next job. So if you wanted to know more about what people to look out for, I would ask you to speak with her. Yet you would probably know -."

"Your wife has hesitations about serving her home kingdom?" Glaurung supplied. The guild leader simply grinned. "I know Cinder quite well. Never met her in person until today, she had eloped with you a week before I was to meet her. That never stopped her peers and of course my constituents from reporting about her quite regularly."

"Sadly I can't say I would be able to help myself as much. After all, as much as I like to keep positive relations with the land of my birth, I have to remain loyal to the place that made me the man I am."

"I see... I see..." Glaurung muttered in thought as they continued to walk, eventually reaching the side of the castle overlooking the ocean. The Emperor took a pause to look over the rolling waves far below the cliff and appreciate the scenery. "Such a beautiful sight... I'll admit, I'm jealous. I don't get to have such a view as this. If it were possible for Emperors to retire, I'd enjoy living in a place like this. Looking over the oceans, calm, peaceful. Serene and gentle yet fierce when agitated."

Hicoth raised an eyebrows at the dreamy statement. "I suppose it is, though I feel as if such beauty is lost to me," he admitted, looking over the waters. "Of course I'm born of fire, ferocity and fierceness. Us reds are never taught to have any shred of compassion from the start."

"Yet you marry a rose by any other name of a red. One who cherishes her Huldra heritage over the ferocity of her blood and design."

"That rose has far too many thorns to be handled by anyone but a draconian!" Hicoth laughed in response, eliciting a grin from Glaurung.

"Much like my own rose at the time. However, I feel like I have drifted off topic long enough." He cleared his throat and turned to face Hicoth, this time taking on the air of nobility he would so regularly cast aside. "About a business proposal, information for information."

"You mean like Fukai?" Hicoth asked, visibly surprised.

"Yes, very much so. Just because our people dislike them does not mean I resemble their every malice. I have information regarding a particularly special bounty. One you yourself may have quite an interest in. Something that would provide quite a healthy challenge for you to hunt down." Hicoth huffed in response, turning back towards the ocean. "Well, hunting them is the easy part, to be honest. Defeating her on the other hand..." The emperor continued on as Hicoth noted some ships coming into view from around a bend. Trading ships from the Empire, it seemed. "Of whom I'm speaking though, of course, is the hellhound."

"Talisan and the Silver Shields had captured her, I've seen the report. They have her locked in custody and are studying her and using her for resources, her fur. Supposedly it's stronger than steel and completely flame retardant. That would make it invaluable for anybody."

"That is the official report, yes, but after my recent visit, I suspect the truth to be far removed from the report. The hellhound is, in fact, Talisan's niece."

Hicoth furrowed his brows. "Why the hell would it be her? How would it be possible!? You're saying a human somehow became both a demon and a werewolf?"

"As well as keeping their sanity." Glaurung continued, causing Hicoth to burst into a fit of laughter. Glaurung smiled and gave Hicoth time to empty his lungs and replace the mirth with reality as the words sank in.

"You're... actually serious? No jest, no joke or fanciful delusion? No... No, you're not the type to resort to those kinds of tricks. You hide details, but you don't outright lie."

"That is true, yes. I don't give out full stories unless absolutely necessary, though in this case what I have said is merely suspicion. What makes this hold weight is the nature of how the Silver Shields were able to repel the most recent incursion upon their headquarters."

"Yeah, I heard the rumours too. They were under heavy siege from monsters, a proper assault instead of a drawn out engagement. They were nearly overrun when the Hellhound showed up and-" Hicoth stopped mid-sentence as the report tumbled out. "You were there during the siege."

"Yes, we were: me, my son and my generals." The pair continued to walk around the castle walls as the Emperor filled him in on the details of his encounter of Talisan and of Lethia. The strange fire she had glowing in her eyes, the sensation of her body so filled with magic he couldn't depict its source. Shortly after she vanished, there was the report of a Hellhound sighting, and she took the demon's fur which, supposedly impossible to ignite, was reduced to cinders. The conversation continued until they reached the doors leading back into the castle proper. Hicoth looked very thoughtful as he digested all the information and evidence.

"This isn't enough information for me to make a move or send a team. But it is enough to raise suspicion and warrant investigation. I think I'll look into this personally."

"I had a feeling one such as yourself would do so," Glaurung said with a smile. "After all, demon corruption is something which should always be a priority for any one of us. This is our world, our home. We cannot risk demons turning it into a hellscape or... whatever sort of plane they call home. Now, I gave you my information, I would like to hear some of yours."

Hicoth thought the request over for a moment. "There would probably be one who may wish to disrupt or perhaps even steal your research. A very powerful Duram mage who goes by the name of Hrumbia. While the mage circles are currently embattled to find a new arch mage to lead them, he seems to be the most powerful by far, yet also the most soft spoken. That, however, doesn't hide his tricky temperament or his powerful casting. Should he learn of your project, he could as easily teleport himself into your study and make off with everything. He can bypass draconian magical security, he is powerful," Hicoth explained, crossing his arms. "That is all I have for you. There are of course bandits and other grey mercenaries who would like to take advantage of such magic, but I hardly know of any grey mercenary who could do much against the might of the Draconian military. That is of course outside of this Hellhound if she is indeed turning mercenary."

"I feel like you give yourself too little credit, Hicoth. I'm sure your own guild could prove an equal to draconic might." Hicoth grinned, taking the compliment in stride. "I have spent too much time on our little walk, my generals are probably getting restless. I can hear the younger ones whining about not getting their wine and caviar now. I miss the old days where our people were not as spoiled. Golden years are as much a curse as a blessing."

"How would a kingdom's golden years be a curse?" Hicoth asked as Glaurung opened the doors and stepped into the archway.

"Because then, everyone's standards become golden, and as soon as reality dips below the gold standard, everyone wishes the leader dead," came the stark reply, before vanishing through the doorway, leaving Hicoth with plenty to consider.

Cinder walked out a short time later, having dressed in little more, adding a pair of spiralling heeled sandals to her appearance along with the silver-steel chain mesh over her bodice. "You look to have quite a bit on your mind. Interesting talk, I imagine?" she asked as she walked over and brought both arms around his chest from behind. Hicoth closed his eyes, enjoying the warmth of his love.

"Yes... very interesting," he replied with a huff before looking back up. "Guess our session will have to wait another time. I've been given a hunt and a mark, though this one is going to be quite the task."

"Really now, what kind of hunt has you this deep in consideration?" she cooed in a sing-song tone.

"The Hellhound, though there is more to it. The suspicion is that Talisan is somehow using the Hellhound, or the Hellhound is using him. There is speculation it's his niece."

"That is quite literally an impossibility for a human to survive such physical, mental and spiritual torment. That's quite unheard of! The only beings that could survive such trauma would literally be the gods themselves!

Though such details wouldn't stop you from following through in this hunt, would it?"

"No, it only entices me more," he replied with a devilish grin. "If this really is a human who has mastered themself as this kind of beast, how powerful are they really!? The Emperor said his son dueled the human in full armor, and she lifted him off the ground with her legs!" Cinder gasped. Draconians in armor weigh hundreds of pounds. Humans had a hard enough time moving in the same kind of plate mail draconians used, even with special training. "Such an opponent who has access to that kind of power. Now THAT is the challenge I have been eager for!" Cinder laughed softly, smiling upon him.

"Well let's get you geared and packed up, hun. You're going to be gone for quite a long time, I imagine. I'll inform the lieutenants. Besides, I'm sure our love making distracts them enough with the sounds of us destroying furniture." Hicoth grinned devilishly as he headed through the doorway and down to the armoury to select what he would bring with him. Cinder meanwhile followed the pathway around the castle to look over the ocean.

She leaned on the castle walls, overlooking the ocean and smiling. She was recounting the day she had met Hicoth and his declaration to the entire arena where the pair had grown up together. "You claimed the arena was too easy, it was making you soft," she said to herself, watching the ocean roll against the cliffs. "People look at your surface and see only turbulent, crashing waves. I look at you and see below the white foam and churning blues. There is so much life inside of you, such passion and determination. It's not to just be the best warrior in the world, but to show you're capable of achieving what people say you cannot." A seagull came and perched nearby. Experimenting with her magic, she willed a bit of moss on the castle wall to sprout a small plant which then produced a tiny berry. It was hardly enough to feed anything larger than a squirrel, yet the seagull took it. Seemingly satisfied, it flew off again, and Cinder watched it go. "Your passion set me free. It alighted my own desires to seek my own path alongside you."

Hicoth prowled through his armoury, claws clacking on the floor as the flats of his feet padded along. He was considering what he should wear if he was to fight such an opponent. He had all the reports from when the Silver Shields were hunting down the hellhound. Silver and holy weapons only, fire and fangs that can rend steel. They never tested draconian steel against her claws, though he wasn't as arrogant to believe that heavier metal could create better results.

Weapons were easy choices. He took short spears tipped with silver points, perfect for throwing or for close quarters. If they were too long they would become unwieldy against someone who could close the distance too quickly. He then grabbed two hand axes trimmed with a silver blade, his more trademark equipment. He had always loved axe fighting, the raw power he could put behind the swing. Going with two axes, if he didn't sunder a shield in a single blow, he could rip the shield away from his opponent and leave them open for a follow up. He had no notion a werewolf would use a shield of course, no reason it should, or 'she' if he was to believe the Emperor's suspicions. Short spears bundled and axes holstered, he still had a difficult time deciding on what armour he should wear. In the end, he decided to at least try the tried and true heavy draconian plate. This should ensure only the werewolves claws could have a chance of piercing him. Just as a nasty surprise, he replaced the steel chain undershirt of the plate with a silver chain, so if she should pierce the full inch breast plate, she should have a more difficult time getting through the silver mesh hidden beneath.

Satisfied with his choice of equipment, he headed towards the stables. He walked past the array of horses his guild members used before coming to a special stable. Opening it up revealed a grey and silver scaled wyvern sitting inside. They were an offset cousin of dragons that didn't bear the same intelligence of the dragons themselves. They were similar to horses in a manner where they could easily recognize people and had enough intelligence to understand rudimentary orders and directions. They sported wings, large enough to glide or float, though they lacked the stamina for sustained flight. A long serpentine body, the scales themselves were slightly rough and jagged. It wore a padded leather saddle with a special metal plating underneath, molded in the shape of the scales. Saddle bags lined either side of the beast's hind legs, already filled with provisions and supplies. Medicine and healing draughts, spell scrolls and camp equipment as well as a crossbow with bolts for hunting. Sensing his master's hunting instincts, the wyvern rustled its scales eagerly before lowering itself for Hicoth to climb on.

"We go towards the home of the Silver Shields, where the investigation begins," he instructed, and the beast gave a growling yelp before leaving the stable. Climbing up the castle walls, it mounted the top of the walls, in view of Cinder. A roar of enthusiasm bellowed from the wyvern before leaping off the walls and gliding off into the distance.

Chapter 12

Lethia wiped sweat off of her forehead as she tried to dig up the remains of the monsters that had laid siege to the castle. The corpses always melted down into nameless liquid, but the liquid always stayed, and according to her uncle, such liquid normally caused havoc if left alone. They had to scoop it up into barrels and ship it off to one of the few Nephele check points in the Northern Commonwealth so they could dispose of it properly. Efforts cleaning and repairing the fortress after the attack took a good few days, and while her superhuman strength and speed helped the process, it was still grueling work. Especially since she could never grasp proper construction skills and how to properly rebuild the wall. A lot of it was druidic magic, but they still needed to use stone and mortar to mount stone properly enough. She then decided to offer help in fixing clothing and uniforms, stitching them back together in preparation for when she had to rely on her own skills to fix up her own uniforms.

Talisan had sent for raw material during the clean-up. Sometime later, a merchant caravan arrived carrying a large assortment of bricks and other building supplies. One of the merchants in the caravan offered a side business selling magic trinkets, deciding to set himself up independently to try and earn his own private earnings. While on break, Lethia approached the merchant curiously to see what he had on hand.

"Greetings, young lady." The duram merchant greeted her, grinning as she looked over his wagon filled with some exotic goods: knives, scrolls, a few swords and axes. She didn't look over the weapons very much, satisfied with her halberd alone. She spotted a few hip pouches and examined them. "Aaah, I see you're looking at the dimensional hip pockets."

"I'm sorry, the 'what' now?" she replied, finally noticing the merchant properly. He kind of looked like a tabby cat with a mix of white and orange fur, though much of it was far less prevalent. He also had normal ears instead of cat ears.

"Dimensional pouches! They are small hip pouches that lead to a magical pocket dimension, which allows you to carry things you normally wouldn't be able to in a backpack or other typical container. These were enchanted by the arch mages and are very difficult to come by, as such magic is quite powerful. As such, I couldn't possibly part with it without quite a hefty amount."

"Sounds like a handy piece of equipment." As she held her hands over them, she could feel something off. She sifted through them before picking one that seemed to have a sensation of magic, whereas the others didn't. Then she realized the merchant's game and put the pouch back, watching him step forward to mix up the bags.

"Of course! People are always asking me for these, though sadly the magic is very unreliable, even for the greatest of mages," the merchant informed her with a sly smile. "I can't guarantee it will work as intended, but they are all absolutely enchanted."

"Well, how much are we talking for one?" There were still many items hidden in sacks and other goods, and as she scanned around, she spotted a tail waving as it vanished underneath the wagon. *The twins,* she realized as she looked back to the merchant. The man chuckled.

"I would have to say perhaps two hundred gold pieces to start, and that's already a generous offer. Mage guilds normally only sell them for a king's bounty." Lethia nodded, then shifted her gaze to the bundles of scrolls, which were laid in sets of three different colors: purple, cyan and green.

"So what are these scrolls?" she asks, picking one at random and opening it up. The merchant quickly stopped her.

"Don't read it aloud!" he exclaimed. "These are magic scrolls, single charge spells put inside magic parchment. If you read it aloud, you activate the spell and the scroll vaporizes." Lethia's curiosity piqued. "Many adventurers always pack a few scrolls with them to deal with magic, and the color of the scroll indicates what kind of magic it is. Though you should know which is which."

"Actually, I don't," Lethia replied with a deep blush.

"Wait, you ARE a Silver Shield mercenary, are you not?"

"I am, I'm Talisan's niece. I just, um, I had a magical accident and so he is helping me learn how to use it," she explained, her eyes giving off small tufts of flame due to nervousness. The merchant's eyes twinkle, seeing her eyes alight. Her flimsy excuse didn't seem to convince him, judging by the open doubt on his face. Lethia didn't know what kind of conclusions he might jump to.

"Well, for Talisan's niece, I suppose I can help out a little bit. See, there are three kinds of magic in the world."

"Oh, I know that much," Lethia interjected with a smile. "Astral, spiritual and nature."

"Correct!" the merchant confirmed, snapping his finger before pointing towards the piles. "Purple scrolls are astral magics, typically energy manipulation or summoning astral beings such as nephele spirits. Cyan scrolls are Spiritual, normally dealing with blessings of the gods or aggressive demon curses. They can sometimes have more direct blasts of energy. Green scrolls are all nature, and have everything to do with manipulating that which can be found in the mortal realm, from growth to shrinking, fire and ice to earth and wind. They work kind of like a game of rock, paper, scissors. Astral magics are above nature, as they are primordial energy. Spirits are those that can bend astral energies to their whim and form what they wish out of it, however they are subject to the laws of nature they create. If that's too much to remember, just think purple beats green, green beats cyan, and cyan beats purple."

Lethia listened intently to the man, rubbing her chin as she took the information to heart. She had been so focused on studying monsters, she had neglected to study magic again like how Lilith wanted her to. "Okay, I believe I understand," she said as she started to look through a few of the scrolls. She assumed her own magic would be considered spiritual as the source was the demon inside of her. It would also help explain how she had little problem dealing with the monsters that attacked. She picked out a few nature and astral scrolls, looking for ones to improve her own physical abilities such as enhanced speed, strength or durability. She also picked out a portal scroll which could allow her to escape quickly if needed. Finally, she picked out an ice scroll and a thunder scroll. "This should be enough..."

"Hmm, a fine selection. I see you prefer to rely on your own skills and enhance them as opposed to using these scrolls as just a quick method of attack," the merchant noted. "Though if you're taking offensive spells, why not round out with some earth and fire?"

"Well if someone's weakness is earth, I'm pretty sure I can use the earth around me to deal with them. Not sure if that's how it works, but..." She shrugged, and the merchant laughed.

"Not at all, but I love your gumption. Tell you what, I'll cut you a bargain," The merchant said just as Lethia saw Felky crawl out from the wagon and hurry off with a sack in tow. The merchant followed her gaze, watching the duram vanish into the crowd with a bag. "Hey! Thief!" he cried out, and Lethia jumped after Felky. She wasn't going to attack her own comrade, but to stand by and do nothing would be suspicious of the guild.

She knew where Felky would likely take his findings, so she headed towards the alchemy room where the twins could normally be found. As she stepped inside, she could see Felky and Telky looking into the bag and pulling out gems. "Hey! Why are you stealing gems from the merchant?" Lethia asked, the fire in her eyes growing a little stronger than earlier. Felky silently looked at Lethia and tossed her one of the gems. "Come on, guys, we're not supposed t-" She found her words caught in her throat as she looked at the 'gem' in her hand, the tell-tale signs of flesh stuck to the edge and it looked like a scale. "Wait..." She looked into the bag they had stolen from the merchant. It was filled with similarly coloured 'gems' that glittered in her vision. It soon dawned on her, these were lamia scales! "I need to go find Ember, she is going to want to know about this." The twins exchanged a look before grabbing the bag and following along.

"We'll go with you, and once you're with Ember, we will inform Talisan and the others. We're going to want to keep everyone clear of the tabby merchant," Felky told Lethia as they walked. Scouring the base, they eventually found the lamia hauling lumber over to where it was going to replace broken portions of the wall. Lethia ran up to her and handed her the scale and explained where it was found. The other members of the Silver Shield overheard and immediately cleared a path as the enraged Ember dropped both trees she was carrying and was off, looking like a bolt of furious red lightning trailing along the ground.

The merchant was showing off some goods to a few other mercenaries when he saw them back off with a look of nervousness in their eyes. He was too slow to turn around to know why they suddenly looked so scared when he found himself dangling in the air. A pair of feral-looking serpent eyes glared back at him as Ember held him up, suspended by his shirt with a single arm, clutching the scale in her other hand. "Unhand me, you brute!" he exclaimed "Someone get this creature off of me!" In response, Ember threw him into the structure of his wagon and shattered the wooden construct with his body. With an arm broken, the merchant tried to pick himself up, only for him to be coiled and gripped within the red embrace of Ember's snake-like tail, muscles and scales grinding against him as she squeezed.

"You have no right to call me ANYTHING, you deplorable piece of hairball waste!" she growled in fury. Lethia ran up in time to see what was happening. "This is a lamia scale! You're smuggling the skin of my own kin!" she seethed, tightening her grip on his body.

"Yes! Yes, fine I am, I admit, let me go!" The merchant begged, eyes shut tight from the pain of his broken arm crushed against his body. His lungs felt like they couldn't pull in any oxygen, and his vision swam. "I can't... breathe, please release me!"

"Why should I even bother? I should just crush you slowly like how you loathsome murderers butcher and peel off my people's skin while they are still alive! Then leave them to die once you have harvested every scale from their bodies." Overhearing this, Lethia couldn't help herself but share in the same fury her caretaker was feeling.

"Enough Ember!" Talisan's voice rang as he approached, flanked by the twins. "Killing this man will not do anything, though death is the justice he deserves. Hilgith will judge him, but right now, we need him to try and figure out where he had gotten his hands on these scales." Ember looked down at the human, her eyes filled with unbridled rage. With a huff, she leaned down until her hands touched the ground, then spun her tail to fling the merchant who rolled painfully along the ground until he was at Talisan's feet. Talisan looked down at him, hands on his hips. "So, I hope you're willing to tell us more."

"I'm a middle man. I just transport the goods from my supplier to the Draconian kingdom. They pay a fortune for these gems, especially raw. That's where they get refined into jewelry and other goods, they know how to make it look like natural stone. Though I hear they like to make entire cloaks of the stuff."

"Who is your supplier?" Talisan demanded.

"Hang on, I got his name right here." He pulled out a small piece of parchment from his pocket. Lethia noticed a hint of purple in his hand.

"Uncle, it's a magic scroll!" she yelled, but before Talisan could kick it out of his hand, he read the scroll aloud and vanished from beneath him. Ember ran off in a roar of frustration. Tentatively, Lethia walked up to her uncle. "Is she going to be okay?"

"Yeah, she just needs time to grieve. lamia treat their own kin like family, even if they are from different tribes. Seeing evidence of their own kind tortured in such a way is a pretty sure way to send one into a berserk state. She knows herself enough to head somewhere she won't hurt anyone."

"What should we do about the merchant's wagon?" she asked, both of them staring at the ruined cart, magic trinkets and goods scattered everywhere.

"Suppose we claim it ourselves as illegal property. Besides, I'm sure we can make use of a few things. I saw you poking through it earlier anyway. Go ahead and take what you want, don't think anyone will object this time around." Lethia nodded and walked over to help clean up the cart. As she did, she grabbed the pouch she had been eyeing as well as a bunch of scrolls. The merchant may have been a cheater and a smuggler, but he wasn't lying about the scrolls or the pouch itself. She found she was able to put all the scrolls inside of the hip pouch, and even her own halberd. Lethia just needed to have the pouch given the same enchanting treatment as her armor.

The merchant fell out of his spell in a clearing near a large structure in the capital city of Githal. Looking up, he recognized the temple of Minerva, home of the Blood Blades, named after the goddess. Hauling himself up onto his feet, he grinned and stumbled his way inside the temple. After interacting with Lethia, he felt like the rumors of the Silver Shield keeping the hellhound was real, and it was the leader's own niece. His own flesh and blood, how horrible it would be for the entire guild if they were caught red-handed harboring a criminal with such a bounty. A bounty requesting her to be dead.

If they were going to ruin him, then he would simply ruin them as well.

After cleaning up the black merchants' wagon, repairs continued as they were, with goods divided up between members based on interest and rank. Many felt like the rookies could use the magic items more than the veterans, so Lethia was able to keep the pouch she had grabbed earlier. Construction meanwhile went ahead as planned and a few days later, the fortress was fully repaired and looked as it always had: wood, stone and nature fused together to form a bastion of ingenuity.

Lethia and Ember sat in their room, meditating. Ember wanted to help assuage her own deep seeded anger. For Lethia, it was just an exercise to explore more of herself and her strange powers with the book Talisan gave her. Eventually, she found a passage that explained that a succubus would change gender based on who they are targeting or who they are with. Lethia only wished the book could explain how to be comfortable having one.

Meanwhile, Talisan was taking his turn patrolling the walls with Autu pacing behind him. Both men held crossbows as they walked around the wall overlooking the roads. Autu paused for a moment as he noticed dust rising in the distance. "Sir, looks like we have company. Shall I alert the guild?"

Talisan watched the incomers for a moment. "Not yet. We will just have to see what's going on. If it was an attack, it wouldn't be so open." The pair made their way down the wall, and Autu headed off to inform other members about the approaching group as Talisan approach the group. He recognized the standard of Minerva's Blood Blades. At the head of the group was a man wearing officer's plate armor. A simple piece of plate over his chest with pauldrons, chainmail covering his arms and a chain skirt beneath the plate. A mixture of swordsmen, spearmen and crossbowmen, all sporting silver tipped weapons marched behind him. Finally, the officer stopped ten feet from Talisan as Autu came out to join him, and a number of Silver Shield mercenaries lined the wall.

"Talisan Azalea, in the name of the Northern Commonwealth and her grace Minerva, you are being accused of harboring a demon and a fugitive with a collective bounty of fifty thousand gold," the officer stated. "You are to surrender the Hellhound for immediate execution, upon which your status as guild leader will be under inspection and the ownership of the guild temporarily placed in the hands of Minerva's Blood Blades. Any resistance will place you and the entirety of your guild under contempt to protect a nationwide threat, and you will all hereby lose status as officially recognized guild members and instead be seen as grey mercenaries. This will also compound with the crime of high treason against our nation."

"What is the source of this intel, who told you all of this?" Talisan asked. The officer turned back and raised a hand, signaling. The black merchant from earlier stepped forward with a wide grin.

"We found this man at the doorstep to our central church, broken arm and bruises. He claims he had called you out on possession of the demon in question, in which your lamian member, Ember Bloodweave, proceeded to smash him against his own wagon of supplies which he claims you stole from him." Talisan glared at the merchant, who shrunk back.

Milly was up on the wall, observing the conversation. She quickly disappeared as she made her way to the quarters where Ember and Lethia stayed. She burst through the door, causing both women to turn their heads in shock as the blacksmith panted heavily. "Lethia, you've been found out. The Blood Blades are here to execute you."

"What!?" Lethia shot up from the floor. "No no no, how? I've been hiding the source of my magic like you taught me. Not even the Emperor was able to sense who I was!"

"I don't know, but that creep smuggling lamia scales is with them," Milly said.

"Either he is trying to make bullshit without realizing it's the truth, or he made a really, really damn good guess," Ember said, her voice carrying a cruel hiss between her words. "We need to keep you here, Lethia. Talisan will be able to talk the situation out."

"I'll keep an eye on things," Milly said before heading back out, and Ember made her way to the window while Lethia moved farther away from it. The two women made eye contact before Lethia went to the back of the room away from the door window up front. Ember made her way to the door and looked out the frame to see if the gates would open.

As Milly returned back to the wall, she could see Talisan looking over an official document that the captain had given him. Talisan grinned before handing the paperwork back. "Funny about sources at times," he said, crossing his arms. "Did you realize the reason why we confiscated his goods, and the reason Ember got angry enough to harm him in such a brutal fashion, was because he was smuggling lamia scales? He used a teleportation scroll to escape from us, and we were going to have him be brought in for trial and either execution or exile. After all, being part of the black market has harsh consequences."

"We shall look into matters after we deal with what brought us here, Talisan. Open your gates and let us in," the officer demanded, and the pair glared at one another. After a few solid seconds, the officer cleared his throat before adding "please." Talisan nodded, and the gates opened up, allowing the procession inside.

"They are coming inside. Talisan couldn't tell them to leave," Ember informed Lethia "We need to hide you somehow, or they are going to inspect you. They probably have warrior priests somewhere in there, and you can't hide demonic magic from holy magic, right?" She bit her lip in deep thought while Lethia thought about her question. She had demon magic, something that priests can discover. She was supposed to be part succubus, so they could claim she had power over them. Looking past Ember's shoulder, she could see the soldiers splitting off to begin combing through the entire compound. Even if Toshiko got her into the underground caverns, they would be able to scour every last inch of it.

With a deep breath, Lethia slowly turned into her hellhound form before looking towards Ember. "I hope you forgive me for this, but I think this is the only way for me to escape and for you all to be spared." Ember opened her mouth to ask what she meant but flames engulfed the room.

An explosion and the shattering of wood, a scream of shock and pain all echoed out at once. Everyone in the compound watched Ember's quarters explode into flames and the front shatter into splinters. Ember was knocked onto the floor as Lethia trampled over her, pressing down on her chest and launching off of her. Her eyes were fully alight as she charged towards Talisan. Acting fast, the mercenary leader pulled out his shield and put it between himself and her as she landed on the silver-plated piece of equipment. It burned her hands and feet, demon influence touching a purified metal. Pressing her weight forward, she then used the shield as a springboard and launched herself upwards along the side of the main fortress. Claws dug into stone and wood as she scaled it higher and higher.

Down below, Talisan immediately began barking orders. "The demon is loose! Gather the silver weapons! Man the walls, it cannot escape!" The Silver Shield mercenaries scattered while the Blood Blades pulled out crossbows and started to fire at the hellhound, silver tipped bolts flying through the air to try and strike her, but she was too high up.

Lethia then made a leap for the southern walls from the edge of the fortress. The jump was one she had never attempted before, and she didn't even think she could make it. Right now, though, if she tried to get on the ground, she would be overwhelmed by numbers in seconds, and she couldn't use her halberd or other equipment. It would show she had been trained here. Instead, she was doing her best to avoid engagement at all costs. Flying through the air, crossbowmen opened up again, a few bolts striking at her limbs, leaving gashes and wounds.

Her jump was unable to carry her to the top of the wall, but she was able to dig her claws into the side. Sliding down a few feet, she got a grip and started to scale the wall rapidly, tearing up the freshly repaired wood. As she got onto the top of the wall, she came face to face with Mason. He held a metal shield and was carrying a silver blade in his other hand.

"Figures this would happen eventually." He growled, brandishing his equipment as other Silver Shield members formed a circle, cutting off her escape down either side of the wall. Mason blocked her way out of the base, leaving her with only the option: to go through him. Saying nothing, she flexed her claws, stiff from gripping the wall so tightly. Mason rushed forward and swung his sword downward, aiming for her arms. The werewolf stepped back, twisting her body sideways to avoid the slash. Mason continued to swing his blade, following with an upward slash and keeping Lethia on the defensive, stepping backwards and side to side. She quickly found herself short on room as she felt the edge of the wall leading back into the base.

Mason made a very exaggerated swing downward, which Lethia took advantage of. She brought a hand up and guided the blade to come down and bury itself into the wood structure behind her. She then grabbed his shoulders, flipped over his head and landed on his back. Kicking off his back, she leapt forward. Spear men tried to cut her off, thrusting at her as Lethia cleared the wall. She free fell down onto open ground and took off, not looking back. Mason ran to the edge and watched her disappear into the distance.

The Blood Blade officer immediately got his group together. "Everyone, quickly, we must get after her!" he exclaimed before turning to Talisan with an accusing look. "So you were keeping a demon here."

"For study, yes. You see, the hellhound shed fur at a very regular rate, so we were able to experiment and make use of it," Talisan explained. "What we failed to pick up on is that this particular demon is a succubus. Certainly doesn't fight like any succubus I've encountered, I'll admit." The officer raised a brow, and Talisan shook his head. "We got complacent, plus I am getting up in my years. I'm not as strong minded as I once was."

"Fine, I'll drop the charges," the officer stated. "You have wounded, tend to them. We shall take the hunt from here." He then turned on the merchant who had brought them there. "Harboring a demon... hardly. Should have known your greedy type would try and spoil the reputation of the Silver Shields." The merchant growled, and Talisan gave him a pat on his broken arm.

"I'm sure he is going to start thinking things over now. Though you're not going to have an escort, so I suggest you get going," he said mockingly.

"I'll have this place burned to the ground for ruining me, just you watch!" the merchant threatened before running out of the fortress walls.

"We won't be having any trouble from him, not anymore. Men like him are usually buried in history," Talisan assured the officer, who cleared his throat, saluted to Talisan, and moved out with his men. With a deep sigh, Talisan surveyed his men as they were putting out the fires Lethia had left, as well as ensuring Ember wasn't too harmed. He caught sight of a terrified

Milly, so he stepped over to her. "Milly, Lilith, I have a favor to ask of you two. Follow Lethia, make sure she's safe."

"What!?" Lilith materialized in mid shout. "You want us to chase down a feral demon!? After she nearly killed a lamia by herself!" Talisan pointed to Ember who looked more shaken than harmed, but Lilith was not convinced.

"She made herself look feral and uncontrolled to ensure our reputation cannot be harmed. That said, at this point, I can do nothing more for her. You are unaffiliated with us, you can do what I no longer can," Talisan explained. "Please, this is the request not of a leader of this guild, but of an uncle wanting my only niece to have a friend." The twins looked at one another for a long moment. Lilith growled and rubbed the bridge of her nose. "I've hardly wanted for much more than my family to be safe, or at least cared for. You're the only two who can look after her."

"Fine... fine. Not like I'd be worried anyway," she relented as Milly nodded.

"We'll make sure Lethia is taken care of, don't worry sir!" Milly assured him with a smile. She could see just how strained Talisan's body was, trying to hold composure over what just happened. There was an unnatural pause before he took a deep breath.

"Good. Go grab Lethia's things, she left her clothes and gear behind. I'm sure she would appreciate having something before she finds her mother."

"What makes you think she would go to her mother?" Milly asked.

"She's alone again and knows she can't return here. She hasn't seen her mother in nearly four years. Wouldn't you miss your own home and family having been ripped from it for so long?" Talisan said, and the twins simply nodded before leaving.

The tabby merchant slowed down as It began to rain on him. He had ducked off the main road to go through the woods. He wanted to avoid any more mercenaries as well as seek shelter. He was in pain, furious, now broke and with nothing. He only had the knowledge his guess was true, but of course, respected mercenary guilds won't believe a now labeled black market merchant. "Curse you, Talisan!" he shouted, failing to notice the ground around him shambling loose below his feet. He continued to walk until he found a massive oak with thick branches, taking shelter below it as the rain continued to pour down.

Reaching for his broken arm, he felt something on his sleeve. He pulled at the thing stuck to his sleeve until it popped off. "The hell?" he muttered before looking at what he pulled off. A small circle with the emblem of a Fukai skull and a knife. His face blanched, and he dropped the marker to the ground as he pressed his back to the tree. "No... no, no no." His eyes scanned the ground. He couldn't see anything, and he realized he couldn't hear anything because of the pattering rain. In a panic, he turned to try and climb the oak, but with a broken arm he couldn't get far. Suddenly, a loud bang erupted, causing birds to panic and flee. The merchant slid down the tree, a smear of blood trailing down the bark. The ground below his body rumbled, and he sank into the earth, erased from the world and never to be found.

Chapter 13

Milly and Lilith relaxed on the open road, listening to the clopping sounds of the horse the Silver Shields had given them. The journey to Floraine had been going rather smoothly so far, and they assumed they would reach the town by around noon the next day. The siblings were passing the time by playing cards with one another, using a magic illusion spell so Lilith could interact with the cards. There was nothing either one of them could bet on, so they were simply playing with no stakes and enjoying each other's company. "You think Lethia is doing alright?" Milly asked as she dealt out cards.

"She's a werewolf, she grew up with an herbalist, lived near a hunting village and is trained as a warrior," Lilith replied rather sharply. "To ask if a werewolf like her is doing okay is like asking if birds are comfortable flying. It would take something monumental to change such a fact." Lilith picked up her cards. "Borus cursed these cards... Milly, I swear you have a gift of dealing bad hands."

"I think it's kind of a talent at this point if it's being this consistent," she replied, looking down at her own hand. "Anyway, I didn't mean physically, I meant emotionally. I know we met her after her uncle began to train her, but he did tell us what had happened to her."

"Yes, yes, cry me a river. Milly, you would cry one for every misfortune you hear about." Lilith complained, doing her best to use the cards she had.

"It's because it's always sad when misfortune befalls someone! We have the tools and knowledge to help people's lives get better. We can make equipment, armor, even prosthetic limbs of some kind. You know I would have made a leg for that man if father let us," Milly reminded Lilith, pointing a finger at her sibling.

"If we let you. We run a business, not a charity," her sister replied as she shuffled the deck of cards. "You're also getting off track. We're talking about Lethia here, not the world."

"Ah, right, sorry," Milly apologized while accepting the hand she was dealt. "I can understand why she would want to return home at this point. I mean Talisan said Lethia ran rampant all over the Northern Commonwealth. Apparently even reaching border towns, the Empire and the um..."

"The Land of the Three Kings," Lilith offered. "Yeah, it's not exactly like she went towards her home. Maybe there was some instinct to avoid it? Again, the spirit locked with her own soul is for all intents and purposes a demonic infant. Time works very differently once we start talking about different realms, and I'd rather not get into the topic right now." Lilith played her hand, then Milly took her turn, showing once again a stronger set of cards. "How do you keep beating me! One on one, you would suspect our win loss ratio would be more evenly split." Milly shrugged in response.

"I wouldn't have a clue, sis, I guess I'm just a bit luckier than you," she said with a smile, and Lilith grumbled.

"Yeah, and if we were making bets, I'd have lost so badly, you would have owned me by now. Moments like these I'm glad you're the kinder one of us."

"You say it as if you're an evil woman wanting to do bad things to me." Milly giggled, and Lilith looks away with a huff. After a moment, she smiled back and shook her head.

"How could I break your heart by doing anything like that," she said quietly, as if trying to ensure the horse they rode wouldn't overhear her.

The horse suddenly stopped and began to strut in place, nervous as it's ears flicked. At the sound of cracking and snapping trees, Lilith faded from view. Nothing overly large, but a creature in a hurry. With a click of her tongue, Milly willed the horse to back up. Within a moment, a purple scaled lamia barreled out from the trees, scaring the horse as it reared backwards. Milly gripped the reins tightly, her strength keeping her on the beast. The lamia turned and darted down the road, as if spooked by Milly. Shortly after, two hunters popped out of the bush bearing crossbows. "You, girl! Which way did a lamia go!"

"No need to ask, the road is torn up." The other hunter said before aiming a crossbow and firing it down the road. The pair began to run after the lamia. Milly started to hyperventilate as the situation dawned on her.

"Poachers! They... they are trying to catch the lamia!" Milly said, torn between decisions. "We... we gotta..."

"Milly no, we are not trained fighters," Lilith said, but Milly took off. "Milly! I said no!"

"I... I can't just... let them kill her!" She replied, knowing she was not trained for this. Sure they had fought in the siege, but that was behind a wall with professionals helping out. Out here they were on their own, untrained. But she needed to help this creature.

"Gods, the werewolf's rashness is infectious. But fine!" Lilith relented. "Then I'm taking the drivers' seat in this." Lilith took control of Milly's body. "Common boy, hya!" She ushered the horse on, and sensing a more confident rider, the horse picked up pace.

The two hunters heard the galloping beast before they saw it: the young ebony woman with a demon eye. "See why you need to keep your trap shut!" The hunter exclaimed before they brought up their crossbow, the bandit trying to reload his. Lilith brought one hand off the reins and fired a bolt of energy, forcing the pair of hunters to dive off to the side. Lilith raced past the pair and down the road. Getting back up on their feet, the hunters both pulled out scrolls and read the spells aloud. Turning to dust, the magic filled the two hunters with the agility of winds, and they took off at a sprint.

Lilith spotted the lamia up ahead, struggling to keep the same pace going. Out of breath, the brown haired woman turned to look behind her, seeing Lilith on horseback catching up to her. Not knowing if this new person was friend or foe, she continued to simply slither as fast as she could along the road, too exhausted to think of ducking back into the foliage. Another crossbow bolt flew past them both, causing Lilith to spin around and watch the hunters catching up. Milly's own astral form materialized. "How are they gaining on us!?"

"Magic! Must be haste scrolls or something," Lilith replied. The lamia saw the sisters were near her tail, so she swiped at the horse. Almost by instinct, the horse jumped over the violet tail to the other side, having been rigorously trained by the Silver Shields. The glittering tail swiped again, and the steed jumped back to his original position. With a few grunts, it managed to get side by side with the lamia. Milly, in her spirit form, drifted down beside the lamia.

"We're friends! Don't worry, we are going to help you," she reassured the lamia while Lilith fired another bolt of energy back towards the hunters. The pair dodged the bolt again but were unable to fire back, as reloading their crossbows while running was not possible.

"Why don't you just crush those two and be done with it, your weight alone is more than enough to kill them," Lilith suggested. The lamia huffed through labored breaths as she fought to bring up a response.

"Poison!" was all she shouted. Lilith got the message quickly enough. Even if the lamia were to use her strength to crush them, they would inject her with a poison to make sure she didn't live beyond the encounter.

"Milly, take over, I need time to cast a disenchantment." Lilith said and allowed Milly to take her body back. In her own astral form again, she floated up and started focusing energies into a spell. She could chant the spell, but she still needed Milly to aim it. The pair of hunters, aided by magic, were getting much closer and were bringing out the poison tipped daggers. "Really hope they aren't using spirit magic." Lilith says once the spell is finished. Feeling the power surge through her body, Milly grabbed the crossbow to focus the spell as she couldn't control it as effectively as Lilith. The spell focused into the holster and fired off like a giant shockwave.

With no warning, all speed the two hunters had in their bodies left, but the momentum carried on. Unable to move quick enough to catch themselves, they crashed hard into the dirt path as the trio continued on and out of view.

After a few more moments of running and riding, they came to a slow stop, allowing the horse and lamia to finally catch their breaths. "Those two hunters will be lucky if they come out of the crash with a number of bruises. I'm hoping a good few of their bones broke," Lilith said with dry contempt. Milly meanwhile hopped off the horse, which went to munch on some nearby grass. The lamia woman had collapsed nearby, chest heaving up and down as she tried to steady her breathing.

"Are you okay? Are you hurt anywhere," Milly asked, finally getting a proper look at the snake-woman. Her features looked softer than Ember's, less like a warrior and also a little younger. She had tattoos of musical notes and a music bar circling her body around her back and stopping below her breasts on either side. On her hips was a violin case clasped shut, a simple, black-painted leather-bound container. Her hair was straight with two yellow ribbons to help frame her face. A silver chain headpiece ran along her forehead as well. Her eyes looked nervous, but too tired to do much else.

She confirmed she was okay with a nod, then curled her large tail up into a spiral and hugged it, looking very uncomfortable. Milly fetched a blanket. "Here," she offered to the lamia. "This may help you rest a little. Don't worry, me and my sister will watch over you."

"Milly, we can't stay, we need to be looking for Lethia!" Lilith reminded her. "You're letting yourself get distracted with this!"

"We can't just leave her to fend for herself-"

"She's a gods blessed lamia! She could wrestle down a draconian war wyrm!" Lilith cut her off before hijacking her body. "We're moving on, we need to get to that damned Hellhound before someone else finds her first." At the mention of Hellhound, the lamia sat bolt upright.

"Wait!" she called out, and the grumpy sibling looked over her shoulder. Shrinking from the rough gaze, the girl gulped. "C-come with." Lilith blinked, unsure if she had just heard right. "He-hellhound... fire wolf, yes?"

"Well in a manner of speaking, yes Lethia is a fire wolf, though, it's just a nickname," she clarified, choosing her words carefully so as to not reveal the secret. The lamia looked a little disheartened before shaking her head.

"Looking for fire wolf," she said again before making a motion of her arms and breathing out in a way to sound like roaring flames. "Big, strong wolfman creature."

"Wait, you mean the actual Hellhound? Why in the world would you be looking for such a creature!?" Lilith exclaimed in shock. The lamia looked down towards the violin on her hip for a moment, hesitating, before reaching for the case. Opening it up, she pulled out the instrument as well as the bow. Silently, she tuned the instrument briefly before setting the bow onto the string and began to play. A low hum echoed as the strings vibrated to produce a melodious tune. "I fail to understand how playing music would-" Lilith lost her words the moment an illusion sprung forth from the ground.

As the music continued to drift on the open road, magic filled the area. Fire billowed and from it, a werewolf stood tall, the fire becoming the fur and hair she wore. Flames billowed from her eyes before motioning a howl, punctuated by a single note held for a brief moment. Then the illusion danced as it depicted the Hellhound tearing through bandits and poachers, fire following her every attack. It showed a depiction of injured lamia watching the werewolf wander off, thankful for a timely rescue. The music turned somber as next, it showed a crowd of them traveling, one by one each vanishing until the last one remaining was the lone violet-scaled girl. The song came to a somber halt and the spell ended, the illusion fading into dust.

The twins watched the entire illusion, completely stunned at the display. "What the hell was all that!?" Lilith finally spoke. "You're a lamia! You're not supposed to have magic! That was literally a symphony of magic you just used!" She cried out, drifting forward to hang over the wilting girl. The Violin in the lamia's hands suddenly glowed brightly as if reacting to her presence.

The violet-scaled woman backed off and coddled the violin, shushing it as if trying to hold back an angry animal. Lilith tilted her head curiously at what she was seeing before making the safest bet she could. "Hang on, is ... is the violin a Nephele?" she asked, a hand coming up to her chin and cupping it thoughtfully. "That would explain a lot."

"Viola," she introduced herself before putting the violin back into its carrying case. Milly smiled brightly, stepped forward and offered her a hand.

"My name is Milly, and this is my twin sister Lilith. She can be a little bit difficult to deal with if you don't know her like I do." Lilith faded away again, leaving the two women alone. "We actually happen to be looking for the same woman. She's a friend of ours. I don't know if she would recognize you or not, it's complicated." Viola smiled, glad to have friendly company. "We know where Lethia... um, the Hellhound is going. At least we have a good idea of where she is going," Milly corrected herself, rubbing the back of her head. "It is safer to travel in a group, so come with us." Viola's expression remained uncertain. The smith followed her gaze down towards her weapon and smiled softly. "Don't worry, I won't turn this on you." Viola nodded, still nervous, and watched Milly climb back up onto her mount. Stroking the stallion's mane, she clicked her tongue, and the trio continued on down the road.

"Don't really agree with picking up stragglers," Lilith noted as they continued down the road towards the twin towns. "Especially a lamia, a tempting target for bandits or grey mercenaries. Adding someone who is a walking gem mine feels like just adding far more risk to our odds."

"We're also going after a demon possessed lycanthrope who could burn us to ashes in mere seconds with a bear hug. You want to complain about dangers now?" Milly replied in a rare sarcastic tone. Lilith fell silent as Viola looked up, confused. "Oh! Right, um... my sister and I can talk in private to each other, though I sometimes forget and speak out loud" she explained with a blush and giggle. "I've been told it makes me look, um, not all together." Viola smiled, and silence fell between them once again.

It wasn't too long before they reached the border of Floraine. Riding into town, they could see a lot of homes were empty save for a few of the local militia. As they peered around curiously, one of the militia men spotted the pair and approached them. Milly could see the exhaustion on his face. It made his features appear sunken. "Hail, you both better leave, or make your way to Huntersden. There has been a growing werewolf problem as of late. You would think after the Silver Shields made an example of the last pack we would no longer have these problems," he said, exasperated. "The only reason we're here is because poor Amelia doesn't seem to grasp the danger."

"Amelia?" Milly echoed as Viola tilted her head curiously.

"Aye, she had a daughter who went missing years ago, werewolf attack. Only problem, even the pack which attacked had no clue what had become of the girl. Lost her husband, lost her daughter, it was too much for her, and she snapped. The guild sent someone to care for her, but she's... well. We owe our old guard mate to keep her safe and to try and give her as good a life as we can." The guard looked over to the house, shaking his head. "It's best you let her be. Family seems cursed in a way. Anyone who gets too close to them gets attacked by werewolves."

The pair asked for directions to Huntersden, then went on their way. Viola stopped at the town's edge and looked back towards the house. Milly stopped her horse and turned to see what was delaying her companion.

"What's on your mind, Viola?" she asked. After a moment of silence, Viola shook her head and turned to rejoin her. "Curious about Amelia?" Milly pressed, but Viola just nodded and signalled that they can continue. Milly couldn't help but wonder why Viola was so confident Lethia would help her. Lilith sensed this thought and communicated with her sister privately.

"Probably a childish fantasy, believing Lethia could do more to protect her kin than the draconians would," Lilith noted coldly. "Silly to put a mortal on a kind of pedestal, even with powers like hers. She is still only one woman."

"Anyone can make a difference if they give people hope, even if the hope ends up being a false one," Milly whispered. "At least there is no way we can let her down... it's going to be up to Lethia at some point."

"You realize you're putting her on the same pedestal, right? She's still a mortal, she bleeds, she hurts, and she is young and inexperienced."

"We're younger than her." Milly shot back. "So don't act like we know better than her when it comes to something like this." She could feel Lilith freeze for a moment before going silent, dropping the topic. The rest of the day's journey from Floraine to Huntersden was of relative silence. Viola was too nervous to speak, and Milly wondered how Lethia felt comfortable walking this path every day. It felt so forlorn and abandoned with the trees growing thicker and leaning over top as if to cage them.

A rustle of bushes made the group pause for a moment and look off the path and into the forest. A tense silence followed, prompting Milly to reach for the crossbow at her hip. It was still light out, so it was unlikely to be a werewolf.

"Milly, you have my clothes?" A familiar voice rang out, and Lethia stepped onto the road. "I've been camping out in the forest for a day or so. When I left the Silver Shields, I left everything behind. Not that I gave myself much choice," she said with a smile.

"Why!?" Lilith cried out. "Isn't this place your old home?! Why would anyone care if you walked in naked! No one cares if you're naked!" Lethia leaned back and raised her arms over her head to expose her torso more. There was a set of scars on her stomach: bite marks. Lilith's expression eased off as she realized why she needed to be dressed. "You're still an idiot for running off without any kind of plan," she added while Milly slipped off the horse to hand Lethia her clothes. Before she could, Viola rushed Lethia and held her up in a tight hug, prompting Lethia to gasp for air. With her eyes lighting up, the twins were worried Viola might experience some burns, though Lethia managed to keep herself in check.

"Hello!" She coughed while being squeezed in overly friendly arms. "Okay, yes, you like me, I get it. Can you set me down so I can breathe? Please!?" she pleaded, and Viola set her down. A light cough and a deep breath later, she looked up. "You are?"

"Viola!" The lamia replied with a bright smile, backing up a little and looking like a child who just met their idol. Lethia smiled back and chuckled at her mannerisms.

"Nice to meet you... you do look... familiar, have we met?" she asked while taking her clothes from Milly. Viola pulled out her violin and started playing, and Lethia got dressed while listening. smoke circled nearby as the melody played, creating a layer around the group's feet. As the notes rose, fire billowed from the smoke, and Lethia saw herself burst forth from the smoke as if she were some vengeful figure. "So, that's amazing, though... not sure what it tells me."

"You apparently rescued her and her tribe at one point, probably during your feral years," Milly explained. "She has been looking for you since, thinking you could save more of her kind. Though..." Milly trailed off as Viola looked finished playing and hugged herself. Her violin emitted a warm glow as if trying to comfort the girl. Lethia bit her lip and understood quickly what it all meant.

"Well," she started while fastening her belt on her pants, "if you stick with us, we can try and help rescue other lamia tribes in our travels. You don't really have anywhere else to go, and neither do I, sort of. I mean, I'm basically home, but I'm a mercenary now so, not exactly going to stay longer than needed. I just wanted to come visit Mom and kind of recollect myself."

"Everyone was evacuated to Huntersden," Lilith blurted in haste. "Apparently, they are under siege from a werewolf pack. We figured you would probably be there looking for friends and family, not that you should be doing so." Milly was about to add the detail that Amelia was left behind when Lilith silently stated 'no' in her head and spoke to her silently, "We don't need a hair trigger werebeast seeing her mentally broken mother and making more of a mess of things."

"Siege!?" Lethia cried out suddenly. "I have to go help them!" Without another word, she was already running down the road.

"Lethia!" Lilith called after her, then growled at the lack of response, the group already following their friend. "That woman is going to get us killed..."

Approaching Huntersden, the guards readied bows and spears at the strange group. One of the spearmen stepped forward. "Halt! State your business."

"You're a new face. Blood Blade mercenary?" Lethia said without hesitating. "I'm Lethia, a mercenary. I heard there was some werewolf trouble, so me and my friends decided to come here to help out."

"Mercenaries?" The guard asked cautiously. "What guild?" Lethia nearly answered with Silver Shields, but hesitated. She knew she couldn't represent them anymore, so she cleared her throat for a moment. "Grey, actually. I had tried to sign up for a guild, but I had some difficulties qualifying. I'm not a bandit or any unlawful person, just, you know how bad the grey mercenary reputation is."

"For good reason, too," the man replied, keeping his spear level. "Relieve yourself of your weapons, and you can enter. Judging by the fact that a lamia is with you, I'll give some credit to you being an honest folk, but it's a skeptical acceptance at best, so behave yourselves." Lethia nodded and handed over her halberd, Milly her crossbow. After seeing Viola only carrying a violin, they let her keep it, and the group entered the town proper.

Lethia looked around once they were past the main gate and felt her heart ache a little bit. Because of the recent trouble, the village looked more solemn than normal. They wandered around town with Lethia as a guide, and they could see everyone looking worried or scared. None of them really gave Lethia a second glance, not recognizing the redhead at first in the vibrant outfit and leather armor. "This place was more lively when I was last here. It was a celebration. They had managed to bag a massive boar harassing trade wagons. Seeing this place now, it's like they forgot all their achievements."

"Welcome to a besieged town," Milly said solemnly. "Not my first time in one, and it's normally not a pleasant experience. Granted, this is a very different kind of siege, it's forcing people to stay awake at night." Lethia bit her lip and looked around. She didn't understand why people were not recognizing her, until she played with her hair and remembered the color change.

Eventually, the group made it to the tavern, which was doubling as a makeshift military headquarters. A few tents were propped up around it, containing weapons and ammunition for the hunters. A collection of silver tipped arrows, bolts and spears laid around, though it wasn't a great amount. The Blood Blades were known for being the largest of all the guilds, but with large quantities came a drastic drop in quality, so they always seemed to be short on funds to supply people with equipment needed for jobs. Milly shook her head at the poor quality equipment.

Inside the tavern the atmosphere wasn't much better. The locals were quiet, simply eating food while the mercenaries stationed there seemed grumpy and on edge. A number were complaining how they were sent out to die in some backwater village or the booze was of poor quality. Lethia had to ignore the comments on her childhood home to keep her emotions in check.

Milly, on the other hand, paid attention to the glum mood. "Everyone looks so crestfallen. Do they think they were abandoned or something?" she wondered out loud, and the bartender overheard.

"More or less. We're a frontier town, normally when a major incident comes up where we locals can't fix it, we are supposed to just duck our heads and leave. We lived here for two generations now and have been one of the most successful ones. Hell, my dad grew up and died running this tavern, and I intend to do the same," he explained, placing the mugs down in front of the three travelers. That's when he gave them closer looks and recognized Lethia through the frame of fire hair. "Minerva's blood! Lethia!?" Hearing her name called out was like a bolt of lightning through the tavern. Her name rolled off the tongue of every local, and the mercenaries were distracted from their grumbling enough to see everyone get up and rush over to the trio. Lethia blushed and laughed as the voices of confusion gave way to relief and mirth when everyone realized one of their own had mysteriously returned from the dead.

The reaction was immediate as the whole village lit up in activity. Word of Lethia's return sparked a fading hope in the village as the tavern began to fill up with the locals, all who wished to see the face of one of their own having returned home. "Alright, alright! Everyone give the woman space!" the bartender ordered amongst the endless questions and concerns. "Just because she's back from the dead doesn't mean she can't die again if you all steal her oxygen right from her face." The crowd eased off, though the tavern itself was pretty full again. "Now, just to ask the question that's on everyone's mind, what in the world happened?"

Lethia let out a heavy breath. She couldn't tell them she was a werewolf, but she could recount everything else.Hearing Lethia was possessed by a demon put the mercenaries on edge. One of them stood up and approached.

"Well now you're all done getting to be so buddy-buddy with the locals, demon. We're going to be escorting you out of here now," he said roughly, gripping the hilt of his sword as if looking for an excuse to draw it. "We have enough to worry about here. I'm not having a demon sit in the same tavern I'm eating at, and Minerva would not hear of it either."

"You aren't gonna do no such thing," the tavern keeper replied, stepping between him and Lethia. Milly instinctively grabbed Lethia's arm to keep her from standing up.

"Are you serious? Werewolves at the door in the middle of a siege, and you're gonna let a demon just waltz inside, openly announce herself and be merry with it? So what if she was a villager here? She's tainted!"

"If she was trained at the Silver Shields, it means she's above such taint," the tavern keeper retorted. "I've known her since her first visit selling herbs, and I've known her family longer."

"So what, ya know her mommy and daddy. An enemy is an enemy, even if they wear the skin of your own kin."

"Tell that to my uncle!" Lethia shouted, her physical strength peaking with her emotions and breaking free of Milly's grasp. "You should know him well since he's the very leader of the Silver Shields, Talisan Azalea!"

"Shut yer trap, you lying wench," the mercenary shot back, followed by an immediate pressure of disgust from the entire tavern. Even his men knew not to talk ill of Talisan Azalea. Sensing any other comment would only see him flogged alive at best, he stepped away from the table and looked towards the barkeep. "Fine, I'll apologize for my behavior, but mark my words, something is wrong with her. No one should ever survive a trip to hell, let alone keep sane for any length of time." With his piece spoken, he returned to his table.

The tension held in the air and refused to dissipate, even after everyone returned to their respective tables. While people were glad to see a familiar face, the news she was demon possessed ended up spoiling much of the mood. Milly looked at the locals' expressions, they were so close to finally regaining some spark of hope. Lilith watched her sister observing the faces and knew her well enough to dread what was about to happen. Standing from the table, the blacksmith walked up to the bar and put down a gold coin. "A round of your best for the whole tavern."

"We're in siege, I can't just-" A second slam of the table, and there were two more gold pieces.

"Give me your strongest," she said as the barkeep furrowed his brows.

"Fine, one round for everyone here," he replied, not certain why he was following along with this. As he poured mugs, tavern maids came to collect them and hand them out. Milly took her mug and chugged the lot. "Good lord miss, ease up! That stuff is meant to be savored, not chugged!"

"Viola!" she cried out. "This place is too depressed and moral is too low, we need to remind these people what it's like to live!" Her words were already a slight slur from the booze. Without hesitating, she started to stomp her foot in rhythm. Picking up what she was saying, Viola fetched her violin, followed Milly's lead, and started to play an energetic tune. Everyone in the tavern took their drinks and watched the two women.

Sounds of her violin rang out fast, hard and full of energy right from the start. Milly walked back over to their table and jumped on top. As Viola's playing grew more energetic, Milly started to dance and sing on the table. Grabbing her flowing dresses, she spun and kicked on the table to the rhythm she had set, her clothing giving the impression of a dancing rainbow of patterns. Viola used the girth of her tail to keep the oak table steady, gripping it firmly to ensure it wouldn't tip over.

As the energy spread over the people, more and more of the locals picked up on the fun mood and started to join in. The noise of the tavern grew louder and started to permeate through the town, drawing in crowds. The barkeep realized what Milly was doing, and started to pour more drinks for the people showing up. The mercenaries were even joining in the makeshift festivities.

Lethia smiled, seeing the tavern alive again like when she lived there. She watched all of her old friends and neighbors laughing, dancing and making merry like they did years ago. Milly finished her song and dropped off the table to an applause from everyone. Viola kept playing her music as the two women sat beside one another. "Thank you, Milly." Lethia sighed, feeling far more relieved.

"No problem," she replied, giving Lethia a playful punch on the shoulder. "Just make sure I have a soft pillow. Drinking and partying like this leaves me with a bad hangover, and Lilith hates it."

"That won't be a problem." Lethia assured her, then asked the barkeep for the finest rooms for them.

Eventually villagers went back home and the mercenaries took up the night vigil as the day came to an end. The full moon was out, and Lethia wouldn't be able to stay human during the night. Milly and Viola were already off to bed, leaving her free to her own devices.

As she made her way towards the outer walls separating the wilderness and the encroaching dangers from the village, she ran into the one person she had been nervous about. The sickly hunter was sitting near the gate making arrows. He was carving a shaft when she came into view. "So..." he started, "what secret are you hiding this time?"

"Secret!?" Lethia asked with a blush. "I already came clean with being possessed, what other kind of secret would I have?" Juria looked up from his craft and she couldn't stop the blush deepening. Nervously, she looked over her shoulder to the sky, watching it get closer to dusk.

"It's how you lie. You tell selective truth and leave details out," he said as he put the finished arrow shaft to the side. Reaching over, he grabbed another piece of wood and began to carve it. "Besides, why would you be in such a hurry to get out of the village on a full moon. If it's to go fight the werewolves on your own, then you're insane as well as possessed, unless..." he looked up at her to finish the sentence. Lethia bit her lip before walking closer to him so she could whisper.

"Okay, you caught me. Yes, there is more to it, I'm a werewolf as well, but not part of the group attacking this town. I couldn't just say it flat out. What do you think would happen?" She closed her eyes. "I'm being honest with you now, and I'm asking you to please keep quiet about it. I can't let people know I'm."

"The Hellhound?" he supplied. "Demonic possession, werewolf. You're the Hellhound that's been terrorizing the countryside, aren't you?" Lethia's face went beat red, and she fought the urge to hide her shame. Seeing her reaction, the elderly man put the arrow he was working on down. "You carry the weight of those actions, don't you? The people that your... beastly half had claimed."

"I... yes, I do," she replied with a shallow breath. "I have a daily reminder about it. The possession, it makes me transform any time I become emotional. I've probably transformed more times thinking about all the people I killed than anything else." Placing a hand over her heart, she breathed out, calming herself. She still had clear memories of the blood and bodies, waking up in the middle of her demonic handy work. It was a pain she always carried.

"I wasn't in control then, but I'm in control now. I realized I can't live this same life anymore, so instead of lying to myself, I wanted to come here to give myself some closure. Now I have an opportunity to do my community more good than I ever have. This isn't me throwing myself into some suicidal death wish. I wouldn't be trying to do this if I didn't have confidence."

"Still reckless for anyone to be thinking they are a one man army against a pack of werewolves," he said, making Lethia laugh.

"Yeah well, I've always been kind of reckless, haven't I?" she teased, earning a chuckle in response, followed by a labored cough.

"Yeah, yeah you always have been. Go on. To be fair, I'm not too long for this world anyway, I'll probably take your secret to the grave," he said with a sigh. "Sickness is finally catching up to me, even with your mother's herbs." There was a tinge of remorse in his voice, making Lethia curious. "Ah, don't fret about me. Guard is still changing. If you're gonna go, then go. You're gonna turn soon anyway, so make it quick." Wasting no more time, Lethia gave him a brief hug before heading off towards the door. Stopping at the guard post to grab her halberd, she hurried out into the night.

✕

Chapter 14

Comfortable with the fact Milly and Viola would do a fine job taking care of her home village, Lethia marched through the woods. The full moon rose up into the sky, causing her to transform. Pausing to put her clothes into the hip pouch Milly brought to her, she continued onward wearing only her leather armor. Halberd in hand, the fiery werewolf stalked the woods. As she predicted, it didn't take long until she came face to face with the horde of werewolves laying siege to Huntersden.

Lethia felt a bit of regret as the wolf pack was easily a small army. According to her studies, they traveled in tightly knit groups of no more than ten or twelve. What she was looking at was a small guerilla army of a couple hundred. "How in the..."

"Who are you?" One of the pack members growled. His large build and brown fur made him look more like a bear, save for his jawline. "You're not one of us, but you're clearly not one of those sheep in the village." This made Lethia's eyes ignite with fury. Sheep!? These beasts were looking at her old friends as nothing more than animals to be slaughtered. "Stand aside, runt. Or better yet, fall in line. We're starting a movement. It's about time us Lycans declared we are our own kind of people. Other races are meant to be fodder for us, why else would it be so easy to transfer this blessing of ours?" Looking down at Lethia's barren torso and still rather human face, he laughed. "Well, aside from your ugly mug apparently."

"Blessing? Sheep?" Lethia exclaimed, gripping her halberd tightly. "You're hardly one to talk, monster. Declare independence by taking over a frontier village? As soon as you do, all of the Northern Commonwealth is going to crash down upon you," she countered with a laugh. "Though I'm hardly going to stand idly by and allow you all to do such a thing."

"You, all on your own?" the wolf challenged, and a series of howls and laughter echoed through the forest from the ranks of the wolves. As the laughter faded, the bigger wolf walked over to stand face to face with Lethia. "You would be turned into a chew toy long before you could even swing your halberd, brat."

Lethia instinctively backed up, trying to keep distance, and as she did, the pack walked forward as well. She ignited her halberd and swung it, causing the large wolf to leap backwards as the rest of the wolves flinched at the sign of fire. "Yes, all on my own. I'm Lethia Azalea, the Hellhound, trained by Talisan Azalea of the Silver Shields!" She shouted in challenge, blade pointing at the group who snarled back at her.

"Azalea?" One of the wolves further back echoed, catching the attention of everyone. The name was repeated again and again, traveling down the line. Lethia kept her stance, weapon pointed forward, though she couldn't hold her curiosity back as her name didn't seem to spur as much hatred as she expected. Finally, the ranks in the back began to split, and the bear wolf turned his head and stepped aside as a large, grey wolf approached. He was in his prime as a werewolf, lean, muscular yet toned like the ideal stalker of the night. There was a strange sense of both wisdom and madness in him, the way he grinned, snout upwards yet his eyes looking down towards her. Lethia saw madness in those eyes.

"You claim to be Azalea," the wolf said. "I am the alpha here, though if you are who you claim," he growled with an amused grin, arms crossing over his chest, "you should be familiar with the name Raziel."

"I'm not, I've never heard of a Raziel before," Lethia said, adjusting the grip on her halberd. The flaming tip was still pointing at the Alpha, who looked down at it. Raising a hand, he experimented with the heat of the flame, bringing it close. Satisfied the fire wasn't a bluff, he shrugged.

"Such a shame. How could you never know of your own kin?" he said, confusing Lethia with the statement before realization dawned on her.

"No, you couldn't be," she retorted. "Mom said my father died, he had gone missing and his body was... never found." She began to understand the pieces of the story. "The memory hurts her so bad, she refuses to utter his name. If you are who you claim, who is my mother?"

"How could I ever forget Amelia," he replied softly. "She was my first lover, and a loving soul. She wouldn't turn anyone away who was in need of healing, or anything."

Lethia found it hard to breathe. This was impossible. Perhaps, she thought, it was a ploy. Everyone knew her family name, especially those hunted by the silver shields. Werewolves have targeted her family before. "Names are openly shared, and everyone knows about Talisan's family. You werewolves would know of us best, so I'm not convinced."

"Ah, of course. Maybe she's talked about the two of us? Maybe how we met," Raziel said with a dreamy smile. "It was so long ago, yet I can remember it clearly. I was on patrol and stumbled upon a dying wolf and her injured cub. They had fallen victim to a trap, forgotten by a hunter. Wanting to do good by Damien at the time, I took the cub from his dead mother and brought him to Amelia. She was moved by my compassion for life despite being a soldier. We cared for the pup, who was adopted by a hunter later on. After, we became a couple, and had you."

"Then you went missing, presumed dead," Lethia said. "You were taken, not killed. It hurt Mom so much, she couldn't bear to say your name." Just saying the words felt like a phantom was stealing the air from her lungs. She thought she had learned fear when fighting the undead.

Then why did she feel as if she was staring death in the face? Why did she see someone who wanted to destroy everything she was? She could still see insanity in his eyes, and it made her skin crawl.

"Yes, now I'm here to finally reunite myself with her and make her into one of us, as well as the rest of the town," he stated as if it was a natural course of action. "As the alpha of this army, we have come to give them all this new life."

"No!" Lethia cried out, stepping back. "I can't let you. I came to stop you, and I will!"

Raziel shook his head with a condescending smile. "Lethia, you silly girl, you're a werewolf like us. You are just hunted down as shamelessly as any other werewolf, it's how society has always been."

"That's... not entirely true, actually," she replied with a nervous gulp. "There was... um, there was a werewolf long ago, who actually was a defender

of a town. I read about him when I was studying in the Silver Shield archive
and-"

"History is over and done with, Lethia. If such a thing led anywhere,
it would have made things different than they are now, wouldn't they? He
may have been an exception that proves society's rules," he lectured her.
"Now, stand aside and let us through. You can't stop all of us. Even if you
fight us here, more of us can still reach the village and you would only be
overwhelmed." In an act of defiance, Lethia slammed the halberd into the
ground and drew a line, igniting the ground and creating a burning streak,
reaching half way up her torso. She then stepped through it and held the
halberd steadily in her hands. Instinctively, all the lycans backed off from the
fire.

Only Raziel held his posture, staring down his disobedient daughter
through the flames, as if staring at her through a door frame.

"I'm not just a werewolf, Father," she declared as number of the wolves
became very aware of who she was. Whispers turned into shouts and
intimidating growls until one of the pack informed Raziel. When he realized
his own daughter was the legendary Hellhound, he laughed out loud as if he
was just given a gift.

"Who would imagine it! My daughter is the Hellhound! The beast
caused such a ruckus throughout the kingdoms!" he howled approvingly.
Lethia tilted her head; she had announced that earlier. Did he not hear her?
Or was he too wrapped up in what madness rules his thoughts?

"Very well, we will delay the attack for tonight. We still have the village
surrounded, plus it wouldn't hurt to starve them out for another week," he
announced, though when his statement wasn't met with the same fervor he
was sharing, his proud smile became menacing. "After all, we always have
dissenters who could easily fill our own larders." Taking the hint, all the other
lycans immediately gave loud, if half-hearted cheers of approval. "There.
Now come with us Lethia, so we may finally spend time together again, as
parent and child." Lethia felt her stomach twist; the invitation did not feel
welcoming at all. Looking up at the full moon, she assumed she had a few
hours left.

"I can spend the rest of the night with you, but I must be back near dawn.
I'm a mercenary now, plus the village will know something is wrong if I don't

return in time. To be fair, it's easy to come up with an excuse as to why you never attacked," she said. 'Plus I really need time to think about everything, if I'm given the opportunity to actually consider everything.'

"Nonsense, you should just stay with us. If they don't know what you are now, they will certainly know long before the week is over," her father pointed out. The wolf pack gathered around her from behind, pressuring her to follow. Finding herself between some sharp rocks and a pretty hard argument to beat, she silently followed the pack. She took comfort in the fact that she was able to buy time for the villages at the very least. However, during the trip to the werewolf camp, it was very clear there was a lot of dissent among the pack of wolves.

The camp they had was actually of some level of military standard. They had made a decent sized clearing with tents, a few hunting stations and medical centers. She could even see some parents and pups running around, families being raised happily together. A clear indication they were indeed people without a home. However, she couldn't help but notice all the looks of unease and wariness they had towards her. Did they not think that she would be worth celebrating? Perhaps, she mused, they thought she had the same madness as her father.

"There are families here, children, young ones needing proper shelter and a stable home. Why do you think conquering a piece of land is going to give you everything you need?" she found herself asking. "I don't know much at all, but even I know the officials who govern the Northern Commonwealth would never let such an act of aggression go. Everyone would be slaughtered to the last child. They would hire people who only look at werewolves as beasts. Even if the official guilds recognized you as having innocent children, they would find grey mercenaries who don't have such a standard."

"They would come upon a force they would never be ready for," Raziel replied, stepping forward to stand beside her. "This is but one camp, Lethia. We are numbered in the hundreds. We have been traveling around, pulling in packs from around the nation, building our numbers in secret. We have also been keeping our hunts to more isolated targets, lone hunters or bandits hiding in the woods. People society would not so easily notice missing long enough for us to make clear." After explaining how his pack had been operating, he took her towards a large bonfire, one of the very few sources of light and heat. "We are big enough now to form our own nation, and if we cannot be respected for it, then why should we respect them?"

"Because that would be how a nation dies," Lethia replied, stepping away from him. "You're not thinking this through. You're just setting yourself and everyone here up for execution!"

"Not if we convert them. They can't deny the will of the pack alpha. They can't deny my strength!" he boasted, everyone in earshot recoiled, having expected something to happen. Lethia realized that her father didn't rule by any moniker of intelligence. The werewolf curse had turned him arrogant, fearless. His rule was violence and he cared not for who it harmed.

"I deny you," Lethia said, and her father stared at her with an expression of shock. As if on cue, the other werewolves started to form a large circle around the pair and the bonfire. "I think it's starting to become pretty clear. You've lost yourself to the beast, and now you're just swallowed up in power and fame. This sense of vengeance and anger you misplaced.You don't sound anything like the man my mother told me was my father. He was protective, thinking of others first before his own desires. He would think things through. You sound like a man so bent on conquest, you can't even comprehend the consequences. You think your unnatural strength makes you immune to any form of repercussion." Lethia shivered as the words came forward, a cold realization that this could have very much been her. Memories of how she lost Yurith flashed in her mind, and her fury grew, replacing the icey fear.

"I am!" he retorted. "I was taken from my family, treated as the pack scapegoat, until I tore out the alpha's throat in my teeth and claimed his role." He laughed, looking down at his claws. "Then I've been dreaming of reuniting my family. Making my love into a werewolf, my daughter. Look at you! Such demonic power! You could advance our kind into something feared the world over! You would not need to be thrown into fights, just give us warriors some of your demonic heritage." Lethia's face blanched at the implications of such a statement. Without thinking, she slapped her father across the face, growling. He hadn't even flinched from the impact, and his manic smile being unchanged awoke a fear in Lethia's heart.

"You truly are insane. I get why Talisan was in such denial when we reunited," she muttered. Looking around, she realized she was completely boxed in with the man. As her father reached down to her, she stepped back and drew her halberd. "I'll challenge you for the place of alpha!" she declared, causing the entire camp to freeze and forcing her to question her own sanity.

"See!? Even you would wish to kill me for more power, to lead this mighty pack!" he challenged.

"No!" she screamed. "I'm going to save you from yourself and your insane machinations!" The flames around her eyes grew intense. She felt the claws from her fingers and breathed. She didn't need to kill him, just incapacitate him. That was the trick, to prove she was stronger than him. 'Gods damn me for being so rash for once.'

"I shall prepare your throne, my princess, the future queen!" Raziel ranted on, and the werewolves howled. "To war, my pack! Go, conquer Huntersden!"

"No!" Lethia cried out as all the wolves howled with enthusiasm and sprinted off away from the camp, galloping towards the village. The sounds of branches snapping and the bark being scraped clean from dozens of razor claws tearing through the woodland echoed, acting as a thunderous wave which would serve to terrify any creature who would hear the approaching wave of frenzied lycanthropes.

All that was left was Lethia and Raziel. The first thing that came to mind was she had to stop the horde of wolves. Turning, she took off at a sprint, panic racing through her mind as her priority immediately became her friends. "You turn your back after declaring your challenge!?" Raziel screamed and followed Lethia into the woods.

Her home and her friends were far more important than some stupid duel. She wanted to buy time until dawn so the attack couldn't happen, yet she caused the opposite.

Gripping her weapon in one hand, Lethia sprinted through the woods as quickly as she could until she heard her father call after her. Looking back, the more experienced wolf was gaining ground on her rapidly, having lived as a werebeast for far longer. He was also not carrying a weapon, allowing him to use every ounce of his strength to gain on her. Lethia looked on ahead, knowing he would gain on her regardless of how fast she would go. Instead, she would try and block him. Snapping her claws to make a spark, her fur ignited, creating a burning ball of flame bouncing from tree to tree. She would make the bark smolder and the leaves burn, leaving a trail of smoke and ash behind her. She made sure her flames burned too hot for any of the dry fodder to catch before burning out, as she didn't wish to cause a forest fire.

Raziel fell victim to the first wall of ash and smoke, the burning air invading his lungs and causing him to miss a branch and crash hard into the ground. This did not deter him as he simply got back up and continued onwards. He took a wide path instead of tailing right behind his daughter, forcing Lethia to have to take sharp turns and a winding route. Now wise of her traps, Raziel was keen to outmaneuver the hell smoke, nipping at her heels when he could. His broken mind only focused on the challenge to his role as leader of the werewolf pack.

Through foliage and over tree tops, the pair ran the race, one to protect, the other to claim dominance. Eventually, they came to a clearing that served as a small arena. Lethia could see far enough through the woods to see the attack on the village had already begun.

Milly was up on the walls, shooting blasts of eldritch energy down at the hordes of werewolves, but they were too fast for her to hit accurately. While her magic could fly faster than any arrow, it still needed a brief time to reach its intended target. The defenders were valiantly trying to keep the werewolves off the walls, but the sheer speed of the lycanthropes was causing them to be overwhelmed in moments.

One of the Blood Blades shoved Milly aside in time to save her from the swipe of a werewolf, only to take the blow himself. She immediately took the shot, throwing the wolf off the wall with a concussive blast of her magic. Seeing more wolves scaling the wall, she immediately ran to the town square where the defenders were quickly falling back. There, she could see a terrified looking Viola using her body to try and shelter a number of families. The hunters and surviving Blood Blades had formed a wall of fire around the town square to help keep the wolves at bay.

Milly reached Viola and looked around, not sure what else she could do. Raising up her crossbow, she continued to simply fire bolts of magic into the crowd of wolves. She was tiring out, the bolts of astral magics becoming less lethal with every shot. Soon, they were only knocking the wolves off their feet temporarily. "I wish werewolves were magical creatures," she huffed. "Then my magic would be far more effective."

Viola looked down at her new friend, feeling helpless, then towards the weaker people she was shielding behind her. Her violin case glowed briefly, so she opened it to examine the instrument. Her eyes stayed transfixed, as if it were silently speaking to her.

Lilith was silently dreading this, watching everything from her twin's eyes. This was the very reason she never wanted to leave home in the first place.

A piercing sound of a violin rang out from Viola. Eyes closed, she simply ran the bow across the strings, letting out a suave of low toned music, starting soft and gentle. "Great, we get to have a funeral dirge." Lilith mocked. The flames acting as a barrier between the villagers and the werewolves began to flicker and twist as winds suddenly picked up. People and Lycans stopped and looked around in confusion as the sounds of the violin grew.

Everything drowned out for the musician. Eyes closed, the only thing she could hear was the sound of the strings of her instrument. Her fingers could only tell the feel and touch of the wood, the vibrations of her strings as she played. The music grew in volume as she played with intensity. Sweat began to form on her brow as playing the instrument seemed to grow more and more difficult, as if sapping her physical strength directly. The flames from the circle of torches grew larger, creating a more intimidating wall. Winds began to howl, drowning out the sounds of the wolves growling. The only sound anyone could hear was the echo of a magical violin singing it's wordless serenade.

Viola played striking notes, and in doing so, torrents of wind surged, scooping up swathes of the lycanthropes and throwing them in the air or to the ground. As if fists from giants, the formless and invisible punches swung through the town, dislodging the wolves from buildings and the walls. Above the rooftops, a cyclone began to form, with the wind currents continuing to dive downward and lift more of the invading beasts off the ground. In a panic, the wolves began to try and clear away from the village and back to the woods. Those caught up in the cyclone were mercilessly thrown outwards into the surrounding woods. Lethia and Raziel stared in wonder at the spectacle unfolding before them, while Milly whispered, "Gods, this is the power of a nephele?"

Eventually, the music reached its dramatic climax and came to an end, and with it, the cyclone vanished. The village was void of any invader, giving the defenders a chance to recover. But half-hearted cheers of victory were soon drowned out by an angry howl echoing through the forest. Viola had only managed to buy them time, not a victory. She had collapsed unconscious, her body, not designed to handle such a torrent of magical power.

Lethia turned her attention to her father. She couldn't stop the horde of werewolves, but now she was given a chance to usurp her father to force them to stop. This was a miracle, but she now had to stop this herself.

Raziel recognized the look on her face and grinned. Finally, she was willing to fight, and he would show his misbegotten daughter her place beneath him. He charged forward and bared claws and fangs alike down at her. Lethia held firm and as he came into range, then lifted the butt of her halberd to carry his momentum up and over her head and into the tree behind her.

Unnatural reflexes kicking in, Raziel caught himself on the broad trunk and simply kicked off towards the demonic wolf. She leapt over his head and struck the top of his head with the flat of her blade. The alpha crashed into the ground hard for a brief moment, only to correct himself while still dragging along the ground. Again, he charged Lethia with the intent of tackling her. Lethia swung the halberd to the side, using the back end of it to try and knock him away from her. This time, he caught the halberd and delivered a haymaker straight to her chest. Gripping the halberd, he ripped it out of her hands while sending her flying backwards across the clearing.

At a disadvantage, she now only had her claws. Raziel was already upon her, his claws glistening in the moonlight as he tore into her without mercy. She felt her flesh rend as he racked them across her exposed midsection, the one place her armor couldn't fully cover her. He followed up with a strike aimed at Lethia's face, which she ducked before delivering her own brutal slash upwards across his chest. The two exchanged a flurry of clawed slashes, drawing blood in equal measure which painted the surrounding area. Yet due to the nature of their curses, both father and daughter would regenerate too rapidly and were too skilled fighters to cause any real damage for the other to yield, at least as long as Lethia held back.

She felt hate and disgust welling up inside of her every time she felt fresh blood on her hands. This was why Talisan couldn't bring himself to harm her, she realized. This was why harming your own family caused such pain. She felt like she was tearing a part of herself into pieces. Yet all she could see was the terrifying visage of bestial rage.

She felt like she was killing herself.

As the pack of werewolves gathered themselves for a renewed assault, they were distracted by the brutal face off the two were undergoing. Black and grey fur tangled together, breaking off with crimson dripping from them both, before once again smashing into one another. The wolf pack quickly noticed, there were only tracks of grey fur littering the ground.

Another brief engagement of claws and fangs before the pair backed off, breathing heavily. Despite the unnatural strength and healing, they only had stamina to fight so intensely for so long. Lethia's torso was marred, bleeding openly for a few moments before her wounds sealed. Recognizing the decision she had to make, she started to whisper to herself. "I know how I can incapacitate him. Minerva..." She shook her head, then yelled. "No, she would have me kill you. I refuse to kill you!"

"You challenged me!" Raziel cried out, wiping blood off of his face and spitting out a fang. "You made your choice, now live with it! Kill me!"

With an idea in mind, she rushed forward at her father, and he met her with another clash of claws. Because they both realized they could only do so much damage without striking anything important, Lethia was going to take a gamble. Taking a few swipes, she intentionally left a spot open which Raziel gladly took advantage of. Swinging down and under, he buried his claws deep into Lethia's side. The mercenary then grabbed his arm and ignited herself. Pain and fear gripped the shocked Raziel long enough for Lethia to take a swing with her claws at his chest and deliver a grizzly blow. With her claws on fire, the demonic heat immediately cauterized the open wound, making her father's ability to regenerate wounds weakened.

Lethia shoved herself off her father, putting the flames on her body out to ensure she didn't cause any more harm. She stood up, eyes wet from tears of pain and having to fight her father, yet mind clear thanks to her training.

"Ha!" she panted, stumbling weakly from exhaustion. "Yield! You, you can't keep fighting with an injury like that."

The battle had lasted longer than she realized. In the distance, she saw werewolves slowly starting to revert to human form as the moon vanished behind the horizon.

She watched her father turn into his human form as well, but to her shock, there was a large, fist sized hole where his heart and lungs should have been.

Still in her demon form, she hurried over, panic settling in. "No! No no no this isn't what I meant to do!" she screamed in terror. "No! Someone! Someone please get a healer! Get my mother! She's nearby, please!" she pleaded but no one moved. "I didn't want to kill him, please! I just wanted to stop him from fighting!"

"Lethia?" Raziel whispered, his breath labored.

"Shut up!" she snapped at him. "Shut up, you madman, and save your strength, we need to get you healed!" Tears fell from her face, boiling from her eyes and leaving red splotches on her father's skin. "You're tougher than this, you're an alpha! This shouldn't be anything to you!"

"Shhh, shhh," he shushed her gently, reaching up to wipe tears from her face. He watched them briefly as they burned his skin, rolling down his hand and arm. Having returned to his human form, Raziel's bestial intentions left. "No... listen... this... this is for the better, in a way. You're right, I am... was... a madman. I'm finally lucid now... though the soldiers always told me to be careful, my own daughter might rip out her old man's heart." He laughed, trying to make light of the situation.

"Shut up!" she shouted "You don't have any right to make jokes! You're dying! I didn't want you to die! I wanted to stop you, I wanted to save you, help you become the man you used to be!" she whimpered, cradling her father. "I thought... I thought I could help you come back... and we could have been a family. You, me and Mom, she missed you.... She has missed you so badly. She misses me too, I know she does. We could have come home together."

"No," he groaned. "Don't be... so greedy. I was doomed long ago when I lost my will to control my feral urges. Yet you... look at you. You're so strong, so full of life, will and determination. So much so, not even the feral curse and demon influence could break you the way it broke me." He gave her a bright smile. "I never wanted you to be a warrior, it's a terrible life at the worst of times. Yet look at this... I can't help but feel some sense of pride. You can weep for me, for the man I was. I just beg you to never... let Amelia see me like this. Simply bury me... someplace she can visit." His arm fell limp as his eyes clouded over. "I've... never got to tell you... I love you... sweet daughter. Grow stronger..." With his final breath, his body went limp in Lethia's arms.

Lethia was now the pack alpha, so one of the men stepped forward. "What will you ha-"

"Shut the fuck up!" she growled into her father's chest. The man flinched but tried to press on. Before he could say another word, Lethia burst into flames, which rose high above the trees. "Back off!" she screamed "Leave! Take yourself and the survivors and leave this country! I refuse to be your alpha!" She looked up, any evidence of humanity in her eyes gone. "If I hear word you or any others hunting another being, I will personally hunt every last one of you down, man, woman and child, until this pack is eradicated." A demonic howl echoed through the woods, even reaching the ears of the townsfolk. "Leave the northern commonwealth and never return! Or so help me, I'll bathe in the blood of you all!"

With the first and only orders from the new alpha clear, they all fled back to camp. The emotional pressure had pushed Lethia to a breaking point, and her nature had become feral. She only had enough consciousness left, gripping her deceased father, to know she shouldn't kill them all. After some minutes, she stood up and carried his body. She never noticed how she wasn't reducing his body to ashes, nor did she truly care at the moment.

With such an explosion of fire and fury, the villagers had gathered up on the walls speculating on what was happening. By this point, the knowledge that Lethia had gone to fight the werewolves had spread. Milly stood on the wall, exhausted, supporting her crossbow on the ledge should the need to continue fighting arose. "Look, the smoke is getting closer!" One of the guards pointed out.

Lethia came out of the clearing, approaching the doors, prompting Milly to scream, "It's the Hellhound!" Her statement sent everyone into panic.

"Wait, she seems different!" Milly cried, calming them, drawing attention to how she was approaching and that she was carrying a body. When she reached the gate, she stopped and waited.

"Open the gate!" a weathered voice called out. Milly and the guardsmen turned to see Juria. "She looks like she's here to deliver something, not to attack. I imagine it was the demon herself chasing off the werewolves." Skepticism did not dissipate among the guards, so Milly took initiative and opened the gate for Lethia. The guards drew their weapons, but one of them recognized the body.

"R-Raziel!?" he exclaimed. "That is him! He vanished years ago!"

"Yes," Lethia spoke, choking on her breath, the crackling of flames hiding the emotion. "He had become the alpha of the werewolf pack. It's why he chose this place to lay siege."

"What happened to Lethia, where is the girl who went to stop them?" someone demanded. "You kill her too?"

"No... when confronted by her own father, I... She could not find the strength to strike him down. She tried to reason with him, barter for him to leave you all alone. She had begged, pleaded. In the end, he challenged her to take his status as alpha, which meant killing him. In the end, she did not have the strength to do it. I admired the woman she was trying to be. So I... I did... what she could not." Silence fell among the villagers. Milly bit her lip, tears forming in her eyes. "He made a final request not to let his wife see his body as is, but to bury him where she can visit. He is sorry he caused you such trouble."

"That still doesn't answer where Lethia is," Another villager said.

"She is escorting the wolf pack to the borders of the Northern commonwealth, where they will leave and make their own home as colonists." Lethia knelt down and laid her father's body to rest on the road. "I will not leave. There is much I wish to fix here, and while this was not the greatest solution, consider this my first attempt at righting my wrongs." Before the village could question her further, Lethia turned and vanished back into the woods. Milly watched her vanish, before looking over the body of Raziel, who looked to finally be at peace after years of madness.

✕

Epilog

It had been a few weeks since the siege on the twin towns. Milly volunteered her services to the restoration of the village by crafting tools and helping construct a local black smithery. With the abundance of wood and lumber the twin villages produced, there was fuel enough for iron tools to be crafted. Viola used the strength natural to lamia to help bring lumber over to rebuild the damage caused by not just the wolves and fire, but also her own magic as the winds had ripped up a few houses. Once the village was back on its feet and self-sufficient again, the trio of Milly, Lilith and Viola headed off down the road. Lilith materialized as soon as they were out of sight of the village.

"Finally, I can speak! Feel so cramped having to stay silent and unseen the whole time." She groaned, stretching her limbs while floating beside her twin.

"How can you have cramps? You're a spirit," Milly asked with a laugh. Lilith rolled her eyes.

"A spirit tied to a human body, so I'm not immune to feeling the effects our body goes through. Plus, I hated being silent for so long, it's so oppressive. At least we can communicate silently, otherwise I would have lost my damn mind." Viola was trying hard not to giggle at Lilith as they traveled. They had left the horse Milly came with in the village, as it would serve them more good at this point. Milly could always ride Viola on the road. "So, we're going after Lethia again, hmm? Any idea where in the world she might be this time?"

"Well, we have some of her fur on hand. I was thinking either we could devise some way to simply track her down, or follow the rumors of where people have spotted either a fire-bound mercenary or a demonic werewolf.

Considering the bounty Lethia has on her lycan form, there are bound to be people after her."

"Tracking a demon is always risky business. It opens you up to be tracked by others and that's how you can get yourself in trouble. With how reckless Lethia can be, I doubt we will have a hard time finding her," Lilith replied and rubbed her brow. "Though why can't we just go home?"

"I wanna see the world! Lethia is the best person to do that with, plus she's the only other person who is comfortable with being around, you know, another demon. Well, outside our parents, anyway." Viola smiled and gave a light nod. Milly smiled back.

"I-It's nice to have friends," the shy girl spoke up, blushing heavily as her voice came out timidly. Milly walked up to her and gave the lamia a quick hug. Lilith rolled her eyes, but then sighed in defeat.

"Yeah... okay, I'll agree there. Even if Lethia is more of a pain in my ass than you are, Milly," she said softly "Reckless idiot, didn't even tell us she was going off on her own. I hope she bloody learns this time not to just ditch us."

"I mean, we're not exactly the best at fighting. I doubt we would even be alive out there with her." There was a pensive pause, but eventually, Lilith nodded. "Right now, she's out there alone, and probably very hurt. She needs us now more than before, and if we could find her once, we can find her again!" Milly threw a fist into the air to punctuate her sentence. Viola imitated the gesture, blushing even more.

The group passed by a Red draconian in heavy plate mail riding a wyvern on the road, not giving him a second look. The armored hunter looked over his shoulder just as his mount paused and sniffed the air. After some hesitation, they continued forward to Huntersden; the trail of the hellhound was still fresh. Who knew where she could wind up next, and what troubles she could find herself in.

As they traveled, they knew they could follow a trail. A trail of rumors, of voices speaking in scared and hushed tones. Of a beast that stalked the countryside, a werewolf, fur as black as coal, skin of Obsidian. Red tufts of fur where flames would dance and fly off of the beast's body. The country would always fear the demonic lycan that stalked the lands.

The Legendary Hellhound.

Don't miss out!

Visit the website below and you can sign up to receive emails whenever Moonlight Soldier publishes a new book. There's no charge and no obligation.

https://books2read.com/r/B-A-XQTX-JLOHC

BOOKS 2 READ

Connecting independent readers to independent writers.